Quirke

and the

Protocol

by

Kaye Reeves

For Joel

Copyright © 2017 by Kaye Reeves

This is a work of fiction. All of the characters, names, incidents, organizations, and dialogue in this novel are either the products of the author's imagination or are used fictitiously.

ISBN: 978-0-9963568-8-6

Cover by Mark Ziemann
(markzman@markzman.com)

Chapter One

9:00 p.m., Sunday, January 31

His sigil, designed and consecrated according to a respected grimoire, hung on each wall and the bedroom ceiling; blue candles and incense of sandalwood, myrtle, and soft tonka beans smoldered in the corners. The day and hour for the rite he'd left it to her to fix, taking into account—he presumed—sound astrological considerations. As universally recommended before important operations, they'd conducted a divination; she'd tossed the coins and obtained the fifty-fourth hexagram, the Marrying Maiden, with the top line moving, which yielded the thirty-eighth hexagram, Opposition. Given the near-perfect salience of the initial image to his aim, he refused to credit the pessimistic augury: "Nothing that would further." They had bathed, separately, and he now awaited her. "There's no performance anxiety like before your first sex magic ritual," Frater Nox had said, and Quirke now understood.

To her, he was vaguer about its aim. "To improve our relationship," he said, when she asked. This discrepancy between his true object and her understanding left him uneasy, but he didn't see why it mattered in the end: Surely improvement couldn't mean something altogether different to her.

At last she emerged from the en suite bathroom, wrapped in a white kimono, her wavy chestnut hair tumbling over her shoulders. She gave him a rueful smile, her eyes rimmed with fatigue as they nearly always were since Ruairí came along. "Have you banished yet?" she asked.

He was taken aback. He understood the lesser banishing ritual of the pentagram to be the introduction to virtually all magical rites, and couldn't imagine beginning this one without her. He was sure that, in his obsessive planning, he'd designated that part for her. "No, do you want to do the honors?" he whispered.

"Sure," she said, a little mechanically. She stepped forward, made the cabalistic cross, and began to draw the pentagrams in the four quarters. Except that—and she was so much more experienced in magic than he that he couldn't bring himself to mention it—he was sure she was drawing them in the wrong direction, invoking rather than banishing. What precisely she might be invoking, he decided not to dwell on.

After the pentagram ritual, the phase of mutual arousal began, and her soft, warm flesh, so familiar and beloved, quickly stirred him. He drew her toward the bed and into his arms, caressing and kissing her neck, her arms, her breasts—every avenue of excitement in nights past. And she returned his kisses—although more slowly and deliberately; was he going too fast? He should know her preferences by now, but for a crazy moment he feared he knew nothing at all about her. Then he chided himself: He should be meditating on the ecstasy that would soon be theirs, not his petty egotistical worries.

When the moment seemed right, he began the next phase, entering her, searching out her eyes, wanting to pour into her all the love he felt. But they were shut tight, and she was not speaking, not making any sound. *Is this the way it's supposed to be*, he wondered? Maybe she was bottling up her magical energies for the next, all-important, prolonged phase. He'd heard some rituals of this kind last hours, though he was pretty sure he wasn't in that league of magician. He remembered to gaze at the sigil on the wall in front of him as he increased the pace and vigor of his movements. She had not yet looked at the symbol, as far as he could tell. Some minutes later, a small voice inside him, whether a cautionary angel or an insidious demon—he couldn't tell—whispered, "Wait," but just then, stimulated beyond any possibility of containment, he came—not more intensely than ever before (as honesty forced him to notice, with some disappointment), but at least he came.

She, however showed no signs of having done so. As soon as he was able, he focused all his attention on her, wanting to bring her to orgasm to complete the ritual. But a glance at her blank, upturned face—her eyes still closed and her mouth slightly open, her breathing light and regular— told him she'd fallen asleep. The places on her skin where his touch usually excited her were now insensible. He lay, still and quiet, next to her until, feeling a chill, he knew it was time to get under the covers.

But first he rose and blew out the candles. Feeling out of sorts at this unexpected end of the working, he forgot both to pronounce the traditional license to depart and to perform the closing banishing ritual, leaving whatever entities the rite might inadvertently have summoned to hang in an invisible miasma over their bed all the night long.

Candles, dozens of them, flickered in the darkness, and smoke of frankincense and myrrh thickened the air. She was kneeling in a pew behind the other girls; veiled, their white bridal gowns gave them the look of angels, or ghosts. Their faces were hidden, but she knew they were happy, smiling, ecstatic to be at last about to pledge themselves to their bridegroom. An eternity of perfect love would be theirs, but she could not take part; she was not yet one of them.

"Receive this ring," Mother Superior recited as the first sister, hand extended, stepped forward to profess her vows, "for you are betrothed to the Eternal King; keep faith with your Bridegroom so that you may come to the wedding feast of eternal joy. Receive this crown of virginal excellence," Mother Superior continued, placing the thorns over the sister's veil, "that as you are crowned by us on earth, so you may merit to be crowned by Christ with glory and honor." One by one, they stepped forward to receive their engagement gifts; then they floated away into the hazy darkness. The chant began, at first barely audible, then rising to a soaring climax: "*Adoro te devote, latens Deitas, quae sub his figuris vere latitas, tibi se cor meum totum subiicit, quia te contemplans, totum deficit.*" She burned inwardly, wanting Him to want her, to offer Himself to her as she wanted to offer herself to Him. Yet suddenly she was alone, and the chapel was changed: In the east, the altar, draped in crimson, pillars on each side, stood atop the third of three stairs all tiled in black and white. Black curtains hung open around the altar, and a strange picture adorned it. She was meant to take part in this mass, not the other, but it was wrong somehow. Her bridegroom was absent. She had only an instant to save herself.

Panic startled her out of sleep. She was in her own bed, with Conal beside her breathing softly. Why did the dream of the convent school keep recurring? If ever there was a time when she could have taken that path, it was long past. She turned onto her side, away from him, but in sleep his arm sought out her waist and held her down.

At eight-thirty the following morning, on a brilliant February Monday in the middle of a long drought, Associate Justice Conal Quirke of the state Supreme Court stood before his bathroom mirror in a white dress shirt, tying a half-Windsor knot in a pink foulard tie. The Chief Justice had appointed him chair of the Committee on Self-Represented Litigants, and he meant to look respectable at the Committee's quarterly meeting that afternoon. For Sadie, he wished he could look young as well as respectable, but at fifty-three his hair was growing whiter by the day, and a recent loss of weight, resulting from his longest period to date of abstinence from alcohol, had left hollows under his cheekbones.

His knot at last satisfactory, he put on the jacket of his navy chalkstripe suit and joined Sadie and the baby, in his high chair, at the breakfast table. Clad for the office herself in a black jersey dress, she seemed to be trying to combine parental quality time with addressing Ruairí's nutritional needs, but judging from the child's peevish expression and adroit evasion of the spoonfuls of squash puree she kept thrusting at his mouth, neither aim was achieving notable success.

He bent and bumped foreheads with Ruairí as the boy burbled something welcoming. Sadie presented her cheek for a chaste kiss.

"I'm sorry the timing wasn't great last night," he said. "I didn't realize you were so tired."

She shrugged. "Neither did I. Don't be too concerned; it takes a lot of practice to do that kind of ritual well."

She was becoming adept at puncturing his ego with the lightest of thrusts. Acutely aware of the limits of his magical accomplishments, he'd probably spend every free moment for the next few days wondering with whom she'd previously practiced sex magic and how much better at it they were than he.

But he forced himself to smile. "The sleep did you good; you look exceptionally beautiful this morning."

She only rolled her eyes, discounting as she lately did his every compliment, and resumed ineffectually chasing Ruairí's bobbing and weaving face with the spoon.

He turned to the kitchen counter and poured himself a mug of coffee but, after glancing inside the cylinder of raw oatmeal standing there, he decided he wasn't especially hungry. What happened, he wondered, to the happiness they'd discovered in each other only a year and a half earlier? She'd long worked as one of the attorneys on his staff when, one night, after a well-lubricated staff celebration at the dive bar across the street from the court, they'd returned to chambers and found themselves tearing off each other's clothes. His previous marriage had long since ceased to exist in any meaningful sense, and that night had brought a part of him back to life, although not without certain personal and professional complications. Leaving his employ soon after the start of their relationship had been her idea, although—because already by then he found it impossible to judge her work impartially—he couldn't see how they could have continued working together in any event. Ruairí, a surprise blessing amid all that, had forced some changes in their routines, as children inevitably do, but it seemed to Quirke that more than routines had changed between himself and Sadie.

Naively he'd supposed magic would help ensure the vitality of their relationship. Before Sadie, he'd never met anyone whose spiritual practice was ceremonial magic, and although her preeminent importance in his life ensured he'd respect her chosen path, once he got past certain popular misconceptions he found himself sufficiently attracted to magic to begin to study it himself. It turned out that magic, at least as practiced in the Ordo Argentum Diluculo, was essentially a mixture of depth psychology, eastern philosophy, and performance art. Properly understood, the magical path entailed nothing necessarily offensive to his intellectual sensibilities as a jurist and philosophy student. Practicing magic had helped him to focus his mind, strengthen his will, and reinforce his native inclination toward tolerance and acceptance. At times he felt strongly that it enhanced his efforts to avoid alcohol and drugs, for which he had a certain weakness. But an order whose holy books adjured one to "drink sweet wines and wines that foam" and "To worship me take wine and strange drugs whereof I will tell my prophet, & be drunk thereof" was bound to generate ambivalent feelings toward abstinence, along with the occasional crazy random thought that he could drink like a normal person and stop whenever he wanted.

And despite his desire to remain sober and dedicate his sobriety to Sadie, he'd slipped, more than once, though not catastrophically. She had remonstrated with him less each time it happened; she seemed to be taking his occasional relapses in stride.

As he was pouring a second cup of coffee, Roísín Dexey—Quirke's niece and Ruairí's au pair—emerged from her room. Tall and voluptuous, her black hair standing up just as his tended to do early in the morning, she pretended to steal Ruairí's nose as she passed his high chair and made for the cupboards. Roísín's arrival had headed off a minor crisis. Several months earlier, in the grip of a mood that looked to him like an incipient case of postpartum depression, Sadie had told Quirke one day that she needed help around the house. Quirke suggested he could support them both if she wanted to be a full-time mother for a while, but, seeing the look of horror on her face, he instead called his sister Kathleen in County Wicklow, in the Republic of Ireland. Luckily enough, her second-youngest daughter, Roísín, was just then at loose ends following the end of a temporary job, and happy enough to come to America to spend a year or so looking after her little cousin. Roísín had a way with Ruairí and an easygoing personality, but it sometimes seemed to Quirke that Sadie remained as downcast and unlike herself after Roísín's coming as she'd been before.

Chapter Two

11:00, Monday, February 1
"Everybody does it," the Chief said. "This isn't a monastery."

The Chief Justice's double entendre seized Quirke's wavering focus. Did she ever employ such a warmly appealing tone with any of their colleagues, or was it something she reserved for him? Given her scrupulous evenhandedness, he doubted she would single him out in this way that, if he didn't know better, he'd have described as flirtatious. Yet he couldn't imagine she'd waste it on the seventy-year-old Justice Ted Kroner or the William Howard Taft-lookalike Justice Windham Farley, much less Justice Carol Wiggins or Justice Sophia Rackrent. On second thought, maybe he was just a little special to the Chief.

His musings caused him to miss her next sentence, and she gave a mildly exasperated sigh. "Look, I'm not asking you to take one on, only to talk to them." He pretended an impassivity that eroded rapidly in the face of her irresistible importuning. "It's just lunch," she said, "and you have to eat anyway."

Quirke inverted his involuntary grimace into a smile as he shifted in the guest chair in front of her monumental mahogany desk. He knew she had enough on her mind without having to listen to small-minded grousing from her colleagues about the occasional social obligation in the workplace. And he supposed lunch with the annuals would prove educational—for him or them, he couldn't yet say.

Annual clerks—an institution in the federal courts, but a practice that went in and out of fashion at the state Supreme Court—were currently experiencing something of a renaissance. The newest justice, former law professor Rackrent, had started the trend by bringing three of her favorite ex-students with her when first appointed to the court a year earlier. Quirke hardly managed to learn their names before they decamped to a more prestigious clerkship in some federal court (or, pressed by balloon payments due on educational loans, to more lucrative employment in Big Law), and were immediately replaced by the next batch of annuals. Several other justices, seeing the sort of clever, tireless young people Rackrent was attracting, started filling vacant positions in their own chambers with annual clerks, sometimes merely as an extended tryout before offering a more permanent commitment. Now there were a dozen annuals on various staffs at the court. Quirke's was not among them: He felt leery of these temp and temp-to-perm arrangements, preferring experienced staff who needed no training and little supervision in the court's sometimes arcane internal procedures. And, in truth, he found confronting all that relentless youthful enthusiasm to be more daunting since Ruairí had come along and made an unbroken night's sleep a thing of the past.

Sophia Rackrent had replaced Allan Hetford, who'd resigned from the court to marry Quirke's ex-wife Eleanor and assume the mantle of general counsel at Marvelocity Industries, Eleanor's father's multinational conglomerate. While at the court, Hetford seemed to find few activities more stimulating than trying to ruin Quirke but, since marrying Eleanor, for reasons obscure his attitude had flipped 180 degrees. He now frequently invited Quirke to lunch—at clubs Quirke had belonged to while married to Eleanor—and Eleanor and Hetford once even had Quirke and Sadie to dinner, in the house Quirke and Eleanor had shared. Everyone behaved well on that occasion, considering Hetford's machinations had very nearly cost Quirke his retention election and Eleanor had declared she'd never be able to unsee a certain photo of Quirke and Sadie violating several canons of judicial ethics on the couch in Quirke's chambers at the court. Relations between the two couples were now so harmonious that Quirke only wished Eleanor hadn't waited thirty years to divorce him.

In all probability, he realized, if he could enjoy a civil evening with his former nemesis and ex-wife, he could tolerate lunch with the annuals.

"All right," he told the Chief. She brightened noticeably. "I'll have Margie set it up. I don't mean to be a pill about it, it's just—"

"I know. Life is short."

"Especially, it seems, for Marcus Dormund. I hear the Governor denied clemency."

The Chief shook her head. "It's too bad."

"For him or us?" Quirke asked rhetorically.

Dormund had been sentenced to death on a retracted confession and circumstantial evidence for the lying-in-wait murder of his former employer in the early 1990s. The court had affirmed the judgment in 2003 and, with the denial of his latest petition to the U.S. Supreme Court the previous week, Dormund appeared to have finally exhausted all his appeals. The District Attorney immediately moved for an execution date and got a death warrant to be carried out on the earliest day possible, thirty days thence. The Governor's press release announcing his denial of Dormund's clemency request stated tersely, "No court has credited the evidentiary premises underlying Mr. Dormund's arguments. Given the facts as found by the jury, I see no legal or moral basis for commuting his sentence." Unless Dormund's lawyers could think of something that hadn't been done before, their client had only a little more than three weeks to live. But Quirke had learned not to underestimate the creativity of the capital bar.

"I thought he might have a fighting chance with the supposed new evidence," Quirke added. "As reported, it sounded a bit troublesome. Enough to give the Governor pause, anyway."

"Not this governor."

"I suppose we'll be seeing a new habeas petition any day now. What'll that be, his fourth?"

"Number three, I believe."

"Third time lucky, you think?" Seeing his Chief give a little yawn, take up her pen and begin to worry it between her perfectly white and even teeth, Quirke rose from his chair. "Well, I'd better go and let you make law."

She nodded and pulled closer an inch-high stack of orders requiring her signature. "Say hi to Sadie and give Ruairí a kiss from me," she said. "And thanks for coming by. It's always good to see you."

"Likewise," he replied.

On the way back to his chambers, he took the stairs two at a time. The Chief's moral support during the darker moments of his reelection campaign and associated events a year earlier had enabled him to maintain his sanity, and conversation with her never failed to buoy him. He now felt able to face Rackrent's dissent to his majority opinion in People v. Quigley, concerning the retroactivity of a particularly obtuse provision of a newly enacted sentencing law. Her dissent was twice as long as his majority opinion, never a good sign.

"Judge? Got a sec?" A young staff attorney stood in the corridor waiting to waylay Quirke as he emerged from the staircase, a mixture of deference and excitement radiating from his freckled face.

Quirke waved him into his office. "Sure, Mike. Come on in."

Mike Frentz was one of the two newest members of Quirke's team, having come over from Hetford's staff to fill the position vacated by Quirke's former head of chambers, Lucas Grieber. Quirke had felt some trepidation at the idea of taking one of Hetford's people, but it turned out

Mike was as different to Hetford (the old Hetford, that is) as day to night. An infectious geekiness underlay his attitude toward the legal system and the court's role in it; if he noticed the foibles of his boss and fellow attorneys, he never pointed them out; refreshingly undefensive, he stood always ready to admit his infrequent errors. He could talk sports with head of chambers John Hendershott as fluently as he could discuss opera with Freddie Osorio, one of Quirke's other senior staff attorneys. Despite his stratospheric law school grades and impeccable post-bar experience, however, at Mike's core still lay a certain naiveté.

"So, what's up?" Quirke asked, sitting down at the conference table and gesturing to Mike to do likewise. The pile of memos, three hundred deep, for the next day's conference still awaited Quirke's attention, and his impatience must have shown on his face.

Mike cleared his throat. "I know you're busy, Judge, but I wanted to tell you I'm prepared to stay for the execution, unless somebody else has already spoken up."

Quirke considered. Of his four staff members, John had the most experience in these matters, but he also had three kids at home, and Quirke refused to rob the family of his presence. Freddie and his husband Derek had just welcomed a baby girl, and Quirke had a rule that parents of infants were exempt from execution duty, though he was sadly powerless to exempt himself. The fourth and newest staff attorney, a refugee from Big Law named Adair Thornton, who occupied Sadie's former chair on the org chart, was as sound as a bell but had no criminal law—much less capital case—experience. Quirke knew he should be grateful Mike had volunteered instead of waiting to be drafted.

"For whatever reason, none of the comrades seems to want to pull an all-nighter here with me and the rest of the crew. It's all yours."

"Thanks, Judge, thanks a bunch. I assume Dormund'll be filing another petition, so I'm preparing by reading the record in the case. Of course, I want you to know I still plan to finish my calendar memo in *Myxilydian* by the first of next month."

"I'm sure you will, Mike; I appreciate your diligence. Let's confer on this again when we know more, all right?"

Looking gratified, Mike left Quirke's office. How little it takes to make some people happy, Quirke reflected.

Margie had to be discouraged from making little name tags for the annuals. Quirke suggested they probably all knew each other well enough at this point in their brief tenures to do without them; she, in turn, tactfully omitted to point out the tags were for his benefit, to avoid embarrassing lapses of memory. Instead she counted and recounted the cafeteria-catered cookies until the annuals had spilled into the conference room and were all standing, laughing and talking, around the table. Quirke cleared his throat.

"Welcome, everybody. Shall we?" He sat down; they followed suit and came to order. Margie deposited the judge's takeout lunch in front of him and returned to her own office and her galley-proofing.

"Even if we've met, in the elevator or elsewhere," he said, taking up half of his turkey sandwich with cream cheese and cranberry sauce, "would you all humor me by saying your names and which of my colleagues you're working for? And a bit about how you got here, if you like? Go ahead and eat, by all means." General rustling and unwrapping followed.

The annual on his right hand, a tall, bearded fellow in a sweater vest, spoke first. "Judge, I'm Ben Grady, working for Justice Corcoran, and last year I clerked for federal District Judge Mark Hawkins. Before that, Harvard Law." Young Mr. Grady turned expectantly to the annual sitting to his right.

A thin Asian guy, whose spidery hands were playing with a large bottle of iced tea and a burrito, nodded to Quirke. "Sanders Chen, Justice Farley, Duke and the Fourth Circuit." Quirke wished Farley's opinions read as concisely as Chen spoke.

"Mia Wolfram," said the brunette in a pink sweater with a deep V-neck to Chen's right. "I'm clerking for Justice Wiggins this year and I'll probably be going to an intellectual property firm in the Valley next year. Oh, and I went to Stanford Law and have a Ph.D. in biomedical engineering from Johns Hopkins."

"Wow," said Quirke involuntarily. As they went around the table, each annual's accomplishments were more impressive than the last's; none of them seemed to have wasted a minute or an opportunity since birth. Thank God at his stage of life he didn't have to account to them; his law school grades wouldn't withstand close scrutiny.

"Anya Holmquist," the last annual, the young woman on his left, was saying. "I graduated from Crowne Hall this past spring and I'm clerking for Justice Rackrent." She focused her gaze on the small container of grain salad in front of her as she spoke. Pale and anorexic-looking, with long, humid, mouse-brown hair partially veiling her eyes, she wore layers of loosely-woven textiles of a kind rarely seen off university campuses. Her voice conveyed an anxious, negative energy, and Quirke felt oddly guilty in her presence.

He'd start with pleasantries; chitchat about what they were presently doing seemed like a safe place to begin the conversation. "Am I the first justice you've had lunch with?" he asked no one in particular.

"Actually, you're the last," said Sanders Chen. "We had the Chief—or she had us—last week."

"You were lucky to have gotten a piece of her time." Curious to hear what they might disclose about his colleagues, Quirke asked, "And which lunch was your favorite so far?"

The annuals consulted each other silently, diplomacy warring with candor. "Justice Rackrent took us to the University Club," Mia Wolfram said at last. "That was pretty nice."

"Hmm," said Quirke. He'd gotten the distinct impression from the Chief that these lunches were uniformly casual brown-bag affairs. But his budget could no longer withstand lunch for a dozen at a club, so the question of what he would have done had he known these were competitive events was a moot point.

"Justice Wiggins made lunch for us herself. She's an incredible cook," said a Rackrent annual sitting directly across from Quirke. His name, if Quirke recalled correctly, was Evan. "It was a roast *en croûte* with frizzled brussels sprouts, whipped sweet potatoes, and *mousse à la vanille* with *coulis de framboise*."

"That's an impossible act to follow." With that kind of culinary skill, no wonder Wiggins was so generously proportioned. "I won't even ask how she managed to pull that off here."

"She didn't," Evan replied. "We all went to her house."

"Yikes." The exclamation popped out before he could stifle it. The thought of a dozen elite young lawyers descending on the loft he and Sadie called home in its present state of disarray unnerved him. Neither of them had the energy to keep the place up these days after getting home from work and spending a little time with Ruairí, and Róisín had let it be known that housework wasn't in her job description.

It was time to change the subject. The only topic on which he felt reasonably knowledgeable being himself, he volunteered: "Anyone want to ask me anything?"

Expecting a question about his favorite dissent or some other legal trivia, he nodded at the woman on Mia's left hand, a tall blonde with a ponytail, Genevieve-something, who'd said she clerked at the Second Circuit last year.

She smiled engagingly at him. "What was it like being in jail?"

All eyes were on him now, and he felt the gulf between himself and them widening, as if he were standing on an ice floe drifting away from the mother glacier. "My God, I assumed all that had long since been forgotten," he said, blinking to dispel memories of the holding tank of the Parmenter County jail. "How did you even hear about it? Most of you were in out-of-state law schools at the time."

Young Grady shook his head. "It was a thing our 3L year. Everybody followed your reddit."

That anxious pre-election month of being the subject of scurrilous blog posts, drinking to forget them, and somehow not losing Sadie through it all came flooding back. Quirke decided to ask his former election consultant and AA sponsor Bobby James, next time he saw him, if he'd known about the reddit. "I followed some of the social media," he said, "but I didn't know I had a reddit."

"You did, Justice Quirke. And there was a separate subreddit for all the conspiracy theories."

"The idea that people found the whole saga interesting enough to post things about mystifies me, but maybe some historical researcher will find that stuff useful someday. Well, to answer your question, Genevieve, it's fair to say the Costante PD saved my life. Whoever decided cops should carry naloxone on raids deserves the Nobel prize in emergency medicine, as far as I'm concerned. And once they figured out who I was, the authorities there treated me reasonably well. Of course, you can find trendier places, places with better internet access, to spend a weekend in than county jail. Any other questions?" If they'd all followed his travails on social media, as they were implying, they shouldn't need to ask him about other sensitive topics. All of that had been thoroughly and publicly analyzed already.

A blonde woman in a horizontally striped dress waved her hand. "Judge, did your experience change your views on drug policy?"

"That's a tough question," he said. "Of course, what the policy on drugs should be isn't our concern here at the court; we take the drug laws as the Legislature gives them to us. I will say that after what I went through, I understand the attraction of narcotics in a way I didn't before." He looked at his watch; his preferred NA meeting had started ten minutes earlier. He'd have to make it another day. "Time for one more question."

"Judge, I understand you were a philosophy major as an undergraduate," said Anya, pushing her half-eaten grain salad away and looking him straight in the eye. He saw a boldness, or perhaps a desperation, in her gaze that seemed out of place. "Do you have a philosophy on the death penalty?"

Aware his audience, unlike him, hadn't yet had the opportunity to decide dozens of capital cases, he tried to recollect the novice's perspective on the ultimate penalty. "The reality," he said, "is only a few of these cases involve novel issues. The rest, we have a duty to decide in line with settled law. Do I have a personal philosophy, you mean?"

She nodded. "You must have had a chance to think about it at some point."

Quirke smiled at her naïve condescension. "I suppose I do, but with the vote coming up, I'd better keep my views to myself." In November, the electorate would have yet another chance to abolish capital punishment in the state. Four years earlier, a similar abolition measure failed by a four-point margin, and this time the polls showed a dead heat. The annuals were, of course, perfectly well aware that anything he said needed to stay within the walls of the court, but given they were here today and gone tomorrow, he didn't want to trust his career to their discretion. If he were quoted as saying he believed death row should be cleared out forthwith, they might as well start a new subreddit devoted to analyzing the trouble—political, disciplinary, and every other kind—he'd doubtless get into.

"With all due respect, Justice Quirke, I'm sure we'd all like to think we decide cases strictly in accordance with neutral principles and settled law, but do you really believe that?"

Her eyes, an indeterminate brown set in shadows that told of poor sleep habits, glared defiantly at him; her forehead was shining with righteousness; her bangs were kinking. Her cohort looked bored; evidently they'd already had enough of critical legal theory in their young lifetimes.

"You don't?" Quirke asked. "What are you doing here, then? Firms pay big money for associates with your credentials." That was uncalled for, he knew. "I'm sorry. Kidding aside, I—"

Ben Grady stepped in to rescue him. "Judge, based on your experience, what do you think's going to happen with Marcus Dormund? You've been through the execution protocol, I gather?"

"Yes, once before, with a guy named Eugene Valence. You may be aware we denied a habeas petition from Dormund a couple of years ago."

"You voted to issue an order to show cause that time, didn't you, Judge?" Evan McCabe asked.

"I did. I was alone on that one. It went all the way up, and not one federal judge agreed with me. Now, if the media's to be believed, Dormund has newly discovered evidence showing somebody else committed the murder. Evidently the Governor didn't find it compelling. Seems pretty likely Dormund will ask us to take a look at it."

"There's not much time," said a Kroner annual whose name Quirke had forgotten.

"I'm sure counsel will step up to the task," Quirke said. "An execution date tends to concentrate the mind."

Chapter Three

5:30 p.m., Tuesday, February 2

Between the tension of the brown bag lunch with the judge and the long walk home with the setting sun baking the right side of her face, Anya's head was thrumming with a fierce ache by the time she turned the key in the lock. The air inside the flat was still and dusty and redolent of kasha, and the only sound was the clicking of a computer keyboard in the kitchen.

There, the day's unwashed dishes and Dane, sitting over his laptop, silently greeted her. She walked straight to the sink and ran herself a glass of tepid water; after refreshing her parched mouth, she turned to him.

"Did you get anything done today?" she asked.

He continued typing for a few seconds, then nodded. "Some."

What Dane did for money she didn't know; she was only glad not to have to hound him for his share of the rent. In comparison with their own sketchy means of making a living, hers must seem, to him and Rusty, quite bourgeois. She wondered if they were aware of the salaries some of her law school classmates were making in their big firm jobs; her roommates never betrayed awareness that, with her spectacular grades, she could have had that, could still have it, too. A Rackrent clerkship was like deferred compensation.

"Rusty said he'd be a little late tonight. There's an organizing committee meeting in the East Bay."

"So it's going forward?"

"Last I heard is Yago'll be here three weeks from now."

"Around the time—"

"Yeah. We're moving forward. We're going to stop it for good. And you're why it's finally going to happen."

She smiled weakly, then turned to the sink, feeling suddenly nauseated. She must have allowed herself to sway a little because in an instant Dane was at her side, his fingertips contacting her shoulder blades.

"Anya? You feeling okay?"

"I'm fine. Long day. We—the annuals—had lunch with...with him today. It was a little weird."

"What's he like?"

She recalled Quirke's contempt for her question about his philosophy and his lame attempts to ingratiate himself with the young attorneys; Rackrent's sarcastic dismissals of his jurisprudence echoed in her ear. "He tries to get by on glamour and charm. For a lot of people that seems to be enough."

"But he's one of the liberal judges, right?"

"What passes for liberal at this court," she said. "He was so proud that he alone voted to grant relief on Dormund's last petition. We'll see whether he's willing to stick his neck out when the next one comes in. Or when..."

Dane grinned. "Dream big."

She returned his smile just as an intense pang reminded her that all she'd eaten since getting up that morning was a few forkfuls of barley salad, spoiled by the judge's sarcasm, at lunch. She had an inflexible rule against eating between meals, and Rusty wouldn't be home for dinner, Dane had said, till later. Her strategy in the circumstances was the same one she'd read that many impoverished third-world people adopt: sleep through the hunger.

"I'm going to take a nap," she said.

Dane studied her. "Hey, I'm about to knock off for today; want to go get a burrito?"

She shook her head quickly. "I'll wait."

"He said it could be—"

"No," she said.

"—Really late. Okay, but...I think you need to eat."

"Obviously. I'm a person. Persons need to eat. And I'll eat when Rusty gets home. Thanks for asking." She turned on her heel and walked down the hall, grit on the bare hardwood floor crunching under her feet, to the room she shared with Rusty. How odd that Dane was beginning to sound like her father.

The sheets and blankets, twisted and graying, hung like dead appendages off the sagging mattress. Rusty hadn't thought to make the bed this morning, not that he ever did. She lacked the energy to do it herself, and now dropped, supine, into the hollow on his side, a little lightheaded. Maybe she was starving, slightly. Maybe she was the only comrade truly in solidarity with the 800 million or so people on the planet who go hungry every day. Or maybe she was still just the anorexic Upper

East Side girl who got involuntarily committed to three different treatment programs before she learned how to fool the therapists into thinking she'd really recovered this time.

Three voices? It was dark and cold, and the lumpiness of the bed impinged like rocks. She rolled over and touched her feet to the floor, waiting till the dizziness cleared before trying to stand. She'd left the door open and could see the lights in the living room, where Dane and Rusty and a woman were talking, laughing. Turning on the overhead light, she checked her reflection in the full-length mirror on the closet door, rubbing a bit of dried saliva from the corner of her mouth and raking her fingers through her tangled hair. She looked like shit, but she couldn't hide here, letting whatever was going on out there just happen.

She deliberately let her feet scuff the floor on the way to the living room, hoping to hear...she didn't know what. Hoping for a sign of recognition, of recollection that she, the nerve center of it all, was still here.

"Hey, sleepyhead," Dane called out at the sight of her. "We were thinking about waking you up, but you seemed so tired when you came in I said we shouldn't, and Rusty said—"

She tried to smile. "Hi. How was the meeting?" Her voice was dry and breathy.

"Great, great," Rusty said. "So, this is Hayley," he said, as the woman sitting next to him on the sofa, a luminous blonde with grapefruit breasts and a small waist, smiled widely at Anya. "She's going to do some organizing work and stuff for us. She'll be staying here for a while."

Anya stared. "Where?"

Rusty glared at her for a fraction of a second. She felt ashamed of her jealousy, but too weak to blush. "Dane can sleep on the sofa and Hayley can take his room. She works with Yago when he's in New York."

She could only look at him dully; it was taking a while for input to register with her. At last she said, "Welcome, then, Hayley. I wasn't planning on more than three for dinner, actually—"

"No worries," said Rusty. "We got some Ethiopian food earlier. Didn't you eat? I told Dane—"

"He told me you'd be late, he didn't—"

"Jeez, I'm sorry. I kind of fucked up the message," said Dane. "I can go get something—"

"Don't be silly," Anya said. "I'm fine." She let herself sink into the sofa, with Hayley, who was still smiling, between her and Rusty. Still somewhere between dream and delirium, she could scarcely tell where her body was in this socialist-revolutionary tableau.

Dane got up from his computer and strode down the hall to the kitchen, returning with a china plate. On it was a chunk of sunflower seed bread spread with vegan cheese substitute. He set it on Anya's lap.

"Would you like a smoothie? We've got strawberries and bananas. A little soy protein and agave, maybe?" Dane stood before her, his hands cupped like a waiter's, anxious to fill her. At odd moments like this when she felt too hungry to help herself, Anya wished she were in love with him instead of Rusty.

"I couldn't, really. I'll wait till—" The dizziness suddenly swallowed her.

When she came to, Rusty's arm was encircling her shoulders and Dane was standing over her, a glass of water in his hand. Hayley was holding her wrist, feeling for her pulse.

"You've got to stop working so hard for the tools, you're killing yourself," Rusty chided her.

"Have you eaten today?" Hayley asked.

"Of course, I—"

"Have you guys got some juice?" Hayley asked. "We need to get her blood sugar up. Her skin's so cold."

Dane again disappeared in the direction of the kitchen. Rusty picked up the plate and held it unsmilingly out to Anya. "Eat."

That was precisely the last thing she wanted to do at this moment; she didn't know whether her stomach, so neglected for so long, could hold anything down. But she had no choice where Rusty was concerned. Or, more accurately, she'd chosen to have no choice when she agreed to embark on a power exchange relationship with him. His role was to dictate and hers to obey.

"Let me go slowly," she said in a voice so low even she could hardly hear it. He nodded. She pinched off a bit of the bread and put it on her tongue, hoping that if she could soften it with her saliva it would slip down easily.

Dane came back with a glass of orange juice. "I hope this is okay. I thought apple juice would be better, but we're out. Here." He squatted at her feet and raised the glass to her lips.

"Thanks," she whispered.

"Could I speak with you, Rusty?" Hayley said.

"Yeah, go ahead," he replied. "These guys know everything."

She frowned. "I don't want to seem mean, but I'm concerned about Anya's health. This operation is going to require strength and concentration. It's clear she's...not in the best state. I'm sorry, Anya. I just know what Yago's going to say."

Rusty shook his head. "She may look like a concentration camp survivor, but she's strong. She'll do what she needs to do. I'll keep an eye on her. Anya, we're going to beef you up."

Hayley groaned. "Wrong thing to say to an anorexic vegan. Let's just say we're all going to pay more attention to your well-being, Anya. If you won't let us do that for the sake of the project, then you need to get out of the way and we'll figure out another way to do it."

"No," said Anya, pinching off another bit of bread and swallowing. "I'm in."

Chapter Four

6:15 p.m., Thursday, February 4

At the sight of his da in the doorway, Ruairí ceased his fretful whimpering and began to kick excitedly in his Jumperoo, stretching forth his plump arms. Quirke scooped him up, made a silly face and squeezed him, planting noisy kisses on his cheeks.

"He can tell time already, I swear." Roísín, in jeans and tall laced boots, finished applying a dramatic dark red shade of lipstick and handed the baby a stuffed dragon from the scrum of toys on the floor. "Started fussing at six, one minute after you normally walk in."

"Sorry I'm late," he said, next kissing Sadie, who had just emerged from the kitchen. "Got a gnarly ASAP a minute before five. How was your day? Latimore behave himself?"

"Mostly," she said, checking her makeup in a compact mirror. "He was in fine fettle at oral argument; I thought the Deputy Attorney General was going to cry at one point. But I was able to mollify him later with a draft opinion in a hairy eminent domain case."

"Have I told you lately that I miss having you in chambers? But my loss was the Court of Appeal's gain. My God, you look stunning. You, too, Roísín. Are you sure this isn't girls' night out clubbing? You'll be picking up half the single straight guys in Sant' Urbano looking like that."

Sadie smoothed her black velvet leggings and cerulean tunic sweater over her slender frame. "Just dinner. I'm a respectable matron; my dancing days are long past."

"You both look about 25," said Quirke.

"I *am* 25," said Roísín.

"I defy you to turn that into an insult," he said. "Now, far be it from me to detain you two; Ruairí and I'll be fine here. Go out and have fun; judge's orders. Where are you planning to eat?"

"Thought we'd try the new Cuban place in the mall on Market Street," Roísín said.

"I hear the food's as good as Mom's. And for the young man—?"

"There's a bottle in the fridge," Sadie answered, "and he'll probably take some Cheerios and mashed banana—look out, he's insisting on feeding himself. And then you'll want to hose him down. Sure you'll be all right here?" She looked as though she were hoping he'd say no. When he merely grinned and nodded, she came halfway to returning his smile. "Bye-bye, Ruairí," she said, letting the boy wrap a hand around her index finger. "Mommy's going out with Auntie Roísín. We'll be back after you're asleep—with any luck at all. Call me if you run into any trouble," she said, almost pleading.

"Get her out of here before she changes her mind," he said, laughing. Still holding Ruairí, who was beginning to look a little doubtful about boys' night in, he waved from the threshold of the loft as the two women headed for the lift.

The restaurant was close enough, and the night still young enough, that they decided to walk. Though Roísín's near-nonstop monologue sometimes irritated her, Sadie felt grateful for it now, as fear was again beginning to take hold of her, tying up her powers of speech. It had started as soon as they brought Ruairí home from the hospital in June. At first it was the fear he'd forget how to latch on, soon succeeded by the fear of overlooking signs of jaundice. Then it morphed into a fear of sleeping through his cries, a patent impossibility. Then it evolved in multiple torturous dimensions, ranging from fear she wouldn't be able to fit back into her work clothes when her maternity leave ran out, to fear she'd never again be able to put two logical sentences together and Justice Latimore would fire her, to fear she'd accidentally become pregnant again. And the latest fear—that Conal was about to fall off the wagon again—had grown so intense she could no longer distinguish it from hope.

In short, she'd forgotten what it was like to relax. Roísín, in contrast, seemed immune to stress. Everything Ruairí did, no matter how far it deviated from the "what to expect" genre of child care literature, found a precedent in her experience minding the kids in the extended family back in Ireland. Living under a visa that restricted her life choices seemed of not the slightest concern to her, and how she might be serving her long-term professional interests by caring for her wee cousin never crossed her mind, if her failure ever to mention it were any indication. And whatever judgments she might have formed about their lifestyle and occult affiliations, she never voiced them to Sadie.

"...D'you know, if you can spare me for a couple of hours sometime I'm going to get a ticket for that photography exhibit at the MOMA," she was saying, apropos of the museum they were passing. "The reviews are brilliant. I'm awful at taking pictures myself, but I love to look at them."

There was a little mental lag while Sadie caught up to what she was saying. "What? Of course. Maybe this Saturday. Maybe we can all go."

"Yeah, good luck dragging Conal out. I've never known such a homebody. Oh look, there's Father."

As they turned from Third Street onto Garrison, she waved at a tall, dark-haired man standing in front of the church opposite. When he turned in their direction and waved back, she jogged across in the middle of the block. Sadie followed, her heart suddenly thumping harder than this little exertion warranted.

"What's the craic, Father?" Roísín laughed. "Out on a date tonight?"

"I was supposed to be," he said, in a voice colored with an unexpected southern drawl, "but my buddy just called to cancel."

Roísín introduced them. "Sadie, this is Father Liam, assistant pastor of St. Declan's."

"Liam Greengold," he said, extending his hand. "Good to meet you."

"Sadie Norrell," she answered, letting him wrap hers in its warmth and strength. His eyes, almost too dark to read, struck a contrast to his pale complexion; his mouth was sensuous, sympathetic. Dressed in black clothes as trendy as they were clerical, he appeared to be in his early thirties. She wouldn't have called his casual demeanor unpriestly, but he was nothing like the priests who'd overseen her convent school. "How do you know Roísín?" she asked him. And to Roísín she said, "I didn't know you go to church." Then, realizing how insulting her remark might sound if Roísín unexpectedly turned out to be devout, she added, "I mean, you didn't tell me you'd found this place."

Roísín laughed. "Didn't want you to think I was trying to convert you. Father, Sadie's my uncle Conal's partner. I'm the au pair to their little boy. They're into the occult, so you're not likely to see them coming round for Easter mass." The priest lifted an eyebrow, but said nothing. To Sadie, she went on: "I was reading a guidebook that said St. Declan's is the most Irish parish in the City so, knowing Ma would ask, and since it's so close, I dropped in one day. Now and again I turn up of a Sunday, don't I, Father?"

Sadie hadn't seen the inside of a Catholic church since graduating from her convent high school some eighteen years before, and until this moment she hadn't realized how much she missed it. Its seasonal rhythms and sensibilities and aesthetics, the intellectual riches of its past centuries, the kitschy imagery of popular Catholicism, and the kindness of the teaching nuns had all made their mark on her psyche at a time when her life was in upheaval. Peter Blake, her high school art teacher and eventual guardian and magical teacher, had rescued her at age fourteen from her sociopathic mother, the same who had, years later, kidnapped and tried to kill Conal. Then a thirtyish, single artist, a practicing ceremonial magician, and an adept of his order (in one of whose holy books she'd later been dismayed to discover the verse "Let Mary inviolate be torn upon wheels"), he'd realized the challenges of assuming custody were beyond him. As his younger sister had been educated by the nuns at St. Anstrudis School for Girls and seemed no worse for the experience, he'd deposited Sadie there for safekeeping until she finished twelfth grade. When Sadie asked his permission to be baptized, he didn't forbid her in so many words, but made her promise to wait and explore other spiritual paths "just to be sure." In the meantime, he made certain she received an excellent magical education, and eventually, her adolescent rebellion spent, she stopped asking to become a Catholic. Now she felt a huge and urgent need to know what she'd given up.

"I'd like to see the church," she said. "But I suppose it's locked up now."

Father Liam smiled and jingled his keys. "We can take a quick peek, if you like. Let's sneak in the side door so our friends on the street don't think we're open for business. Not that we don't enjoy having them visit," he added. "It's just getting them to leave." He led them around to the Alma Alley side of the church and up a short staircase, and then opened a heavy door with iron fixtures.

"Don't worry, there's nobody but us. Stay here," he said. "I'll go turn on some lights." He disappeared into the darkness, his footfalls hushed by the thick carpet in the aisles.

Standing there in the dark, letting go of the tension of the street and the stresses in her life with each exhalation, she caught the familiar smells: warm wax from spent votives, hints of incense, furniture polish, paper and ink. As her eyes adjusted, she made out colored gleams from the stained glass in the clerestory above their heads and the rose window at one end of the space. Suddenly the lights in the chandeliers started coming on, back to front, revealing a Gothic-style space with clusters of green marble pillars, oak pews, and a blue apse leafed with gold in which the high altar sat flanked by tall green plants in marble cache-pots. Along the aisles, a dozen saints' statues stood sentry, and along the walls hung bas-relief stations of the cross.

In a moment, Father Liam came jogging back toward them. "Welcome to St. Declan's," he said.

"It's beautiful," Sadie said. "Being here really takes me back."

"Oh? Roísín said you were 'into the occult,' whatever she meant by that; were you raised Catholic?"

"Not exactly, but I went to a Catholic boarding school."

"Sounds chilling enough to put anybody off the Church," said Roísín.

"Not at all," Sadie protested. "I loved it. I would have become a Catholic if—if circumstances had been different."

"There's still time," the priest observed.

Sadie found herself speaking before she could think. "Since your date stood you up," she said, "would you care to join us for dinner?"

"Yeah, Father," Roísín seconded. "Come along with. We're going to Bembé's."

"The food's incredible there. You're sure you don't mind me tagging along?"

"Course not. Love to have you," Roísín insisted.

"We should probably head over, then, or we'll never get a table. But, Sadie, I'd like to show you around the church one day when we have a little more time. There are some historical artifacts dating back to the Gold Rush that you might find quite interesting."

"I'd like that, thank you, Father. Maybe this Sunday. Or—I'm sure you're too busy on weekends; next week sometime, maybe. If that works for you." Did she sound as awkward as she felt? She had to make him understand she wasn't just making small talk.

"Call me Liam," he said, his opaque brown eyes on her again. "I'll go turn out the lights, and we can make our way to the restaurant. Be right back."

Sadie stared after him as he retreated toward the space behind the altar where the light switches evidently were, and when she looked back Roísín was studying her. Another worry: If she didn't take care how she looked at and talked to him, Roísín would start to think she had designs on the priest.

"Also known as Father What-a-Waste," Roísín whispered.

"I imagine so," Sadie said neutrally. "He seems quite nice."

"Rumor has it a pretty lash was furious when he announced his vocation."

Sadie would have liked to hear more, but this was the wrong time to pursue it. The chandeliers began to snap off, and their eyes hadn't even adjusted to the darkness when, a moment later, Father Liam returned to their side. This time he was shining a pocket flashlight at the red-carpeted floor in front of them.

"Sorry to cut short your first visit to St. Declan's, Sadie, but shall we go?"

"Well, you're not a bit hungry, are you, Father?" Roísín teased.

"Stupidly, I forgot to eat lunch," he explained.

"My thighs wish I was that stupid," Roísín sighed. "Let's be off, then."

For the few blocks to the restaurant, and during most of the meal, Roísín and Father Liam kept up a steady banter, their conversation roving from parish news to his recent trip to Rome and Venice, to movies they'd both lately enjoyed. Roísín dispatched her *ropa vieja* and he did justice to the house *plato vegetariano*, while Sadie, suddenly tired and feeling almost mute outside the bubble of their shared energy, picked at her *arroz con frijoles*.

As they awaited the arrival of *café con leche* and caramel rum flan at the end of the meal, he turned to her. "I have to apologize for being so rude. St. Declan's gossip can't possibly interest you."

"Not at all," she said. "I'm afraid I'm just not up to making sparkling conversation—the baby's been waking up twice every night again lately, and it's taking its toll. I probably should have stayed home tonight and taken a nap, but I was practically pushed out of the house. I'm getting to be rather a bore. Roísín, don't you say a word."

"Oh, I will, though: Wonder Woman. Sorry, two. I don't know how you do it, even with a deadly au pair like me to help out. You know, Father, Sadie's a fantastic lawyer as well as a great mum. She used to work for my uncle. You remember I told you he's a judge? Not just any old judge but a Supreme Court judge."

"Doing law at the highest levels," he said, nodding. "On no sleep, it must be challenging."

Sadie smiled, grateful for the recognition. 'Mostly I just hope nobody notices when I'm not making sense, or at least has enough sympathy not to make fun of me."

The server brought their desserts; Sadie sipped at her coffee. When Roísín temporarily left the table for the restroom, Sadie called for the check.

'What's my share?" Father Liam asked, opening his wallet.

"You're my guest," she said.

He raised an eyebrow again. "I really can't let you—"

"But I insist. You were so kind to go out of your way to unlock the church. And it's been a pleasure having you join us." She gave the server a credit card.

He smiled in surrender. "Thanks."

"Not at all. But I do want to take you up on your offer. Of a tour of the church," she added. "If you were serious."

"Of course, I—"

"There's something I need to talk with you about," she said, abruptly.

He took his phone from his pocket and tapped into his calendar. "Tuesday half past noon all right?"

Chapter Five

6:30 p.m., Friday, February 5

As a typically chaotic evening at the loft dwindled into nightfall, Roísín had gone to her room to study for her driver's license test; Sadie was sitting at the kitchen table, Ruairí at her breast; and Quirke stood over the stove, idly watching orecchiete boil. He reckoned he had the dullest duty of them all, then chided himself for indulging in yet another access of self-pity. After being called on it at a few NA meetings lately, he'd come to recognize the bubble of the thought forming, and sometimes he could even dissolve it before it unsettled him. Tonight was not one of those times.

Lunch with the annuals had left him ill at ease, both with them and within himself. Their questions reflected their evident opinion of him. He was a mere novelty, a celebrity; that self-contradiction, an outlaw among jurists. The juicy details of his drug-saturated kidnapping ordeal, not his jurisprudence, was what interested them. Lately all his opinions had involved bread-and-butter sentencing questions, straightforward interpretations of obscure administrative regulations, and tedious attorney fee issues, nothing important or splashy. On the other hand, he was consistently getting majorities, if not the whole court, behind him. Was the Chief giving him these cases because she doubted his ability to handle the strain of the constitutional blockbusters, the big tort law game-changers? He supposed he'd never learn the truth—questioning her assignments wasn't a done thing.

And his home life had changed. Thoughtful conversations with Sadie had become rare lately, and energetic, uninhibited sex, of the kind they'd lived for in the old days, even rarer. Often, he wondered if her feelings toward him had changed. A year before, they'd talked of marriage. Or he had; come to think of it, had she ever actually agreed to marry him? It was academic, because now she was saying they ought to wait, he should work on his sobriety—which stood at a precarious three months and three days—before they took a step like that.

That she was objectively correct only made the craving flare again, closely followed by more self-pity. He knew he needed to face it squarely in the company of a bunch of other addicts in some church basement in the Tenderloin, and soon; pretending it wasn't there, that he was cured of it, was the surest road to disaster. If he told Sadie how he was feeling, she'd shoo him out the door to the closest meeting and tell him not to come home until he'd worked a step or two over coffee with Bobby. She deserved a guy who was immune to that temptation, and his current, likely doomed, strategy was to pretend he was that guy.

He tossed the chopped kale into the boiling pasta water and turned to the leeks and creminis awaiting his knife on the counter. Behind him, Ruairí gave a satisfied burp.

"Roísín says his latest thing is trying to escape his playpen and crawl away, but he hasn't quite got the speed yet," she said. "We need to think about baby-proofing this place."

"Assuming that's even possible. We'll probably just have to keep devising bigger and better methods of incarceration." How like life in general, he thought. "You never told me about your night out," he added. "Did you and Roísín like the Cuban place?"

She smiled before looking up. "It's as good as they say."

"Well, then, let's all go there sometime." *Include me*, he silently beseeched.

Sadie of a year ago would have heard his inner voice, but tonight she did not respond to it. Instead, she asked, "How's the pasta coming? Shall I go get Roísín?"

"Another ten minutes." He threw a few sliced fennel sausages into a skillet with the vegetables. "Did I tell you it looks like Dormund's on? Sometime in the next month, probably."

"I'm sorry. I know you thought that case should have gone down differently." Years before, when Dormund's prior habeas petition had come before the court, he'd complained to her how thin the prosecution's case had been at trial, and how intriguing the filaments of new evidence seemed. He'd had her write a memo urging the court to issue an order to show cause so that the claims could be thoroughly aired at an evidentiary hearing. Nobody bit. Eventually he acknowledged that, from a strictly legal standpoint, his colleagues were right: The petition hadn't quite come up to the mark.

"I suppose you'll have to be there," she was saying.

"You know the protocol."

Just as the prison had its protocol to ensure the execution went off smoothly, so too the court had its own protocol. At midnight on the appointed date, the justices solemnly gathered in the Chief's conference room, listening on an open phone line to the execution chamber at the prison until the condemned prisoner's death was pronounced. They could handle any conceivable legal business surrounding the execution remotely, in the comfort of their homes, but this death vigil had been enacted for every execution, going back beyond memory.

The last time, Quirke had gone home afterward, drunk a pint of bourbon whiskey, and slept through half the following day. He hadn't determined what his coping mechanism would be this time.

Standing over the stove with the wooden spoon in his hand, Conal looked the picture of domesticity and sobriety. If only she could trust him to remain so. But three months earlier she had finally realized that he was an alcoholic, and alcoholics will relapse. The first time he'd slipped, while she was pregnant, it had been a glass of wine over brunch at the house of a couple they were friends—not very close friends—with. He'd drunk seemingly without thinking, and stopped when he noticed the look in her eyes. That night he'd knelt, in shock and shame, at her feet and apologized, over and over; she'd only told him to call his sponsor, Bobby. The second time, a few days before Ruairí was born, he had a couple of double whiskey sours, his old usual, at a bar association dinner honoring the justices. He came home and, when kissing him she smelled the alcohol on his breath, he laughingly owned up to having fallen off the wagon, assuring her it wouldn't happen again. The last time, after leaving him in charge of Ruairí for an afternoon's shopping, she returned to find him passed out on the floor beside the baby, asleep in his Jumperoo, and a half-empty bottle of bourbon. The next day, she insisted he pay his niece's airfare from Ireland to come and be their au pair. Although she didn't say so explicitly, he must have understood the only acceptable alternative was his moving out.

At that moment, she knew it would happen again. She couldn't guess when or what might precipitate it, but he would drink and get drunk again because that's what alcoholics do. And, in all likelihood, one day he'd do worse things, because he liked heroin even more than bourbon whiskey. That was when the idea of marrying him receded from the realm of the imaginable and fear became a constant, taunting companion.

"Sadie—" he began.

"I'll get Roísín," she said, rising with the now sleeping baby in her arms.

Chapter Six

6:15 p.m., Friday, February 5

The sight of the cream-colored, black-bordered envelope sticking out of the slot amid the rest of the day's mail made Anya cringe. Recognizing the stationery instantly, she bent to retrieve it. There, written in the upper left corner in her mother's turquoise ink, was evidence Anya wanted to keep secret: 79-1/2 East 79th Street, New York, NY 10075, her childhood home address. Why had Mother written her? She'd instructed her to text or email only. The last thing Anya wanted was for Rusty to see that zip code, that pricey address. He already believed she hadn't been deeply enough involved in the struggle, and this letter would only confirm that view. She stuffed the envelope in her purse and brought the rest of the mail—a shopping circular, a utility bill in the name of the master tenant, whom she'd never met—inside.

Dane came walking hurriedly toward her, impaling her with an earnest stare, although the sounds of voices coming through the open door of the bedroom she shared with Rusty won the battle for her attention. "Hey, Anya. What's up? Wasn't expecting you back until later."

"Tonight's the meeting, right? I thought I'd try to tidy—to get things organized."

"Oh, yeah, of course. I—"

Rusty emerged from the bedroom, clad only in underwear, and coolly smiled as he made his way to the bathroom at the other end of the hall. Someone was still talking to him from the bedroom. Dane, reddening, blocked Anya momentarily.

"Fuck off, Dane," she spat. "Just fuck off. No, fuck Hayley. Or on second thought, it looks like that's already been taken care of."

"I'm sorry, Anya. Really sorry." Humiliation colored Dane's fair complexion, his bony shoulders drooped, and his eyes now searched the floor.

"Why should you be?" She took a step, then stopped, thinking she'd never be able to pass the doorway of the room where Rusty had just fucked the irritatingly pretty visiting socialist. "Why should anyone be? It's not like he's my property." She threw the scraps of mail she was holding to the floor and left the flat.

She walked for hours but didn't get far, only circling the next block just out of sight of the flat. Her rage transported her further in her mind, back to the squalid little studio she'd occupied while studying obsessively in her quest for the top spot at Crowne Hall Law School; before that to the dorm room, her oasis, in Worth Hall at Swarthmore, where if she wasn't reading 19th century political philosophy she was running in place for hours at a time, burning the flesh off her bones; and finally back to the kitchen at East 79th Street, where she'd have found comfort—and comfort food—had she been able to tolerate it. She could have tried to explain to her mother—who was quiet, kind, precise and rational above all—how she found herself involved with this infuriating man who used her, took her for granted, and slept with another woman, a prettier, more womanly woman who he thought was more politically evolved, in their shared bed. But Anya doubted she'd have succeeded. She couldn't at this moment think of a plausible reason for her situation.

The sensible response would be to get out for good, but on an annual's salary it would be tricky to manage; the average rent on a studio in Sant' Urbano was two-thirds her take-home pay. Mother and Dad would gladly provide financial help, but she couldn't face availing herself of it, not yet. She could quit her clerkship and get a job with a big firm, but she didn't know if she had the energy, and the idea of working 80-hour weeks to make some tech entrepreneur a billionaire or litigate on behalf of obscenely rich corporations was even more demoralizing than being taken advantage of by an unappreciative sexist revolutionary.

Exhausted—she must have burned a good 300 calories, nearly as many as she'd taken in today—she turned her footsteps back toward the flat. When she let herself in, past thinking anything, the meeting was in progress in the living room. No one even looked at her as she sat down on the arm of the sofa where Dane was sitting. Rusty occupied the armchair beside the window, Hayley sitting cross-legged at his feet. A man in a faded black t-shirt and jeans whom Anya had never seen before was standing in front of the fireplace, holding a lit cigarette, talking. His Manhattan accent reminded her of her high school history teacher, an avowed Marxist who was the butt of endless jokes among his privileged students.

"So, where it went wrong was the security aspect. I know you're thinking, how obvious. But it wasn't at all obvious at the time that this guy, who really had a tremendously acute grasp of explosives manufacture, who'd shown his loyalty and trustworthiness in a whole bunch of different ways, was about to experience a psychotic break. Although it turns out he'd been dismissed from his previous college for just that. This, incidentally, is why there's no such thing as privacy rights in the struggle: It's for everyone's protection. So, part of the purpose of tonight is to make it clear we expect that if you learn something that would make a difference, whether about yourself or somebody else in the group, it needs to be raised. And by 'something' I mean any fact relevant to your decision to put your life in the person's hands. Raise it, raise the thing. There will be discussion. If a decision has to be made, it'll be made. You might not see the relevance to the struggle of who you're related to, who you choose to sleep with or work for or buy your drugs from, but now...especially now...I'm sure you see what I'm saying. No secrets." He laughed.   "No disclosure could possibly piss Yago off as much as withholding will."

Anya suddenly felt filthy with secrets. They all knew where she worked and the position she held, but every specific thing she did at the court, the name of every case, her judge's thinking on the cases, everything was confidential. She could be fired for saying a word to an outsider. The same would be true wherever she might work as a lawyer: Confidentiality was a given. And work was only a beginning. Her family, where they lived: She needed to keep them private. Her medical and psych history: She'd rather jump off the bridge than give it up.

She tried to speak, produced only a grinding sound, cleared her throat and tried again. "So, what's the consequence?" she asked. "For nondisclosure."

"I can't answer that. Depends on the circumstances."

"Well, I totally support this policy because I want to stay alive," Hayley said. "I've seen what happens when people hold back sensitive stuff. One thing Marco didn't say, but of course everyone understands, is that telling eliminates the leverage of a secret. No one can make something out of something that's no longer confidential information. I'm going to bring something to light here, to show my good faith. Rusty and I were lovers a long time ago, back at school."

While Rusty gazed approvingly at Hayley, she looked evenly at Anya, who felt disconnected from them all. She said nothing, certain there was more to follow. When the silence had gone on uncomfortably long, she laughed. "And was anyone going to mention that your relationship seems to have relaunched recently?"

"You practically walked in on us this afternoon," Rusty said. "You already know that. But it doesn't affect you and me."

"Oh, really?"

"Come on, Anya, this is—"

"And anyway," she said, furiously, "aren't we ever going to talk about the bomb?"

Chapter Seven

12:15 p.m., Tuesday, February 9

Sadie stepped hesitantly into the vestibule of St. Declan's, a buzzing cloud of flies the first test of her resolve. The white marble holy water fonts had collected bits of urban detritus, but the tract racks were freshly stocked with the weekly parish bulletin and a variety of pamphlets: "Your Child's Baptism," "Marriage Preparation at St. Declan's," "Rite of Christian Initiation of Adults: Is RCIA for You?" and "St. Declan's Catholic Book Club Selections for Spring." Beyond the inner door lay the dimly lit nave of the church and, at the far end, the sanctuary, where a mass was now being said to a handful of congregants. Squinting at the altar, she thought the dark-haired man in the purple chasuble—she marveled at her memory of the word—must be Liam. She told herself she'd watch from without in order not to disturb the quiet proceedings; in truth, she was afraid the statuary would pitch off their pedestals and the stained-glass windows pop out of the walls if her pagan presence were to breach the sanctity of the ritual.

Unable to hear what the celebrant was saying from her vantage point in the vestibule, his disappearance from the chancel took her by surprise. As the few worshipers—mostly elderly, mostly women—exited their pews, genuflected and then turned and moved toward the doors, she deemed it safe to enter. An organist was playing a meditative theme to the dust motes that were now the only other moving things in the church.

Passing the banks of votive candles at the rear, she walked up the aisle and stood in front of the communion rail, wondering how to get hold of Liam. He'd said only that she should come to the church at this date and time, not where precisely they'd meet. Finally, as she was considering going back outside to phone him, he reappeared in his street clothes and crossed the sanctuary to meet her.

"Sadie, hello." He looked gratified to see her and shook her hand, holding it for a moment. "I'm glad the place didn't scare you off. Shall we go have a sit in my office?" She followed him through the chancel into a warren of small rooms, closets and offices. Apart from a woman working at a computer in one of them, who took no notice of Sadie, they were alone.

His office lay at the end of a narrow hallway. Light filtered through a small, high window. The space not occupied by bookshelves and a high-backed guest chair was filled with a black wooden desk ornamented with Gothic carvings, which looked as though it might have stood in that spot since the construction of the building. Over it hung an incongruously primitive-looking cross of reeds, its arms offset at the corners of a woven central square. He let the door stand open.

"Please sit down." He gestured toward the chair. "St. Brigid's cross," he said, noticing her gaze. "A parishioner was kind enough to bring it back from a trip to Ireland. She's still considered pretty hot there."

Sitting opposite her behind his desk, he waited for her to speak. She searched for the words, wondering if what she needed to say would disturb him, whether this appointment would end with his demanding she leave and never darken the place's doors again.

"It's not every day a non-Catholic makes an appointment with me," he said, gently prompting. "But I like it when they do. Some of the best conversations happen then. You'd be amazed who finds this place."

The pressure of her obsession finally overcame her nerves. "Sometimes I have no idea where I'm going, what I'm doing," she said. That wasn't at all what she'd planned to say, but she could only continue to give voice to the feeling. "It's strange, because a magician's supposed to be all about accomplishing her true will, but the longer I'm in this world, the less I'm sure of. I'm afraid of ruining my son with this...not knowing."

He nodded slowly. "I've never tried to raise a kid, but I hear it's pretty daunting."

His evident sympathy encouraged her to go on. "People worry about the most trivial things—cloth versus paper, getting into the right preschool—but what I can't stand is the thought that I might be guilty of...of moral neglect. Of missing that instant when he needs...something only I can provide him with. And if I'm so confused that I don't know what I'm supposed to be looking for, how can I ever get it right for him? The minute after he was born and I looked at him for the first time, all I could think was how opaque, how unknowable, how separate and inscrutable he is. I'm sorry," she said, wiping tears away with the back of her hand. "I'm the most unnatural mother."

"These are pretty high-level fears," he said. "And so, the ways you used to manage all this seem not to be working anymore; is that right?"

"I don't know if they ever did. Magic is supposed to help you develop vision and strength and whatever, but I...I tried like forever to get it and...."

"Get what, exactly?"

"Knowledge and conversation of my holy guardian angel," she replied. At his look of surprise, she added, "It's an old-fashioned term signifying a certain level of...you might call it enlightenment, or self-realization, or something like that. It's not the ultimate magical attainment, that would be more like becoming a bodhisattva, but it's supposed to happen somewhere along the line and you're supposed to be in conscious contact with your own divine nature."

"Your own divine nature? But people are so changeable."

"That's it, that's the problem. I can't get any kind of handle on myself. It doesn't help that 'Do what thou wilt shall be the whole of the Law.' Not at all. It's terrifying. It doesn't mean 'do whatever you want'; it's more like 'let everyone do their true will without interference,' but still."

He shook his head. "The way you're describing magic, it sounds sort of like Buddhism. Not quite what I imagined."

"There's a lot of Buddhism in the kind of magic I was taught. But, honestly, I'm a fallen-away magician. I barely go through the motions." She wanted to tell him about the failed sex magic ritual, but felt sure he'd find it beyond the pale.

"Is your husband—"

"We're not married. That's the other awful thing."

"I'm sorry, of course. So, he doesn't want to get married? Or can't?"

"No, quite the opposite. He asks me every day. I feel like a horrible person, but I just can't marry him."

"Are you already married to someone else?"

She laughed. "I've never been married, never thought I'd find someone who wanted me, but...."

"You don't love him." He said it gently, without judgment.

She hung her head, tears filling her eyes. "I loved him so much—or thought I did, when it was just a fantasy. He was my boss; he was married and miserable. One night we...we overindulged and wound up almost having sex in the office."

"Almost?"

"Long story. We were interrupted, and it became a minor scandal. He's a very eminent judge, far above anything I could ever aspire to, professionally. But he...he's also...I hate saying negative things about him."

"I can see you care a lot about him, but you've discovered he's not perfect."

"This is like under the seal of the confessional, right? The thing is, he's an alcoholic. And he's, if not an actual drug addict, at risk of becoming one. I know there are plenty of alcoholics and addicts who manage to get clean and sober. And he has—for short periods—but I don't know if or when he'll ever really commit to it. One day I came home and found him passed out drunk next to the baby. I mean, that's the line I just won't cross. I grew up in a home, if you could call it a home, where I wasn't safe because of drugs and alcohol and abuse and...he's not like my mother, not at all, but I realized at that point I can't trust him—I want to, but I can't—and I just cannot marry him. I should leave, but it's so hard. I'm afraid it'll make his addiction worse. I know that's stupid—if I can't make it better, I can't make it worse, either—but I know it'll cause him pain."

"Wow, I'm sorry. No wonder you feel so conflicted."

"God, no, *I'm* sorry. You're probably wondering what all this has to do with you. I've been...looking for something. Wondering if I can find the strength to do what I need to do by getting closer to God. If there's some way for me to do that, I mean, if I could somehow find out what God wants for me. And I keep thinking of this place."

"You mean the Church?"

"I suppose I see it as a shelter against the storm. Maybe that's a fantasy, too."

"You're too smart to expect instant peace of mind, but, you know, there's a lot here." He laughed. "I don't want to sound like I'm trying to sell you a 24 Hour Fitness membership or something, but...I'm sorry, I interrupted you."

"It's just that this would be another slap. He's a cradle Catholic who studied philosophy. He's probably considered himself an atheist since high school."

"A slap to him if you become a Catholic, you mean?"

"Is that even possible? I must be anathema."

"Sure, it's possible. And no, you're not anathema. But I should mention, next time you come here—you will come back, won't you?—be sure and ask for me. Not all priests will talk to occultists. Father Bridges would probably throw you out if he knew your background."

"Seriously? Thanks for the warning. I'll be sure to leave my pentagram at home. I feel like I've outgrown it at this point anyway, and I should give it away, but Conal gave it to me." She paused, thinking of the silver and moonstone symbol she'd worn so often and lately set aside. She stood. "Thank you, Father. Talking with you has been...really freeing."

He smiled. "Do call me Liam."

"And yes, I'd like to come back. I'll sneak out of the house on Sunday. Say I'm going out to get cigarettes, and come to mass instead. Bad joke—I don't smoke."

"On the other hand, he'd certainly sit up and take notice. But a straightforward conversation's probably a better idea."

"I know. Thank you, Liam. Talking with you has been so reassuring. Maybe there's hope for me, after all? Anyway, I'd like to talk with you again."

He rose and came around his desk, and his big hands clasped hers. "I say the eleven o'clock mass every Sunday, if you want to catch me."

Walking along Fifth away from St. Declan's, she felt an interior lightness and spaciousness that was all new, and that seemed to beam onto and transform the urban streetscape into bright potentiality everywhere she looked. Liam had been kind, as she'd have expected of any decent priest, but what amazed her was that he'd understood, even as incoherently as she'd expressed herself. He seemed to appreciate the difficulty of her situation and had even invited her to come and talk with him again—she hadn't expected that. He'd allayed her fear that Catholicism was a place forever prohibited to her, but had exerted no pressure, even though he must think ceremonial magic a shady place to linger in. She felt blissfully grateful and, now that he'd lowered the barriers, eager to talk with him again.

Chapter Eight

2:00 p.m., Tuesday, February 9

The electric harmony of the Bell of the 'Loin carried over the sounds of sirens, delivery trucks, and hip-hop wafting from the open windows of cars in passing traffic. Tad Laker ground his cigarette into the cracked, stained sidewalk, entered Peace Current Methodist Church, home of the Bell, and filed down to the basement with the other addicts for the two o'clock meeting of Narcotics Anonymous. They all took seats on the mismatched folding chairs; it was unfortunate the meeting was too small to offer refreshments, because he'd been struggling with hunger and caffeine deprivation since awakening an hour earlier. The secretary called the meeting to order, welcoming the handful of veterans and the new face or two, and invited an elderly man named Pete to read the preamble.

The old dude's reedy tenor recited the words they'd all memorized: "Narcotics Anonymous is a fellowship of men and women who share their experience, strength and hope with each other that they may solve their common problem...."

Tad's attention was already wandering. Scanning the room, he saw that his sponsor—or temporary sponsor; the guy had insisted, as a condition of agreeing to take him on, that he keep looking for a sponsor with more sobriety—again wasn't in attendance. This irritated and frightened him a little; he'd been looking forward to the chance of being treated to a coffee, listened to, and maybe fed at one of the cheap Vietnamese restaurants in the neighborhood; the chance of that was gone now. And whenever an expected face fails to materialize at a regular meeting, the thought of relapse crosses every recovering addict's mind. Nothing scarier, nothing upends the foundations quicker, than your sponsor going out and using.

Then again, Con wasn't your typical sponsor. He hadn't said exactly what he did for a living, but Tad had seen him walk down Lamden Street after meetings and go into the state building, so maybe he was some kind of bureaucrat, except he had a sense of humor. He dressed well, not flashy but tastefully, and when not laying the Big Book on him was always quoting ancient philosophers; once, he'd given Tad a book on the Stoics. He didn't talk much about his Higher Power or anything too overtly religious; that was one of the things Tad liked best about him. Tad didn't care to be hit over the head with dogma; a certain amount of it was inescapable in the program, but he never went out of his way to encounter it.

Pete was now reciting the Twelve Steps, and Tad tried to focus. Con had said something about working the Eighth Step with him—"Made a list of all persons we had harmed, and became willing to make amends to them all." Tad wondered how he was even supposed to remember who to put on the list, since he reckoned most of the harm he'd ever done had happened while he was too strung out to remember. That was just one of the questions he needed to ask Con.

He slipped out to the street to phone the number Con had given him, telling himself he should show a care for somebody else for a change and maybe, just maybe, Con could use a call from a fellow drug addict right now. But his voice mail picked up, and Tad's anger flared irrationally. Was Con even working the program anymore? You could see the guy was a high bottom junkie, if he was even one at all. "Con, it's your sponsee. Tad. Missed you at the two o'clock at Peace Current. Where the hell are you? Just called to see if you're okay. Well, call me, aight? I'm stuck on the Eighth Step and I need your help. You did do an Eighth Step, right? Okay, talk to you later. Keep coming back, it works if you work it." Mouthing the slogan, he hoped Con would be able to detect the irony in his voice.

Taking a closer look at his phone, he noticed he had a voice mail of his own. Could it be a business opportunity at last? "Hi...Tad? Saw your listing in the Clarion and was wondering if you're available for...escort services tonight. I'm at the Wentworth, sort of at the dodgy end of the theater district...but then you probably already know where it is, right? Hey, maybe you could call and let me know your availability. I'm at 322-119-6642. Oh, and my name is...Fred. Hope to see you later, eh?"

Hallelujah! he thought. *A commercial traveler, and Canadian, by the sound of him. Bound to have wads o' cash burning a hole in his pocket. Well, some of that sweet moolah's gonna be mine tonight. Better go get cleaned up. He sounds cute, too.* Phone at his ear, walking briskly back to his room at a hotel considerably more downscale than his date's, he said, "Hi, Fred? Got your voice mail. You ready for a good time?"

Having a plan for the evening took his mind off heroin for a little while. In the shower, he kept reminding himself the fee would keep the roof over his head; a night on the street for lack of rent money was never far away. After showering, he considered and ultimately decided against shaving, settled on a black T-shirt and jeans, polished his cowboy boots, and pulled on his leather jacket. He waited at the corner outside his hotel for a bus, then watched as three, crush-loaded, passed him by. It was that time of day, next to impossible to catch a bus unless you boarded closer to either end, and he decided to walk to the Wentworth. The boots, secondhand, pinched, but he supposed he'd have plenty of money for a cab home after.

Fred had said he was in room 818, and Tad wasted no time finding it. The hotel was laid out in a big circle, and he walked the entire circuit of the eighth floor before realizing 818 was in close proximity to where he'd gotten off the elevator. When he finally spotted it, the door was standing open a hand's breadth, country rock music playing softly within. He pushed it open and entered what appeared to be a corporate suite, the inoffensively decorated living room and a kitchenette immediately visible, the bedroom apparently off the short hallway in the back.

"Fred? Hey, it's Tad. You here? Taking a shower, maybe? I'll just make myself comfortable, wait for you." He pulled the door closed and sat down on the sofa, then stood again, sidling up to the kitchenette, where a bag of Cheetos spilled onto the counter beside a two-liter bottle of Coke. Helping himself, he tried to eat silently. Satisfied after a few moments' snacking with still no appearance by his date, he spritzed himself with breath spray and cleared his throat.

"Dude, hey, everything okay back there?" Still no response. "Hey, uh, you need any help? Hey, I'm just gonna see what's up, aight? Now, don't freak out, I'm harmless." He walked toward the bedroom, hoping Fred didn't pack heat, then figured with airport security these days he was probably safe.

The bedroom door stood ajar; the room was dark, blackout drapes drawn against the afternoon sun. "Fred?" In the dimness, he could see only that the bed seemed to have been used, and at last flipped the light switch.

"Aw, fuck."

The poor sod had started partying a little ahead of him. There was a regular pharmacy on the bedside table, and Fred, or whatever his real name was, was lying on the bed, a piece of latex still tied around his upper arm. Tad didn't have to look hard to see that Fred had stopped breathing. He was short, a bit overweight, and balding; not quite as cute as his voice, or maybe it was the way death de-animates everyone's features; but Tad nevertheless felt they could have had a good time together. "Calgary's gonna miss you," he said quietly to what was left of Fred.

Even as his superego told him not to touch anything, the id in his hands was sweeping the pills into his pockets. His forty-two days of recovery clamored, *Remember us?*, while he stuffed a paper bag he found on the floor next to the bed with the syringes and narcotics littering the top of the desk in the corner of the room. He told himself it was for the folks back in Winnipeg, so they wouldn't have to learn how far into addiction their late lamented boy had sunk. Once he'd thus cleaned up, he pulled a tissue out of the box in the bathroom and wiped down everything he'd touched. Then he was out of 818, waiting to catch the elevator as the music continued to drift out into the corridor.

Back in the dingy precincts of his own crib, Tad paused to take an inventory, literal in the case of the drugs and figurative in that of his sobriety. Evidently Fred hadn't planned to do much sightseeing, as he'd accumulated a week's worth of multiple psychoactive substances for himself and several companions. There were vials of Nembutal, Seconal and Xanax, Adderall and Benzedrine; a baggie of crystal, small in quantity but evidently high in quality; a bunch of blotter papers representing a good two dozen acid trips; and several bindles of what looked like it might be reasonably fine heroin. The stuff had serious street value. Or it could supply a fabulous party for a day and a night. Or it could stock a rockin' personal medicine cabinet.

But what about his forty-two days? It had been harder than a motherfucker to kick the stuff the last time; he didn't have the strength to even think about doing it again. Starting to use again would, in all likelihood, lead him sooner or later down the same path where poor old Fred ended up. And, of greater immediate significance, he was on probation. Practically speaking, the cops could go through his shit any time they wanted. Not being a lawyer, he didn't know exactly what his exposure was with all this stuff in his possession, but they'd no doubt try to prove he was selling, and that would mean big time in the big house for sure. He needed Con's advice more than ever.

Chapter Nine

7:00 p.m., Tuesday, February 9

One in the living room, another in the kitchen, and yet a third in the master bathroom. Glossy brochures depicting gravid young women in floral sundresses, radiant with happiness, ecstatic shirtless men palming neonates like softballs, slumbering pink infants swaddled like burritos in crocheted blankets. Discreet slogans and italicized testimonials. Allan Hetford felt a word cloud forming in his head—'fertility' and 'baby' in the biggest font of all—and began to hyperventilate.

Eleanor had been dropping these and other hints for weeks, ever since the night Quirke and Sadie and their child had come to dinner. Though he'd pretended to be oblivious to her reaction, there was no mistaking the longing in her eyes as she watched the young mother nursing the little fellow, or the eagerness with which she accepted Sadie's offer to hold him. He'd even caught her gazing bemusedly at Quirke, as if wondering what life might have been like had she gone ahead and procreated with him when she had the chance. The very idea of begetting a child sent shivers down Hetford's spine. Yet making Eleanor happy had become the *summum bonum* of his existence, and he knew he was powerless to deny her this thing if she was really determined to do it.

He heard her footstep on the stair and turned toward her as she entered their bedroom. At the sight of him, her face bloomed with the enraptured smile that said, so improbably, that she thought him the most wonderful thing that had ever happened to her. All evidence to the contrary notwithstanding, including his malicious and very nearly successful mischief against Quirke's retention campaign during the election a little more than a year previously, she believed him to be a great and good man. She even had his father-in-law, Gene Scorchner, the CEO and Hetford's boss at Marvelocity Industries, believing it as well. Only too aware of how close he'd come to disgrace over his conduct, and of how absurdly fortune had rewarded him despite his wrongdoing, Hetford had dedicated himself to living up to Eleanor's image of him. He'd resigned from the court and devoted his legal acumen to the tireless furtherance of Gene's business interests, joined more nonprofit boards and dispensed more tax-deductible donations than he could count, and dedicated body as well as soul to her joy and fulfillment. He'd put his own interests far below hers on the to-do list of life, with the predictable result that he no longer had the taut, sleek, soigné look of the bachelor Hetford.

Instead, as he daily observed in diminishing dismay, he looked like what he was: a balding, slightly overweight, thoroughly domesticated middle-aged general counsel who happened to adore his wife.

She now threw her arms around him and kissed him just like the first time. "How was your day, darling? Did that antitrust clearance you were telling me about come through?"

He rolled his eyes. "Turns out there are a few glitches with the Zigmobi merger. As I told Gene, we really ought to withdraw and refile the Hart-Scott-Rodino report. It'll save time in the end, but it wasn't what he wanted to hear. I'm afraid I'm not his favorite person today."

"I'll sort him out. Daddy ought to remember you're the legal expert."

"No need for you to get involved, dearest." As she had lain down on the bed and begun smoothing the duvet in gestures of invitation, he cleared his throat. "Aren't we expected somewhere tonight?"

"I sent our regrets to Clyde and Rowena."

"Why? I thought you—"

"I wanted to have a little talk."

"With me?" Where had that squeak in his voice come from?

"Of course, with you. Honey, do you mind?" She got up and gestured toward a tufted chair in front of her dressing table; he sat upon it, his gaze alternating between her sylphlike form in her columnar white dress and his reflection, pale and perspiring over his shirt collar, in the mirror.

"I know you've noticed the literature," she began, "and it's so considerate of you to let me bring it up in my own way."

He tried to manage a smile. "You mustn't feel compelled—"

"But I do feel a compulsion. Not from you, of course, but...have you ever known, just *known*, you were meant to have something? And that you needed to have it *now*?"

There was a time when he'd felt that way about his Tesla, but what she was talking about was orders of magnitude more significant. With no aftermarket to speak of. He could only nod apprehensively.

"Because I don't seem to be getting any younger, no matter how much laser resurfacing I have done." She averted her eyes, frowning.

"Nonsense, you're the most sublime woman under the sun, of any age," he said, taking her hand in his.

"Allan, darling! You're cold. Let me get you a sweater."

"I'm fine. R-really."

She looked searchingly into his eyes. "Allan, I want a baby."

His stomach lurched. "Dearest, are you sure—?"

"I know it'll change everything. And everything's already perfect. But somehow—it defies logic—but I know everything will be even more perfect. With a baby." When he remained silent, she brushed her hand against his cheek. "I suppose this might seem to come out of the blue," she began.

"Not entirely," he said. "I could see how deeply you were affected by the sight of Quirke's little lad nursing at his mother's breast the other night." Did that sound like an admission he'd spent the night ogling Sadie's tit? Perhaps he could rephrase it. "It's remarkable to see what happens when the last people you thought were parent material have a baby."

"Yes! That's exactly what I was thinking," she said. "And what our friends could be saying about us in a year or so, seeing us with a baby of our own."

"Dearest, a few questions occur to me. You're—"

"I know, Allan, I'm almost 50—past the age when these things happen without significant tech support. But you read about women older than I having babies all the time. There was the one in Spain—wasn't she well over 60?"

"You're—" He'd been about to say she was so gorgeously, perpetually, rigorously in shape that he could scarcely imagine her body swollen with child. Fortunately, he was thinking fast enough to be able to avoid implying he thought she'd look ugly pregnant. "So, you've ruled out surrogacy? I mean, dearest, the physical ordeal—"

"I haven't ruled anything out," she said flatly, raising a shudder in him. She was dead serious. "I want a baby. By any means necessary." She gazed at him, her grip on his hand tightening.

He swallowed. "I—"

Her eagerness to hear him echo her desire was palpable. And yet he'd never imagined himself a father, never envisioned a tyke toddling next to him, calling him "Daddy" in a tot's duck voice. The idea of becoming a parent had always seemed too much like death: a forced ceding of territory, a visible acknowledgment that his time on life's stage was nearing its final act as his successors, who would someday lay him cold in the ground, grew up and claimed the world he and his cohort had in the same fashion wrested away from their fathers. But it wasn't as if not reproducing would spare him that fate. If anything, he supposed, a childless man died more definitively dead. And since he'd had the great good fortune to marry a woman with the dream and determination of making a child with him, he concluded, why fight it? If Quirke could do it...

"You'd make a wonderful mother," he said at last. "Absolutely wonderful. But...don't you have a thousand questions?"

"Not really," she said airily. "Of course, they'll come up, and when they do, we'll find experts to answer them. People have been doing this for a while." She sat on his lap, slipped off his necktie, and began to unbutton his shirt, all while kissing the top of his head.

Thoughts of something related to but distinct from parenthood were now straining urgently to be acted on.

Later, as they lay together in bed, Eleanor gently stroking his flank, Hetford brought up the subject that had now begun to obsess him. "Do you think we might just have—"

"I asked my doctor," she said. "He gave me an FSH—follicle stimulating hormone—test and said the chances of me conceiving naturally were extremely remote. I'm sorry, Allan."

She looked so forlorn he enclosed her tightly in his arms. "There, there. We can fix this. That is, there's a fix if you're certain, really certain—"

"Do you mean it? Of course, I'm—"

"—Certain you could curtail our little getaways, put up with the colic and fussing and teething—not to mention the diapers—"

"We'll have nannies, of course."

"Of course, but in the end...in the end there'll only be the two of us...and the child. And sometimes, I understand, they don't turn out quite as one anticipated."

"I want a little boy who looks just like you," she whispered, squeezing him around the middle.

Any lingering resistance Hetford was feeling melted, her want becoming his, but he deemed it prudent not to reveal this as yet. Instead he said, "Perhaps we should borrow a baby for a day or two, just to be sure having one around suits us. And that we suit a baby."

"That's a fantastic idea," she said. "But how? Everybody we know who had kids has sent them off to college already."

"I'll give it some thought. Maybe we could babysit for someone at the office."

"Darling," she cooed, "you're the Tower of Pisa."

Chapter Ten

3:10 p.m., Tuesday, February 9

On the bench, it had become clear that Sophia Rackrent was determined to wrest the crown for most long-winded questioning from the hands of her predecessor, Allan Hetford. Three times during a single argument she'd interrupted counsel, and once even Justice Farley, to interpose queries of unparalleled tediousness and tangential relevance. Quirke was forced to keep pinching his right forefinger with a medium-sized Acco clip to stop himself from interrupting her right back. Glancing surreptitiously over at the Chief, he saw on her face only her typical engaged impassivity and thought, not for the first time and not without admiration, *A Chief out of central casting*. Finally, he could bear Rackrent's numbing interrogation no longer and leaned into his mic to cut to the chase.

"Counsel, I think what Justice Rackrent is asking, far more eloquently than I ever could, is, what is the rule you want us to adopt?"

At the podium, appellant's counsel looked at him with the gratitude of an explorer toward a kindly native chieftain who has just fished her out of a pool of quicksand, and launched into the argument she'd prepared.

Now it was the Chief who interrupted, saying, "Counsel, you're out of time, but you may answer Justice Quirke's question." A few minutes later, counsel submitted and the Chief adjourned the session.

Back in his chambers, Quirke shed his robe and checked his voice mail. Sadie had called to inquire when he'd be home that evening; she knew he'd spent the day on the bench and would forgive a quick text message reply before he went to conference the cases with the rest of the court in the Chief's chambers. Then Tad had called to ask why he hadn't shown up at the 2:00 NA meeting, after having told him they'd work the Eighth Step together. In fact, Quirke had simply forgotten about oral argument when he'd made the plan, but promised himself he would call back to reschedule with Tad as soon as he had a minute. Quirke's reservations persisted about having agreed to be Tad's temporary NA sponsor when his own sobriety was manifestly so tenuous. Of late, a chronic, low-level, edgy dissatisfaction plagued him more often than not; memories of the bliss of the first few drinks of the day, the euphoria of his first experience with heroin, even the last hit off his last spliff, periodically flashed back in hallucinatory temptation. Getting clean and sober had been the best thing he'd ever done, except perhaps having Ruairí, although of course having Ruairí, and most likely having Sadie in his life, too, would have been impossible had he not given up getting wasted. His pink cloud now dissipated, he wondered how he was going to keep saying no for the rest of his life. "A day at a time," Bobby always said. He ought to give Bobby a call, too, but he was due back in the Chief's chambers in less than two minutes.

Tad had left a second voice mail, and this one left him staring open-mouthed at his well-ordered office.

"Con, Con." Tad sounded out of breath. "You won't fucking believe this. I went to meet a guy…a date…and he was fucking cold, man. As in deceased. Poor fuck overdosed. He had this huge stash sitting right there in the hotel room, out in the open, man, and, like, I don't know what I was really thinking but I found myself scooping the shit up, stuffing it in my pockets and zipping the fuck out of there. So, like, you want to party? No, no. Just kidding, but, you know, I don't know what to do. It ain't a great idea for me to be holding this shit. I got forty-two days. I'm on searchable probation. What the fuck should I do? I gotta talk to you. Call me, aight? Like now? Please, I need my sponsor. Right. Now."

"Holy shit," said Quirke involuntarily. In the small office adjacent, he heard his assistant, Margie, pause in her filing. He moved to the door and pulled it closed, tapping his phone to redial.

"Tad? Con."

"Man, thank you."

"Sorry I couldn't make it to the meeting. Where are you?"

"Back in my room."

"So, who—"

"Like I said, a date. He was an out-of-towner, a Canuck, I think. I only talked to him once, on the phone. By the time I got to his room, he was…aren't you going to ask if I was traumatized by seeing him like that?"

"I already know the answer. Have you used any of it?"

"Somehow, miraculously, no. Can you—"

The absurdity of the suggestion made Quirke laugh. The Commission on Judicial Behavior had disciplined him once before for considerably milder misbehavior, and he could kiss his career goodbye if he were to come anywhere near Tad's stash. He shouldn't even be talking about any of this. "No," he interrupted, "I can't take it off your hands. I just can't. Don't even ask."

"But what am I—"

"You say you're on probation? You had a lawyer in that case?"

"Yeah. She wasn't worth sh—"

"She might not have been Clarence Darrow, but she can give you advice right now. Call her."

"Well, as it happens, I did. I mean, I tried. She's on vacation."

"Was this the PD?"

"Do I dress like I can afford to hire my own lawyer?"

"Well, look, they've got about a hundred deputies, they can spare somebody to talk to you."

"That's right. But not till a week from Thursday."

"Shit."

"You can say that again. Just tell me, Con, what would you do if you were in my position?"

A raft of sanctimonious thoughts floated through Quirke's mind, but in the end he knew there was a nonzero chance he'd have grabbed the stash on his way out of the dead guy's room himself. The point now was to help Tad extricate himself. "This isn't legal advice I'm giving you, but there's a lot to be said for flushing."

"I don't know, Con." Tad's dramatic sigh came across clearly.

"What do you mean, you don't know? You know you don't want to be the slave of dope again, right?"

"I know, man, it's just...okay, well, for one thing, I'm in a shared-bath situation here. People are going to think I got a nasty bug if I'm in the can long enough to dispose of all this shit."

"Jesus Christ, just how much—never mind. Look, you could flush in stages. All right, if flushing's not practicable, put it in a paper bag and toss it in the trash outside. The point is you need to lose that stuff." When there was no immediate response, Quirke asked, "Tad? You still there?"

"You're totally right, Con. Your judgment is spot on. I'll do what you say."

"So, you'll—"

"I'll get rid of it."

"By—?"

"Look, I'll do it. Okay?"

It was Quirke's turn to sigh. He could go round and round with Tad indefinitely, but there was no way to verify his actions over the phone, and Quirke was late for conference already.

"Okay. Text me when it's done. So, we'll talk next Wednesday after the 2:00?"

"Sure, you bet. Hey, thanks for pulling my feet back down to the ground."

"And right after you get rid of the shit, you go find yourself a meeting and a real sponsor."

"Spoken like a real sponsor. Thanks, and see you soon, okay, man?'

"Remember to text me."

Tad's predicament drove all thoughts of Sadie out of his mind, and he grabbed his benchbook and dashed up the stairs to the Chief's conference room without having responded to her voice mail. Once again, he felt he'd gotten in over his head being involved in what he still insisted to himself was a purely provisional, mutual self-help relationship with Tad. On the bright side, talking to him, thinking of the various imperfect ways the scenario could spin out, knocked the romance out of mind-altering substances for him, at least temporarily.

The Chief looked up with mild irritation as he walked in, as did all his colleagues save Sophia Rackrent, who seemed immersed in a well-worn copy of Alvin Plantinga's *Warranted Christian Belief*. "My apologies," he said. "Urgent call."

"Before we begin," said the Chief, "Ward tells me Marcus Dormund's lawyers just filed a habeas corpus petition. Ward has some other information to share with us as well."

Quirke hadn't noticed Ward Freitag, the Clerk-Administrator of the Court, sitting in a guest chair at a respectful distance from the conference table. The court never had an audience for its postargument conferences, and past practice dictated that Ward deliver his message and depart, so the justices in turn might confer on the cases and wrap up their business for the day.

Ward rose and approached the conference table. "So, as the Chief indicated, Dormund's attorneys filed a petition on his behalf this afternoon. It's 472 pages long, with nine volumes of exhibits. It appears to present an assortment of claims centering on some allegedly newly discovered evidence."

"Whose is it?" Justice Wiggins asked. No justice currently at the court had been serving when Dormund's initial appeal had been decided.

"Justice Kroner inherited the case from his predecessor. The central staff has offered its assistance, should it be needed. As you're probably aware, the U.S. Supreme Court denied cert in Dormund's federal litigation, and not quite a month ago the superior court set an execution date—February 25th. A little over two weeks from today."

"You have your work cut out for you, Ted," Justice Corcoran said as

Justice Kroner groaned.

"We can stay the execution if we have to," Quirke noted.

Justice Farley shook his head. "That's the last thing we want to do. It'll only encourage them to bring these frivolous petitions at the last minute."

Quirke's unsettled mood wouldn't permit him to let it go. "We won't know if it's frivolous until we've—"

The Chief intervened. "Anything else, Ward?"

"We need to know whether to ask the Attorney General to file a response to the petition. Justice Kroner?"

The most senior associate justice scowled. "Dormund's been here twice before. If staff can't look at one of these things and tell whether or not it's got any merit without the AG's help, then we need new staff."

"So, should our office let the AG know no response is requested?" Ward asked.

"That would be nice, Ward, thanks." The Chief nodded, and Freitag left the room.

Chapter Eleven

10:30 p.m., Wednesday, February 10

Long after sunset, the living room had grown dark but for street light filtering through the windows and ambient cigarette haze. Yet they lingered, Rusty at one end of the sofa, Dane on his laptop at the other, and Anya on the floor at Rusty's feet, a cup of cold green tea beside her. Rusty was focusing his attention on her in a way he hadn't for many days, yet this was not entirely comforting. "So, you'll be there the night of?" he asked her again. "You'll have access to him?"

Anya nodded, irritated at his repetitive interrogation. She wasn't yet sure how she'd unobtrusively gain access to Justice Quirke on the night of the execution. She knew he'd be at the court, like all the other justices, and to ensure her own presence wouldn't be questioned she'd volunteered to assist her own judge despite her inexperience with capital cases. She needed only a pretext to be in Quirke's immediate presence, and to get him to the street outside the state building, at the appointed time.

Rusty pressed her. "So, you're going to, what, just hang around his office at 7:15? Go in and chat?"

"Something like that," she said, glad her face was too deeply shadowed for him to see the uncertainty she knew she must be registering.

"We need a more solid plan. Get him to let his guard down, go out and eat with him," Rusty said. "This is no time to get all anorexic. Hell, fuck him in the courtroom if that's what it takes. Didn't he do that with his last clerk?"

"I wish you'd stop saying I'm anorexic," she said. "And there's certainly no need to fuck him. I mean, the idea's...repulsive. I—I'll just find out which of his staff is there that night and—and get myself invited out with them." Saying it made it sound so easy.

"That sounds better. We're not talking, like, bodyguard-size staff, are we?"

Anya tried to visualize each of the Quirke staff attorneys. She remembered none as being particularly intimidating-looking. "That won't be an issue."

"Not martial-arts experts, are they?"

"I wouldn't know. But they certainly won't be expecting—Look, I have no control over who's there that night, but I'll carry out my end of it.

Is everything else going to be set?"

For the first time, Rusty questioned Dane. "Will the device be ready?"

Their comrade nodded. "Anya," he asked, between clicks, "did you bring me that book?"

"It's in my backpack. I'll get it."

She got up, turned on a lamp to light her way, and from the bedroom retrieved the fat volume of the second series of the Federal Reporter she'd taken from the judicial branch's law library. Stealing it had proved trivially easy, since the library was thinly staffed and nearly deserted most of the time, they'd apparently never needed to put electronic tags in the books, and security never checked people leaving the building. Back in the living room, she handed it to Dane.

"This'll be perfect," he said. "Thanks."

His was the first thanks she'd received since they'd begun this operation. "You're welcome," she replied. "How do you make a space for the thing?"

"The bomb, you mean? Basically, you glue a few pages to the front cover for the lid, paint glue all around the outside to make it like a solid box, and after the glue sets you measure an inch from the margins all the way around the top page, take your Exacto knife, and just cut through as deep as you need it to go. This is a good size; there'll be plenty of room inside. I can make you a book safe, too, if you get me another book."

"Oh, no—I didn't mean—thanks anyway," she said. The idea of ruining a book, especially a repository of law, merely to store possessions disturbed her.

"One thing I've wondered," Dane said, "is why Quirke. I mean, of all of them, how was he picked?"

Anya drew in her breath, but was surprised when, instead of cross-examining Dane, or questioning his loyalty, Rusty blandly answered. "He's the one everybody's heard of. Taking him will have the biggest impact, no pun intended. You know, people, this project is a way for us to stop the death penalty. We have the power to kill it, here and now. Think about that: Never again will an innocent person be executed in this state. No waiting and wondering if the voters are capable of resisting the reactionary tough-on-crime arguments, come election time, and end it themselves. Other states are gonna follow. And our stature's gonna go up, way up, in the International when we manage to do what no one's been able to do in this state in forty years. You remember what Hayley said? How Yago was very impressed? And this is just the beginning. When the people see an example of direct action like this, how can they not be inspired? Public ownership of utilities, single-payer universal health care, worker ownership of business enterprises—one by one, the parasites are bound to die, be killed, disappear, or be transformed. Buddy, you'll be able to tell your grandchildren you were there in the beginning."

"Yeah, but do you really think the Governor's going to commute all the sentences—Anya, there are, what, nearly 800 people on death row at this point? Do you think one action's going to move the needle that much?"

"It'll be one pretty dramatic action. Anyway, I thought you were down with the plan." Rusty, chagrined, jumped to his feet and began to pace, his feet blindly striking the legs of chairs and tables in the dark. Anya could only marvel that he'd engaged with Dane's doubts this long; if she'd been the one voicing them, he'd have shut her down, ridiculed her, painted her as a spoiled bourgeois, despite all her sacrifices. She wished he could see himself, see how badly he was treating her. She, without whom this action that was going to lift them above all the other extreme left-wing groups could not occur. She knew he could imagine her performing badly but not refusing to perform at all. When, exactly, had he become so certain of her?

She stood again and looked at the darkness where their faces were. "I'm going to bed," she said, tentatively.

Dane stopped keyboarding and shook his head. "Man, it's just...with the magnitude of the risk, I wanted to see if you really believe in it yourself."

"Never doubt it, dude, never doubt."

Chapter Twelve

1:00 p.m., Thursday, February 11

Delivering the draft opinion in *People v. Hargreaves* to Justice Latimore, Sadie's heart began to accelerate. "Mind if I take the afternoon off, Judge? I'll mark it down as a half day of vacation."

The judge looked over his reading glasses and nodded. "Thanks, Sadie. You've earned a break; see you tomorrow. Say hi to Quirke for me."

"Will do," she assented, though she forgot his request even before she powered down her computer. Moments later she was breezing out of the state building, striding south toward Market Street and beyond, to the rectory at St. Declan's. She was largely oblivious to the unsavory aspects of the neighborhood, and happiness quickened her footsteps to a pace that few of the broken-down street folk she passed could have matched even had they wanted to accost her. Since Ruairí came along, she'd rarely experienced the luxury of attending only to her own desires, and the anticipation of this appointment made trivial the fleeting selfishness of naps and shopping trips to which she'd limited her self-indulgence. Her last talk with Liam had lifted her mood for days. She was sure it had helped her relate better to Conal and be a better mother to Ruairí. Really, she was doing everybody a favor by seeing him.

The noon mass had ended a half hour earlier, so she bent her path toward the rectory office and asked after him. The receptionist, who took no particular interest in her (she must not come across as being obviously one of those disreputable occultists, she thought happily), rang Liam's office.

"Please have a seat," the receptionist said, after a moment. "His line is busy, but I've left him a message." She resumed folding bulletins.

Panic filled her mind. Could he have forgotten? She was only a tiny part of his world, after all. *Breathe*, she reminded herself. Waiting for him, she studied the photographic portraits of St. Declan's last six pastors, hanging on the office walls. Redoubtable men all, especially the incumbent, Father Bridges; she fancied him the type who in an earlier era would have considered it his duty to burn her at the stake.

She stifled a giggle, converting it into a cough, as the receptionist glanced at her. At last she heard the footsteps she was already coming to know, and tried to look serenely pleased rather than eager to see him.

"Sorry to have kept you waiting, but we've had a death in the parish this week, and the family needed to check in about the funeral. My office is this way," he said, leading her past the receptionist toward the interior of the building. "Same room, but you came a different way last time."

"You're sure I'm not taking up too much of your time?" she asked once they'd sat down under St. Brigid's cross, desperately hoping he'd reassure her to the contrary.

His reaction was gratifying. "I'm never parsimonious with time when it comes to converts. I was like you, once, searching."

"You're a convert? What were you before?" she asked, thinking she could have phrased it more elegantly.

"Full-Bore Church of God and Jesus," he said. "I'd be amazed if you'd heard of it. It's a tiny little Pentecostal church in the south." She must have looked a little doubtful, for he continued, "Whatever you're thinking, you're probably right. Snake-handling, relentless bible study, speaking in tongues. When I was thirteen—"

The rest was overwhelmed by an ear-piercing fire alarm. He rolled his eyes, then reached across the desk to take her hand and pull her to her feet, yelling, "Let's get out of here."

The receptionist and sacristan were standing in the office, looking exasperated. "Third time this week," the former complained. "Father Bridges had the alarm company out yesterday."

"Well, they're going to have to make another trip," Liam shouted. "I'm taking my appointment outside."

Once they had turned up Fifth Street and put some distance between themselves and the blaring noise, he slowed his pace to something closer to hers. "Are you up for a walk? I wouldn't mind burning a little energy."

"I'd love to," she said; she wouldn't have turned down any suggestion he might have made. "You were starting to tell me something about when you were thirteen?"

He smiled. "You're paying attention. I was about to say that's when I spoke in tongues for the first time."

"That's amazing. So, is there a particular vocabulary or syntax or grammar when you speak in tongues, or is it all sort of like the linguistic version of a prime number?"

He laughed as they ran across Market Street as the walk sign flashed a warning. "It's actually Dothraki."

"What? Wow, that's—very funny."

"Now it is, but there was a lot of pressure on each of us to do it at one point or another. Having to fake speaking in tongues was one of the main things that drove me to leave Pentecostalism. I'm not saying everybody fakes it, but that's one gift the Holy Spirit sure didn't give me."

"And how did you become a Catholic? I'm sorry, it's probably none of my business." They headed toward the Financial District, with its narrower streets, shaded by the height of the office buildings on either side, and happened to pass Smee's, a popular local coffee shop known for brewing an array of unique blends by the cup. She stopped, and he followed suit, smiling expectantly at her. "Can I buy you coffee?" she asked.

"I'd enjoy that. So long as we can keep walking afterward; I find it conducive to thinking. Plus, if I show up back at the rectory too soon they'll probably just ask me to look for the short in the alarm or whatever's causing the problem, and I'd much rather talk with you."

His words thrilled her out of all proportion to their significance but, caught up in the moment, she didn't think to question herself. Inside Smee's, music and the intermittent racket of espresso machines and milk steamers precluded serious conversation, and she could barely hear his request—"You pick; something kind of chocolaty, just black"—over the din.

They sipped their drinks on the pavement before resuming their walk. "I'm not ducking your question," he said. "How I came to the church was through a college girlfriend."

Not gay, she reflexively noted. "Where was this?" Sadie asked.

"University of Tennessee. I was a conservation biology major and took a religious studies class for a distribution requirement. Met a young lady freshman year, one of the relatively few Catholics at the school, and when she invited me to come to mass with her, I couldn't say no. Many things about it drew me in, what you talked about the other night and other stuff as well, and pretty soon I was more involved than she. I was baptized that year, much to my parents' chagrin. By the time I graduated I was sure I was meant for the seminary."

Sadie felt unaccountably mischievous. "How did your girlfriend take it?"

"I'd like to be able to say we remained friends, but...."

"I'm sorry, I shouldn't be prying."

He shrugged. "She told me I was the lamest excuse for a priest she'd ever seen, and if I didn't wash out of seminary I'd be defrocked within five years."

Sadie's mouth formed an O. Recovering, she said, "Well, see? You proved her wrong."

"My five-year anniversary's coming up next summer, assuming I make it, and—"

A wiry little man, pursued closely by a shoeless woman, bolted out of a shop as they were passing by, nearly bowling them onto the sidewalk. The woman halted beside them, apparently not willing to risk her bare soles on the pavement. "Hey! Stop!" she yelled. "What do you think you're doing, asshole? He stole my purse!"

Liam tore after the man and, some fifty yards ahead, tackled him onto the pavement, his superior mass pinning him down despite the miscreant's constant thrashing. Sadie already had her phone in her hand and was calling 911 as she ran toward them. The victim retreated into the shoe store; when she reemerged, once again shod, she retrieved her purse, which the thief had dropped along the way, and started off down the street in the opposite direction.

"Wait!" Sadie called. "Aren't you going to wait for the police?"

She looked back at Sadie as she marched away, tossing her hair. "I don't want to get involved."

Sadie coughed in disbelief and hastened to Liam's side. "Well, for fuck's sake, look at her," she railed, unable to restrain herself. "After you risked your life, she won't even stay to talk to the police."

Seeing the witness and the physical evidence walking away, the thief began to yell at Liam. "Get up off me, dickhead, or I'll file a complaint. You got no proof of nothin' and your girlfriend just called the cops. Let's see what they say when they get here and you're on top of me, huh?"

Both men scrambled to their feet, panting, the thief glaring at the priest. Suddenly he cuffed Liam on the side of the head and bounded down the sidewalk, disappearing around the nearest corner.

Liam rubbed his ear ruefully. "No good deed goes unpunished."

"Oh no, you're bleeding," Sadie exclaimed. "Wait, let me—." With tissues from her purse, she reached up to blot away the blood. "Your jacket's torn. And I'm sorry I let fly with that language."

He laughed. "I've heard worse in the rectory." He closed his eyes and submitted to her ministrations for a moment. Then he looked down at her in some alarm, asking, "Do you feel like we have to wait for the police?"

She paused in cleaning him up and considered. "I could give a rough description of the guy, but they probably won't be able to do anything with it. So, unless you think we need to—"

"I'd just as soon not. Bridges has been after me lately to act more peaceable, and this episode kind of doesn't fit with that narrative. Here, I'll take care of it." He took the bloodied tissue from her and, with an arm lightly touching her waist, drew her on.

They circled back toward St. Declan's, walking more and more slowly the closer they drew to the church. They talked of their respective undergraduate experiences, of law school and seminary, and of their first impressions of Sant' Urbano. She was keen to learn everything about him that he might care to disclose, but hesitated to ask about his family, knowing his next question would be about hers. Hearing in any detail about her antisocial mother could only taint her in his eyes. But then she told herself she was being ridiculous, that nothing he might think about her would affect her personally, since he was a celibate priest and presumably dealing with imperfect people was his business.

He stopped in front of the rectory and continued to chat, seeming to put off reentering its walls. At last he smiled sadly. "Sadie, I've really enjoyed talking with you. But I have to tell you that our RCIA class is nearly over." She must have looked confused, as he continued. "Rite of Christian Initiation for Adults. The convert class. Anyway, Easter's only a few weeks away, and the new class won't start until the fall."

She felt like crying, though not because she couldn't stand waiting for the right time to be baptized. Any magical rite had to be performed in an auspicious season; this she knew well. But without the excuse of her investigating the possibility of conversion, there would be no reason for them to meet. How painful it was to think of never seeing him again, of never again hearing the sweet twang of his voice. And, she thought angrily, how stupid she was being in the circumstances. "I understand," she said. "I'll let you go, then. It was wonderful meeting you, Liam. I wish you all the best, and a happy anniversary in advance." She clasped his hand in farewell, but as she backed away he held on.

"Wait a minute, I didn't mean...Listen, Sadie, I'm always happy to talk. Or see you. It doesn't have to be about the conversion process. I'm here if you want me."

He sounds as lonely as I feel. "In that case, maybe...maybe we'll talk again," she said. Smiling once more, he nodded and released her hand.

When next she looked up, she found herself standing on the worn concrete staircase at the top of one of Sant' Urbano's best known hills. She'd covered four miles and twice as many neighborhoods' distance from the rectory, and was now in one of the toniest parts of town, not far from where Conal had lived when he was married. On either side of the street enormous houses stood, their windows facing the bridge, the moody waters of the bay, and the headlands beyond. The sky was now darkening, the sun sinking in a hot angle in the overcast sky as residents in their cars began to return home for the evening. Miles away, at the loft, Ruairí would be hungry, but Roísín was there to care for him, and Conal would be arriving soon. But the thought of them soon slipped out of mind, and she remained on the hilltop lost in recollection of Liam as lights came on singly and in clusters and the air grew chillier. Only when darkness had fallen fully and she noticed herself shivering did she turn her steps toward a bus stop to make her way back to her present life.

Chapter Thirteen

11:00 a.m., Friday, February 12

She declined Conal's phoned invitation to share a brown-bag lunch in his chambers. "Justice Latimore's been on me about this case," she explained. "Please don't be annoyed at him. It's got a gnarly sentencing issue, and he's right, I've been mulling it over too long. I need to start writing."

"You always had the best work ethic," he said. "Only Mike comes close to you. You'll be home tonight, won't you?"

"Sure, of course. Why wouldn't I be?"

"I love you, sweetheart."

"Till tonight."

She flattened appellant's opening brief on her desk with the heel of her hand and typed the case information into the opinion template on her computer, feeling as though she deserved the same sentence appellant had received. If she'd been able to bring any reasonable degree of focus to her job for the past week, she wouldn't be in this time bind. But her thoughts had been constantly on the priest and not on whether the five-year or the ten-year gang enhancement applied to Hugo Davisson, Smog Town shot-caller. She kept hoping Roísín would have suggested going to Sunday mass, but the not particularly observant au pair had instead gone hiking with friends on Sunday morning. Various appointments of her own prevented her from attending St. Declan's weekday mass except on Wednesday, and instead of Liam at the altar it was flinty Father Bridges; recalling Liam's warning, she turned on her heel and left before he looked in her direction. As she tapped out the statement of the case her nerves tautened, and she kept committing typos. Now, added to her cellular-level desire to see Liam was anger at feeling the need to conceal it from Conal, anxiety that he'd see it despite her efforts, and—worst of all—a trace of pity for him that began to widen like a crack in a settling wall.

Every hour or so, too, she rebuked herself for dwelling on this fantasy of Liam instead of taking some definite action with respect to Conal, either committing to him and working on the relationship or, as seemed more and more inevitable, telling him it was over. But was it over? He still behaved nearly as ardently as ever; it was, after all, she who'd conceived and then convinced herself of the idea that things were falling apart. But whenever confusion threatened to overwhelm her, she recalled the image of him lying on the floor, passed out next to the baby and a half-empty bourbon bottle, and knew she couldn't spend the rest of her life, couldn't make another baby, with a man capable of doing such a thing.

Even Freddie, so loyal both to her and to the Judge, when she'd confided the incident, didn't try to reinterpret it for her. "Of course, you'd never feel safe again," he said. "But for everybody's sake, get it over with quickly. Go far away for a while if you can."

The day dragged on, and her attention had wandered so far from Davisson's case that she couldn't tell whether two Supreme Court decisions cited in the briefs were saying the same thing in different words or were truly inconsistent. And the worst of it was that she'd once understood it well; she wrote one of them while on Conal's staff. With a cry of annoyance, she flew out of her chair to the window, and cranked it open.

Several minutes in the teeth of the cold afternoon wind, staring out unseeingly at Foltz Street traffic, served to chill her skin but only tempered her need. She held her phone tightly. *If he answers and seems like he doesn't like me calling, I'll never bother him again.*

"I was afraid you wouldn't call," Liam whispered.

"Hi," she said, matching his tone. "It's Sadie."

There was a low chuckle. "I know."

Her heart soared; calling him had been the right thing, the only thing, to do. "Am I interrupting?"

"I'm in a parish council meeting. Bridges is boring us to death with his budget."

"I'm sorry. I was going to see if you wanted to meet for coffee or tea or something."

"Yes. Can you give me twenty minutes? Where are you?"

"I'm at the office, but I can—." On second thought, he sounded even more desperate to escape than she. "It's in the state building, Foltz and Golden Gate. I'll treat you to a bubble tea."

"I don't know what that is, but I'm down. Meet you out front of your building in twenty?"

"Yes, yes. Yes."

He laughed. "Same here. See you soon."

They sat in the back corner at Sweetly Tea, where anyone could see them. He was wearing chinos and a stylish grey sweater, and exuded effortless youth and strength and energy and sexiness. Chatting humorously about church business, movies, and the neighborhood around St. Declan's, he so totally held her attention that Conal and the entire Supreme Court could have come and ordered tea without her noticing. She could feel the color rising in her cheeks and the joy of being with him making her eyes shine. He kept pronouncing the red Thai bubble tea amazing.

"It's really good to see you," he said at last.

"I was about to say the same thing," she said. She looked at the wobbly little veneer table, at her lonely hand lying halfway across it, and suddenly her pulse began to pound in her ears. She looked up and met his rapt gaze.

"I have to tell you something," she murmured. Lifting his eyebrows, he leaned closer.

"It's hard...what I mean is..." What she was about to say would probably terminate this wonderful interlude, but she had to acknowledge this feeling aloud before a return to mundane reality could make her believe it didn't exist. She took a deep breath. "I'm having a hard time not telling you how much I care about you."

"And why shouldn't you tell me?" he asked quietly.

"Because it's wrong of me to...to interfere in your life this way."

"Let me decide if you're interfering." His hand was covering hers. "You're trembling." Leaning across the table, he kissed her, softly at first, then searchingly; when she opened her eyes, she could see he wanted her.

"Is this normal for you?" she asked. She wasn't sure what she meant, but he nodded.

"Yes. And no. I never stopped wanting a woman's presence in my life. For me it's been the hardest thing about being a priest—not that I've had a particularly easy time with poverty or obedience, either. If you're asking whether I've had other women since I was ordained, the answer is no, although there were a couple of close calls in my last parish."

"But you didn't instigate it."

"I believe I can truthfully say I didn't. It took some fairly extreme effort, but I let the opportunities pass."

"Until now."

"This is different." He shook his head. "I can't put it into words yet, but...I'm starting to wonder if I made the right choice. I've known guys—other priests—who had girlfriends or boyfriends as a pressure valve, something on the side to make the irritations and deprivations of clerical life tolerable. But I'm not going to use you that way. I've also known some guys who live married to their, quote-unquote, housekeeper in all but name, waiting for the church to come to its senses. I don't want you to be that. I want to live my life whole-heartedly, the way I was meant to live it, honestly. And when I—if I—decide to spend my life with a woman, I'll make her my wife the old-fashioned way."

"Until then—?"

"Well, there's the rub. If I get caught, there'll be consequences. I've seen some priests get transferred, reassigned, even sent to mental health facilities."

"What, for dating a consenting adult woman? That's amazing, considering all the cover-ups of abuse of kids. But I suppose I see their point. Without discipline, the institution would soon become unrecognizable. The faithful would lose confidence. And yet you don't want to slink around trying to keep it secret. I thought my life was complicated, but...I'm sorry, Liam."

He pulled her chin toward him and kissed her, long and deeply. "Are you saying you'd rather not get involved in this? I'd understand if that were the case."

"No!" The vehemence in her voice drew stares from other tea shop patrons.

"Then never be sorry for reminding me what it feels like to be a normal man; I was a fool to forget it. Sadie, if you can put up with the status quo for a while, till I figure out what the hell I'm supposed to be doing with my life, I would be grateful beyond all belief."

He could have asked her to wait for him until the church abolished the celibacy requirement; her answer would be the same. "I'll be here."

"And I understand things may change for you in the meantime. If your relationship with your baby's father is healed, then that—that's something I could only rejoice in for your sake. Of course, I'd be miserable and I'd want to leave Sant' Urbano forever, but—"

She stopped his speculations with another kiss.

The loft was in its usual early evening state of mild chaos. In the kitchen, Conal stood at the stove, stir-frying ginger and garlic; Roísín was collecting toys from underfoot; and Ruairí, covered in yogurt, was babbling in his high chair, waving a spoon. Sadie slipped in unnoticed and made for the bedroom. She did not turn on the lights, but lay on the bed, trying to find some still point in herself. Inwardly, her thoughts—if these utterly consuming, ecstatic nonverbal sensations could be called that—

kept revolving back to Sweetly Tea and Liam's kisses. She remembered barely anything of the remainder of the afternoon. He said he'd call her, and, even when back at her desk, trying to sort out the gang enhancement issue, she'd been able to think of nothing but him.

Conal entered the room and turned on the overhead light, yelping in surprise at seeing her. "When did you come in? I didn't hear you."

"Just a minute ago," she said, although it was more like a quarter of an hour. She shut her eyes against the glare. "I should have checked in."

"Headache?" he asked. "I'm sorry. Can I bring you anything? Aspirin?"

"No, thanks." She wanted only privacy for a little while; then she could face her domestic role again.

He looked at her for a moment, his eyes widening; she knew what he was thinking. "Sadie, are you—." He sat beside her on the bed, his hope palpable.

"No, I'm not pregnant. Sorry to disappoint. Just tired—it's been a long day. If I never get another gang case, I'll die happy. Rest is all I need. I'll spend some time with the baby as soon as...as soon as I've rested a little. Is that okay?"

"Anything you want, sweetheart." He leaned over to kiss her, his lips cold and thin compared with...but she couldn't start comparing, or she'd go insane. "I'm making kung pao chicken," he continued. "After that, how about a massage?"

"You're a dear." Her words sounded weirdly old-fashioned, as if pronounced by somebody's maiden aunt. "I'll join you guys soon."

But it was hours later, nearly nine o'clock, when she awoke, disoriented, in darkness and left the bedroom. Conal was alone, reading memos at the dining room table. He looked up, smiling wearily, as she approached. In the cone of lamplight from overhead, she saw how the years were beginning to tell around his eyes; how his hair, curling to the nape of his neck, was whitening; how thin he was becoming.

She sat down opposite him. "I'm so sorry, I just passed out. I guess I missed the baby."

"Yes, he just went to sleep. Here, I'll get you some food." He started to stand.

"Don't, I will. Have you eaten?"

"I had some."

A few months before, she'd have tried to entice him to eat more, tried to build him up and fill him out. She'd loved all of him, even the middle-aged spread that had somehow disappeared without her noticing. Now, feeding him was in some way too intimate, too proprietary; his flesh was separate from her, didn't, after all, belong to her. Even to comment on his weight loss would be too personal. And the feeling of separation was entirely reciprocal: She bridled at the thought that he might consider her body to belong to him. If it wasn't already another's, it was surely her own to bestow as she willed, and at this moment she felt connected to him only through their child.

"I see you're working," she said.

"Getting ready for oral argument next week. We're in Le Streghe this time, and I have to fly down on Monday morning. I'll be sorry to leave you, but Roísín will be here."

The Supreme Court customarily held oral argument sessions three times a year in Le Streghe, the biggest city in the state, an hour's flight from Sant' Urbano. In the past she'd dreaded his absences, but this time the prospect of time alone thrilled her. "It's not a big deal," she responded. "I can manage things with Ruairí for a couple of days. We'll miss you, of course," she added. Did the words sound as mechanical to his ears as they did to hers?

"The feeling's mutual. I'll be back on Wednesday night; maybe we can celebrate?" He smiled lasciviously.

She returned his smile, thinking not of Wednesday, but of a plan for Monday evening that was already taking shape in her mind.

Chapter Fourteen

7:50 a.m., Monday, February 15

Breakfast and the normal accompanying pandemonium were under way at the loft on the Monday following. Waiting for his Judicial Protection detail ride to the airport, Quirke sipped his coffee and picked at a slice of toast while studying his benchbook at one end of the kitchen table, Ruairí petitioned shrilly for release on parole from his high chair, and Roísín tapped away at her laptop at the other end, putting the finishing touches on a paper for a class she was taking at City College. Sadie had put more effort than usual into her appearance, having donned a black pencil skirt and a red and pink sweater that fit her closely. She had to force herself to keep the tune she was humming *sotto voce*, and she found it impossible to contain the bounce in her step. As she rounded the corner of the table, Quirke caught her by the waist and reeled her onto his lap.

"I wish Grimes weren't about to pick me up. I wish I were going to be here with you tonight. God, the Le Streghe sessions are always interminable," he murmured, kissing her neck as she sat immobile, like a feral cat caught in porch light.

"It's just two nights," she pointed out. "Isn't it nice to have a little time with your colleagues at night once in a while, getting treated like big cheeses by the bar associations down south?"

He looked at her as though she'd just suggested it might be pleasant if the court all shared a cup of E. coli with the local attorneys. "Evidently I've been doing a lousy job lately of reminding you how I really like to spend my evenings," he said. Just then his cell phone rang: Grimes was waiting for him on the street. "Alas, I must say *au revoir* now, my love. Roísín, thanks for pitching in for the next couple of days; I'm sure Sadie will appreciate it—"

"Actually," said the au pair, "I'm traveling myself, up to the wine country for a couple of days with some mates to celebrate getting this paper done; didn't Sadie tell you? She said I—"

Sadie jumped off his lap. "It's fine, Conal, really. I finished that awful gang case, and Justice Latimore knows I'm taking off. You know Roísín deserves a break, and there's no earthly reason why I can't get along by myself here. Single moms do it all the time."

He looked at her skeptically. And, she knew, not without reason: She'd been vocal about having no help on those rare nights when he and

Roísín happened both to be away. "You're sure?"

"Of course. Don't give it a second thought. Ruairí and I'll have a great time binge-watching Thomas the Tank Engine. I hope everything goes well in Le Streghe." She bent to kiss his cheek. "You'd better go; it'd be embarrassing to have to get counsels' waiver of your presence if you miss your flight."

"I suppose so. Goodbye, sweetheart. I'll call you tonight—if I can get away from this odious dinner early enough."

"No worries. I'll probably turn in when I put Ruairí to bed; we can talk tomorrow after you get off the bench."

He stood and kissed her amorously, then gathered his benchbooks and carry-on. "Till Wednesday, then. Bye, Roísín—have a good time. Don't do anything I wouldn't do."

"Of course not." The au pair winked. "Fortunately, that leaves a pretty wide-open field."

A weekday governed by infant rhythms was unusual for her and not without its challenges, but Sadie found the Monday spent with Ruairí to be unusually frictionless and pleasant. After Conal and Roísín departed on their respective travels, in mid-morning she and Ruairí went to the park, where she pushed him in a bucket swing until her arms grew tired; she let him taste a blackberry popsicle and play in a sandbox with other infants and toddlers, of whom he, a born urbanite, seemed wary. Fascinated by the bamboo growing in planters along the exterior walls of the bathrooms, he pulled back when she brought him close enough to touch it. About lunchtime they went grocery shopping; later, while he napped, she made him pureed squash scented with cinnamon and nutmeg and glossy with butter and brown sugar. For herself and her guest, she set to work on pork tenderloins with asparagus and balsamic strawberries; she whipped heavy cream and put a brut rosé to chill in the refrigerator next to a flourless chocolate cake. It would be a delicious, if perhaps a little heavy-handedly romantic, dinner. After feeding Ruarí his formula, rice cereal, and squash, which he tasted with dawning amazement—belatedly she thought of his father's addictive tendencies and wondered if she should have gone easier on the brown sugar—she changed into a dress of stretchy maroon lace and heels. At 7:35, as she held Ruairí, about to put him down to sleep, the doorbell rang.

He stood before her, smiling, a tissue-wrapped bouquet of tall purple tulips in his arms. "I know you said 8:00, but I couldn't wait any longer to see you." He bent to kiss her—even with heels on, she was nearly a foot shorter—then stepped back, awaiting an introduction.

"I'm so glad you're here, come in." When he'd crossed the threshold, she shut the door and kissed him again as the baby twisted and thrashed in her arms. "Ruairí," she said, clutching his feet to stop him kicking, "this is Liam. He's our friend."

The baby scrutinized him with guarded skepticism, if not outright hostility, while Liam greeted him mildly. "I'm very happy to meet you, Ruairí. You sure do favor your mommy."

Sadie's smile brightened. "Do you think so? Most people say he looks just like Conal."

"Maybe so, but to me, the resemblance seems obvious. Here—your hands are full—can I put these in water for you?" He held the tulips in front of his face and played hide and seek, eliciting no reaction from the baby.

"They're spectacular, Liam, thank you. Sorry, he hasn't got object permanence yet."

"Oh, he knows I'm behind them; he just doesn't know what to make of me yet. Well, Ruairí," he said, emerging from behind the blooms, "I look forward to getting to know you."

"I was about to put him to bed. Do you mind if I just—?"

"Of course not. I'll wait in the kitchen for you, if it's all right," he said, gesturing at the table. Then, looking around, he whistled. "You didn't tell me you lived in a train station. It's amazing."

She laughed. "It is pretty spread out. I'll rejoin you in a few minutes."

Twenty wasn't her idea of a few, but Ruairí fussed and demanded no little rocking and lullabying. When finally he lay asleep in his crib, she checked the baby monitor and returned to the kitchen. The tulips stood commandingly in a cylindrical glass vase in the center of the table, and Liam sat on the bench beside it, his face resting on his hand as he watched her approach. Adding to her mental list of his wonderful qualities, she admired his easy resourcefulness and that he didn't need to occupy every vacant minute with smartphone consultation.

He smiled. "Found the vase under the kitchen sink; hope you don't mind my poking around."

She assured him of the contrary, and while their dinner was warming in the oven she poured them each a glass of the brut rosé. The thought crossed her mind she'd have to get rid of the bottle before Wednesday;

for Conal's sake, she never kept alcohol around the house, and the presence of an empty bottle would raise questions. She sat on the bench next to Liam and, before she could speak, he pulled her onto his lap, kissing her with an unabashed hunger. Neither of them looked up until the oven timer buzzed; then, breathlessly and with some reluctance, she got up to serve the food.

He ate well and complimented her, while she was too keyed up to do much but move the meat around her plate and nibble at a strawberry. They finished the bottle of wine. "Shall I open another one?" she asked. But he was already carrying her away from the table.

Later, as night advanced, they lay entwined together under the covers. "I fantasize about this more or less constantly," he said. "The feeling of you in my arms, in a place where we can be together, nothing and no one coming between us. I don't want to scare you, but I'm starting to need you a lot. And you hardly know who I am."

She curled closer on his solid, hairy chest. "Then tell me who you are."

He was silent for a moment. "I'm a guy who cracked a lot of jokes in class and drove my teachers nuts, though they didn't seem to hold it against me in grading. A kid who pretended not to like video games because my parents couldn't afford to buy them for me. A guy who always thought I was going to work outdoors, for some reason, though I read more books than any ten kids. A boy who earned lots of merit badges in the Scouts until I took it into my head to quit in protest over the gay scout leader issue—I don't know why, exactly; no gay men were clamoring to lead our troop or anything, but it seemed wrong to me."

"That was brave. Did you get a hard time for it?"

"I was the biggest, strongest kid in the outfit and everybody knew better than to give me any shit. But my folks were always a little suspicious of me after that—like, what the heck is he going to crusade about next?"

"And what was your next crusade?" she teased.

"Well, for a while there was veganism."

"God, I'm sorry—here I've been stuffing you with pork tenderloin. I wish you'd told me."

"Darlin', if I were still a vegan, I wouldn't have kept it from you. And, in case you want to know why I'm no longer a vegan—"

"I want to know everything about you. Wait, that sounds creepy, doesn't it?"

"It doesn't sound creepy; it sounds like...well, I'll wait to hear it from you," he said, kissing her again. "The simple reason is that I couldn't do it perfectly, and I was spending all my time sweating over cruelties that were more or less out of my hands while paying no attention to the little, everyday cruelties I was actually responsible for. I suppose you could say I'm just not sufficiently evolved for it yet; maybe I'll go back to it someday. Oh, and thank you for not saying how amazing it is that a hillbilly can be so progressive."

"Do you think of yourself as a hillbilly?"

"Hell yeah. Kentucky born and bred."

"Then I must be one, too." She'd never before thought of the epithet as a badge of honor, but if he claimed it so proudly, then so would she. "I was born there, but we moved away when I was still a baby. My mother had a lot of reasons to leave." She'd intended to keep Laudie out of this relationship, to leave her origins a mystery for the time being, but his openness made her want to be as honest as he.

"Tell me about her."

She took a deep breath. "This is the biggest risk I've taken with you yet. But if you have second thoughts after hearing about her, then better sooner than later."

He laughed. "What is she, some kind of criminal?"

"Every kind of criminal," she replied, straining in the darkness to see his face and not the upwelling mental images she'd sought to forget. The slutty clothes Laudie had made her wear at fourteen—the roving hands and tongues of Laudie's meth customers—Conal's blackened eyes and bruised ribs—the Facebook page of the inconvenient half-sister she'd never known, whom Laudie had "accidentally" shot. "She tried to pimp me out, among other things. She shot Conal up, trying to kill him, and in the process gave him a taste for heroin that's probably going to do him in someday. She murdered—actually murdered—three people, including her husband, her lover, and the half-sister I never knew. Just talking about her makes me sick. At least she's where she belongs right now, locked up tight in state prison. She's not going to hurt anyone again anytime soon." He held her close as she tried to stop the tears that were dampening his chest. "I'm sorry, I...." She couldn't restrain a sob, and he held her closer than ever.

"Oh, Sadie, Sadie, no, I'm sorry. You're even more admirable and amazing than I realized, to have survived all that. If you can, if you want to, tell me more. Tell me how you made it through the abuse."

She cleared her throat and forced herself to continue. "Two of my high school teachers—a lovely woman named Leila Hennigsen and Peter Blake, the guy who owns this train station, as you put it—took me out of the situation, or I'm quite sure I wouldn't have survived. Or at least I wouldn't bear any resemblance to what I am today. They became my legal guardians and sent me away to school. It was a Catholic boarding school, and I thrived there. I've had a fondness, sort of a longing, for the Church ever since, although Peter didn't want me to convert. One day I'll introduce you to him. He's been like a father to me."

"What about your biological father?"

"I never had one—Laudie, my mother, never said his name, if she even knew what it was. I haven't begun to tell you how she contrived to make ends meet while I was a child, and I don't feel quite up to it tonight. So, you see, my origins are about as sketchy as they could be. Not someone you want to take home to meet your mother."

"I'll be the judge of that. But you've done incredibly well for someone who's been through experiences like that. How did you end up becoming a lawyer?"

"More or less by accident, piecing together mismatched snippets of education until I'd gotten a degree from the least intimidating law school in the state and somehow, miraculously, passed the bar exam. And then I took advantage of lucky opportunities that I'd never have acquired on my own merits to land a job on Conal's staff. Which I gave up when we got involved."

She half-expected him to render some sort of verdict, but he only sighed. "My people are boringly normal by comparison—apart from the snake-handling, anyway. My dad made cabinets and wood furniture. Mom trained as a nurse but took care of me and my siblings. There were four of us, two girls and two boys. Big extended family. We'd have great reunions every summer at my grandparents' place out in the country. Though we didn't have a lot, I was a happy kid, pretty much, though, as you may have guessed, with a tendency to find myself at odds with authority."

"Your family must have been surprised at your vocation."

He grunted. "Like I said, the prevailing—well, okay, unanimous— view was that it wouldn't last. And the Full-Bore Gospel folks don't have a lot of use for Catholics, did I mention that? We're not really Christians to them."

"So, would you say you're estranged from your family?"

"I'd say the relationship is strained rather than estranged. I haven't given up hope of regaining the closeness we used to have."

Just then a thin cry came from the next room. Sadie got up, took a kimono from the closet, and turned to Liam. "I thought he was so precocious when he was sleeping through the night at three months, but there are these little regressions along the way. Don't go anywhere," she said, laughing. "I'll be back."

In his room, she lifted Ruairí from the crib. "There, there, precious one," she whispered, hoping he didn't sense her resentment at having to leave her lover's embrace. As soon as her arms enclosed him, his thumb found his mouth and his cries ceased, but, wanting to induce a sound sleep to last into the morning, she carried him to the kitchen to prepare a bottle. The LEDs on the appliances read 2:18.

"May I, please?"

Liam had put on underclothes and ventured into the kitchen. "I have nieces and nephews, never dropped a one." His size and muscularity would have assuaged any concern about his ability to maintain a grip on an infant, and she gave him her son, watching as he snuggled the baby into the crook of his elbow and held the bottle at just the right angle. Ruairí took a few more pulls at the nipple and relaxed into sleep. Then Liam handed her the bottle, smoothly carried the baby back to his room, and lowered him into his crib.

In bed afterward, once more satisfied and spent, he held her close. "My sister told me these middle-of-the-night feedings were why she had Irish twins—twice."

"Do you want children?" She'd intended not to ask any question that even hinted at a desire for commitment, but the words were out of her mouth before she could filter them.

"That depends, now," he murmured, kissing her hair. "Under the right circumstances, I would, no doubt."

Faint traces of dawn were only beginning to be visible through the skylights when she awakened to the sounds of his stirring in the bedroom. "Sorry to run, but I have the 7:30 mass this morning." He sat on the side of the bed, tying his shoes.

"Can I make you coffee?" The prospect of parting was incomprehensible. It was less than twelve hours since he'd arrived, nowhere near long enough, and she wanted him so much she hardly trusted herself to speak.

"Sadly, no time." He drew on his jacket.

She sat up, sharply awake now. "Can I see you tonight? He isn't home until tomorrow afternoon, and—"

"Sadie." His hand caressed her cheek and pushed aside her disordered hair to leave a kiss there. "In my whole life, I can't remember a more wonderful night than last night with you. I hope you believe me when I say I hate to leave you, but I'm going to do what I have to do today. And then...This has gone so far, so fast, that I...I know this is going to sound cold, but I need some time for discernment. I need you to give me that. So, I can't say when we'll meet again."

He may as well have torn out her beating heart, she thought; the pain was shocking, paralyzing. "But I—"

"I don't want to be halfway with you and halfway a priest. That's just not enough of either. I can only speak for myself, but maybe you'll agree. Goodbye for now, Sadie, my love." Another kiss, the tenderest one yet, and he left the room. Seconds later, the front door opened and closed again, and she was alone with the inexorably increasing daylight.

Chapter Fifteen

5:00 p.m., Wednesday, February 17

She tried to time it so that she'd be out when Conal arrived home, and so spent Wednesday afternoon trundling Ruairí, fleeced and blanketed, in his stroller all over the northern half of Sant' Urbano, staying far away from St. Declan's. A few times she knelt to rub his cheeks and hands, fearful the fifty-degree temperature might give him hypothermia, but he was remarkably insensitive to the cold and, as ever, curious about everything in the world. In the course of their travels she went into a Smee's in the Financial District, ordering a latte for herself and hot water in which she warmed a bottle for him. They stopped to watch antique trolleys in the colors of the transit systems of different cities clattering up and down Market Street and seagulls clambering over an enormous fountain that resembled the castings of a giant worm. She bought a soft pretzel from a sidewalk vendor, only to toss it on an already overflowing trash can when her heart rebelled against the idea of taking nourishment. Finally, dusk began to overwhelm the western sky and she could put off her homecoming no longer.

She felt acutely the duty to tell Conal...what, exactly? That, once and for all, she would never marry him? That she no longer had the same feelings for him as before? Even the most painful truth, that another man occupied the place he formerly had in her heart? He deserved better than to be deceived, certainly. But any confession would lead to questions, and Liam's situation wasn't hers to disclose. Roísín was a parishioner, and would inevitably find out if she said a word to Conal; even if she promised to keep it to herself, Sadie didn't like the idea of relying on her discretion. And how horribly manipulative a revelation would be. There was no reason to rush into any declaration, since—true to his word—Liam hadn't called, and wouldn't call, she knew, until he'd sorted out his life...in which she might or might not ever have a place. Should she tell Conal there was someone else, but refuse to name the man? Provided he didn't look at her phone log, Liam's identity was probably a safe secret...unless she'd made some stupid mistake, which was entirely possible in her current shambolic mental state. She was getting a headache trying to think it through, and suddenly wanted only to be at the loft—her home since forever. That was another awful aspect to all this: Conal would have to move out, and then who would take care of him?

But her key was in the lock and the door was being thrown wide.

Conal was holding her tight, kept holding on, as though she was even then pulling him back from the edge of a cliff. He smelled of airports and, despite the layers of clothing between them, felt smaller, bonier, than she remembered, or perhaps only in comparison to Liam. Finally, he let go of her and lifted Ruairí out of the stroller squeezing him, kissing his cheek. The baby drooled happily.

"I missed my family," he cried. "I missed you both so much."

"We're very glad you're back," she said, striving for a bright smile. "But he needs a change. Let me—"

"I'll do it. Come on," he said, pulling her toward Ruairí's room.

She watched him as he replaced the baby's diaper and asked him the anodyne, automatic questions about the Le Streghe session—how was the trip? Any surprises at oral argument? Did anybody get a word in edgewise with Justice Rackrent?—until he interrupted, saying, "Let's put Ruairí down for a few minutes." Indeed, the forced march in the afternoon's cold air must have tired the baby, for he'd fallen asleep, and Conal first carried Ruairí to his crib and then grasped her wrist and led her to their bedroom.

No, no, she thought, as he peeled off her jacket and sweater and T-shirt and jeans, kissing her everywhere. But, though her mind simmered with notions of refusal, her body responded to his touch, and he so obviously drew pleasure from trying to make her happy that she couldn't bear to withhold herself.

Later, as they lay together in the gathering darkness of the evening, he answered all her rote inquiries and chatted about court doings. She was so preoccupied by memories of Monday night and Liam—already they were fading, like a pastel sketch too often probed by covetous fingertips—that he had to repeat himself.

"What have you and Ruairí been up to? And what has he done for the first time since I left?" he said again.

"That's a good question," she said, ashamed to realize the last thing she'd been thinking of in the last couple of days was observing the constant little novelties in the baby's life. "He tried a blackberry popsicle the other day."

"And?"

"He seemed to like it. On the other hand, he's not keen on the bamboo in the park."

Conal stroked her belly. "That's odd. Why?"

"I don't know. Too tall, maybe?"

"Speaking of tall plant life, those are spectacular tulips."

Liam's tulips. "Yes, aren't they? I couldn't resist." She rolled away from him to hide the pain she couldn't dissemble. "Are you hungry? Shall I make something to eat?"

"Not yet," he whispered. "Stay with me a while." His arms locked around her waist and his lips hovered over her neck. She held still, suppressing a shudder.

※

10:20, Wednesday, February 24

In mid-morning, while the court was engaged in its weekly petition conference in the Chief's chambers, Sadie visited Quirke's staff. She showed Margie the latest pictures of Ruairí, said hello to John Hendershott, and waved to Adair and Mike in their offices. Last, she entered Freddie Osorio's office and shut the door. Freddie had long been a close friend and confidant of Sadie's, a role he'd discreetly maintained when she and the Judge became lovers but that was becoming more awkward and uncomfortable with every new revelation of the progress of Sadie's relationship with the priest.

This time, in particular, Sadie's distress was distressing him. She could not sit for more than five seconds at a time, instead pacing around his office and staring disconsolately out the window onto the Foltz Street traffic, obsessed with the priest's decision to suspend contact. Ordinarily Freddie empathized deeply with the lovelorn, but this time he was unable to contain a flash of irritation. "Try, at least, to see it from his point of view," he urged. "He's having to decide whether he was all wrong about God calling him. If he wasn't, I mean if he was right when he got ordained, then this is just a test. And if he was wrong, then what the hell was it that was calling him? It's kind of a big deal if you believe in that stuff. I don't mean *you're* a test, honey, but—"

"I get it. I hear myself, I know I sound completely selfish and self-absorbed, but there's never been anyone like him in my life. And never will be again."

Freddie came to the window where she was standing and took her by the shoulders. "I remember a time not long ago, when you were over the moon for someone else," he whispered. "Someone who still—"

She shook her head, tears starting to well up in the corners of her brown eyes. "Don't, Freddie, please. You can't make me feel guiltier than I already do. Believe me, I'm in hell."

At that moment, there was a familiar rap on the door, which opened to reveal the Judge, back from conference and summoning his staff, as he did every week, to go over the results. "Sadie," he said. To Freddie the imploring quality in his voice cut like a recklessly wielded razor.

She walked away, her head lowered. "You're all busy, and I'd better get back to work or Justice Latimore will be calling and haranguing you."

Freddie gathered his papers and prepared to join the rest of the staff in the conference room, but the Judge lingered in his office, staring into the hallway after her.

He turned to Freddie. "What's new?" he asked, leaning against the desk, his tone superficially sunny.

"Oh, you know. Same old, same old." Freddie put on a smile, hoping it reached his eyes sufficiently to fool the Judge.

"Do you think she...." The Judge trailed off, unable or afraid to disentangle the crucial question from the snarl of feelings within himself. Then he stood and moved toward the door, his file of memos weighing on his hip. "Sorry, that's unfair. We'd better get this over with; everybody's waiting."

Chapter Sixteen

2:00 p.m., Thursday, February 25

"What you're saying saddens and disturbs me," said Father Bridges, his fleshy shoulders slumping as though under a resented, if not entirely unexpected, burden. He gazed across his desk at the young woman sitting opposite. "Tell me what led you to this conclusion."

Roísín switched Ruairí to her other knee, perfunctorily wagging a small stuffed animal at him, but he seemed to disdain the distraction and stared in some trepidation at the man with the rubicund complexion behind the desk. "I feel awful telling you all this, Father, not keeping it in the family, you know. But it's not a purely private matter, is it?"

"Certainly not. You have no reason to feel guilty; in fact, on behalf of the Church I'm grateful to you. And, until it's clear what needs to be done, your information stays with me. You say you haven't told your uncle—?"

She shook her head. "He's a really important judge, and I don't want to be upsetting him unless it has to come to that. You're the first person I've spoken with, other than my ma."

"Start at the beginning. How you first came to suspect, how you confirmed your suspicions, and so forth."

"Yes. Well, I'm guilty of introducing them—Sadie and I were walking by St. Declan's one evening and Father Liam was standing outside. We chatted with him; since she hadn't seen the place, he gave us a peek inside the church, though it was locked up. Then she asked him to come along to dinner with us. It didn't take a lot of coaxing, I must say. We had a lovely time, and at the end she asked to meet with him. She seemed quite...determined to get a private audience."

"Do you remember the date this happened?"

"I'm thinking it was early February. Afterward she didn't say much to me about him, but I know she came to mass a couple of times—she's not Catholic, not even Christian—"

"Jewish?"

"Pagan, Father. She's a witch, or sorceress, or like that."

His fearsome eyebrows knit together.

"Initiated my uncle into all that stuff. Of course, he's Catholic, but they've never baptized the baby." Ruairí began to suck his thumb as the priest frowned at him.

"Living with them, I can't help noticing that their relationship—Sadie and my uncle's—isn't what you'd call perfect. Not that they fight; but she's distant, and he's always trying really hard to please her. Last week, he was away in Le Streghe for court business. Sadie suggested I take a little time away myself. Bit of a surprise, that was, as she normally demands all the help she can get with the house and the little fella. But, since she offered, I took the opportunity for a trip to the wine country with friends. When I came back, there on the kitchen table was a vase full of the most gorgeous purple tulips you ever saw. Well, taking the recycling out the next day, I happened to see in the bin the wrapping from the flowers, printed paper and a bow. They were from Fleurtation at the 50 Fifth—you know, that extremely upscale florist at the hotel round the corner from the church? There was also an empty wine bottle in the bin—another item we don't keep round the house, as my uncle has a bit of a problem. Well, that seemed a little odd, so I went into Fleurtation and, lo and behold, they still had some of the tulips. The shop girl saw me admiring them, and I told a bit of a fib, pretending to be the recipient of the tulips. She remembered the sale—goes on and on what a lucky girl I am to have such a sweet, attentive, handsome boyfriend. The way she described him, there couldn't be any doubt it was Father Liam. He'd asked her loads of questions about the language of flowers and all that. She even asked me if he proposed, fancy that. Said she can always tell when a man's about to pop the question."

Father Bridges shook his head, his pouchy eyes glittering darkly. "Have you spoken with...Sadie, you said is her name?"

"It is, and no, I've not. Didn't think it was quite my place. I called my ma, though; she's Uncle Conal's older sister and a no-nonsense type, and she said you'd know what to do."

"I'm very much obliged to her. And to you. I'm sure this has been difficult."

Roísín inclined her head. Ruarí, sensing the interview might be drawing to a close, began to twist and squirm in her lap, and Roísín had to grip him more tightly to prevent him slipping off, which caused him to fight even harder for his liberty.

"This isn't the first thing that's given pause about Father Greengold's judgment and character. But I'll leave it at that. Thank you, Roísín. I'll pray for peace and healing in your family and household. See you on Sunday?"

"I'll try, Father." She gathered the baby and his equipment and left the pastor's office.

Father Bridges leaned back in his chair, his arms folded across his ample belly, musing. His young associate had arrived only a few months before with a reputation as a charismatic guy, a thoughtful preacher, someone capable of revivifying the parish. He'd already started a book and film club and taught a couple of cutting-edge bible study classes, and St. Declan's was acquiring some buzz around the archdiocese along with a small and growing number of younger regulars, the Church's lifeblood. Yet there had been cautionary notes along with the praise from his previous pastor. Some of the parishioners in his last post had complained he was too often seen with one or another young female eucharistic minister, and there had been some sort of ugly or at least embarrassing rivalry between them. It had been thought wise to transplant Father Liam into new soil. Unfortunately, if what Roísín said was true, he seemed to have wasted no time in getting up to the same sort of thing at St. Declan's. And with a pagan! As well, Father Bridges couldn't help noticing an inappropriate streak of aggression or temper in his associate, along with a tendency to break into language decidedly unsuitable for a parish priest. Father Bridges had seen several similar instances of clerical laxity in his time, most of which had gotten fixed with appropriate and timely intervention, the remainder being cases of men who never had a real vocation in the first place. And, not to be forgotten, there was the fact of Father Liam's being a convert; maybe the diocesan formation committee should have taken a closer look or postponed his ordination until a more thorough process of discernment could be undergone. In any event, something had to be done before St. Declan's became notorious for harboring a priest who cuckolded an important judge—if it was even possible to cuckold a man content to be living in sin with a witch. Hopefully, Father Bridges mused, Conal Quirke would one day find his way back to the Church and be done with occultism and all such unholy practices. Perhaps, depending on how pastorally he handled the situation, that day would soon arrive.

He strode out to the front office. "Susie," he asked the secretary, "is Father Liam in? Would you tell him I need to speak with him in my office?"

"Sure thing, Father. I think he's just finishing up a pre-Cana session with a couple in his office."

"Terrific," said Father Bridges, an unwholesome note of irony creeping into his voice. Based on what Roísín had just told him, Father Liam could teach significant parts of the marriage preparation curriculum from his personal knowledge. "Send him in as soon as he's done." While he waited, Father Bridges busied himself with an Internet search and made a series of phone calls.

Several minutes later, Father Liam breezed into Father Bridges's office, settled his tall, strapping frame in one of the visitors' chairs, and unwrapped and began to suck on a starlight mint from a bowl on the desk. "What's up, Norb? I've got an appointment in ten minutes. Couple wants me to baptize their baby."

"That's fine, Liam, but I've just had a troubling talk with a parishioner. Roísín Dexey. You know her, I think?"

"Yes. I hope nothing's seriously wrong?"

"She's a fine young woman with enough sense to come to me with her concern instead of spreading it around the parish. You know where I'm going with this."

A blush rose on Father Liam's cheeks as he averted his gaze, frowning. "I think so."

"So it's true you're having an affair with the mother of her uncle's child?"

"That may or may not be the right word for it, but—"

"She came to me rather than confronting the woman or her uncle, for which I'm thankful. Obviously, Liam, when people bring these things to me, I have to act."

"I suppose you do," he said, remembering his conversation with Sadie in the tea shop.

"This isn't the first indication you have a fit problem in this role," Father Bridges went on. "We've talked about the language and aggression issues. And, of course, there was the situation at Holy Redeemer."

Father Liam stiffened visibly. "What's your point?"

"I'm relieving you of your responsibilities here for a while. Trying to be proactive, I've made arrangements for you to get some treatment—"

Liam shot out of his chair and leaned over the desk. "Wait a minute here. Isn't there a little thing called informed consent? I'm not a piece of broken property to be shipped off to get fixed."

Infuriatingly, Father Bridges only laughed, his hands flying up past his shoulders and coming to rest on his belly. "Certainly not, but you seem to be proving my point."

"So, the presumption is that a 'fit problem' consisting mainly of my loving a woman is a sickness that needs treatment."

"I've known men who benefited greatly from the program at St. Casimir's. They spoke glowingly of how the therapy helped them reconcile themselves to the necessary sacrifices. Every last one said he was a better priest for it." Father Bridges studied Liam over his glasses. "It's your choice whether to go or not, but either way you're taking a few weeks' leave to think about it."

Liam, already on his way out, paused in the doorway. "I won't need weeks."

Sadie knew perfectly well her recent behavior was deplorable, that she was acting like a deranged woman. She stayed away from the loft as much possible; when being at home was unavoidable she tended to snap or drip passive aggression at Conal, Roísín, and even the baby; and when asked what was the matter, she remained sullenly silent. Roísín pointedly wondered whether she was on her period; Conal's face disclosed his stoic hope she was, instead, going to make him a father again; and, to her shame, Ruarí only kept quieter and more hesitant around her than usual. But it was Liam's silence that was causing this madness, and it was that, ultimately, that she was determined to end. She had to speak with him, or she didn't know what she might do.

She'd dreamed three nights in succession of being in a rowboat in the waters of the North Pole, with Conal floating wordlessly away on a glacier like a polar bear on its way to extinction, and finally knew she had to tell him, regardless of whatever Liam might decide, that their relationship was over. The timing of this epiphany was awkward, as the Dormund execution was set for this evening and the protocol required Conal to stay at the court long into the night. That afternoon, however, while at her desk in Justice Latimore's chambers putting the finishing touches on a draft opinion, she decided the confrontation could be put off no longer. After going home to relieve Roísín, who had an evening class, she would bring Ruarí to the state building and have it out with him.

First, though, she would go to St. Declan's and give Liam a piece of her mind. Before she was through talking with him, he would damn well understand she couldn't take the cruelty of his radio silence, that his principles were stealing her sanity, that he was killing her with his bloody time of discernment. She would also make him understand, unless she was struck dumb first, that she loved him with all her heart and would be his forever if he wanted her. She felt acutely the recklessness of her plan, but was little more than an observer of her own actions at this point.

Thus, as the afternoon drew near its end, she shut down her computer and left the state building, her steps carrying her along the familiar route to St. Declan's.

She arrived at the parish office a few minutes before the close of business. She didn't have to check her reflection in the front window to know her hair looked like she'd been badly startled and her demeanor entirely lacked the tranquility she liked to project in religious settings. But these trivial concerns would not cause her to waver from her purpose. Breathing a little too heavily, she told the secretary she needed to speak with Father Liam.

The secretary, whom Sadie had encountered here and inside the church on several occasions, but who had not, to date, introduced herself, eyed Sadie coolly and replied as she lifted the receiver of her telephone, "Who shall I say is asking?"

"Sadie Norrell."

No sooner had Sadie pronounced her name than a cacophony of bulky flesh rising from a squeaking chair resonated in a room just off the reception area and the tread of heavy footsteps approached. A beefy man of late middle age, dressed in black trousers and short-sleeved shirt with a Roman collar, stood before her as if to bar entrance to the hallway leading to the priests' offices. His thick white eyebrows seemed fixed in mid-forehead, his gaze bore down on her like that of a jail deputy monitoring a particularly treacherous inmate, and his purplish lips worked a little and then curled into a rigid smile. "I'm Father Bridges. May I help you?"

She had never stood this close to the pastor. From the feeling she was getting from him, she fully believed Liam's warning that he'd eject her for being an occultist. Still, she would not be intimidated. "I'd like to speak with Father Liam, if he's here."

"I'm sorry, he's unavailable." Father Bridges pulled himself up to his full height and crossed his arms over his gut. He pointedly did not offer himself as an alternative to his associate.

She inferred this new unavailability would be permanent, at least where she was concerned. "May I ask why?" she asked, trying not to let her voice climb to a higher register.

He spread his feet like a gangbanger standing his ground against a rival. "Father Liam is on a leave of absence."

Her heart skipped and thudded. "Why? Since when?"

"I'm sure you'll understand it's a private personnel matter." Not relaxing his stance, he stared her down. After some seconds rooted to the spot, in surprise rather than defiance, she turned and fled.

Chapter Seventeen

2:15 p.m., Thursday, February 25

"Sure I can't run down to the cafeteria and get you something, Judge?" Margie looked up at him from her desk, that annoying newfound solicitude evident in her rosy countenance.

Of late his assistant was behaving in a peculiarly maternal way, seemingly determined to see he never missed a meal. Did he look that malnourished? He supposed he'd lost some weight recently. Or so Sadie had mentioned, once or twice. Coming from her, it was no compliment, but his former appetite for sweets and other junk had dwindled and he was no longer getting thousands of calories a day from alcohol, so a certain amount of shrinkage was inevitable.

"Thanks, but I'd like a little fresh air," he said. "It's been a long day already, and if I don't see the sky for a few minutes, I'll...well, I'd just like to get away. Call if you need me for anything."

"Oh, I wouldn't think of disturbing you, Judge. Have a nice late lunch, then." She pushed her glasses back up her nose and returned to her cite-checking.

Lamden Street was relatively quiet in mid-afternoon. Crossing the street, passing the federal building and various residential hotels—which one of them was Tad's, he wondered?—he stepped carefully past the puddles that tended to appear regardless of the weather, over the flattened, rotting fruits and vegetables that had escaped the local restaurants' compost bins, and around the less identifiable hazards that proliferated in the neighborhood. The brisk wind pushed a few high clouds across the sky, which was otherwise clear, promising continuation of the early spring they were experiencing. It would have been a good day to walk the length of Lamden Street, through the Tenderloin and the Geary corridor, into the Heights—his former neighborhood—and down to the bay. If he kept on this path long enough, he'd find himself at the bench in Aquatic Park where, only a year and a half before, Sadie had found and claimed him when Eleanor kicked him out. The memory of his regeneration in her arms sustained him now, when something indefinable had shifted between them and he'd begun to feel he was no closer to connecting with anything than when he was numbing out every night on bourbon whiskey.

But confronting the reality of that shift was too distressing just now. Even were there not innumerable things to do at the office, he would not go to Aquatic Park today.

In his preoccupation with the past he almost missed his favorite banh mi shop, just south of Geary, but, suddenly noticing where he was, he went inside and examined the prepared sandwiches in the refrigerated glass case.

Only a sparse selection remained at this late hour. "I'll take those two *banh mi thit nuong*," he told the clerk. He couldn't have said why he bought both of them; one was more than sufficient for him. Lunch in hand, he turned south again on Lamden and headed back to the office, making one more stop at Sweetly Tea for a tapioca red Thai.

Inside the building, he took the stairs rather than the elevator and, still mentally revisiting happier times, absentmindedly found himself on the floor above his own chambers. Funny, he thought, how he could tell he was in foreign territory; the ambient sound and energy levels were noticeably higher up here than on the third floor, probably due to the larger population of annuals. When Hetford had been at the court Quirke had tended to avoid the fourth floor, and when Rackrent moved in there seemed no reason to depart from his custom. But now that he was here, he thought, he might as well pay the Chief a visit. Odds were overwhelming she'd be knee-deep in administration, too busy to chat, but it was worth a try. Putting on a cheery front, he walked into her chambers. "How's every little thing?" he asked her assistant.

Margo, on a telephone call, looked up at him and grinned. Cupping her hand over the receiver, to his surprise she whispered, "Hi, Justice Quirke. Go on in."

"Sure it's okay?" he asked. When she nodded emphatically, he rapped on the inner door and entered.

In the several seconds it took him to cross her office—the most spacious at the court, naturally—the Chief, sitting behind her immense desk with the afternoon sun slanting in through the windows giving onto the plaza, continued to study her computer screen. At last she smiled at him, which he took as a tacit invitation to sit in one of her guest chairs. "Brought you lunch," he said, realizing he was still holding onto the banh mi. He took out one of the sandwiches and handed the bag to her.

"You're an angel. I've been too busy even to ask Margo to bring me something. What is it? Never mind, I don't care." Without ceremony, she unwrapped and started in on the *banh mi*. "Thank you so much," she said, a manicured fingertip pushing a shred of carrot into her mouth. She smiled gratifyingly again at him. "It's kind of you to think of me."

"Boba tea? I took a sip," he warned.

"I'd love some."

He took another sip from the straw, sucking up one of the oddly addictive chewy black beads, and passed the cup across her desk. She accepted it and took a long pull on the straw. Sitting in the warm golden light in this metaphoric pinnacle of the state judiciary, he suddenly recalled a time when the Chief was his adversary. It had to have been almost a quarter of a century before. She'd been a raw junior Sant' Urbano deputy district attorney, and he a defense attorney with a few years on her, newly installed in his own private law practice. They'd faced off over a robbery case in which he was representing one of the defendants.

"I mopped the floor with you," he mused.

She started; then her surprise gave way to a wry smile. "Were you thinking of Robinson and Lowrie? At least I put Lowrie away."

"Points for remembering my client's name."

"How could I forget? It was like my second jury trial. I got a lot better at it, you know."

"Oh, I know. Your career took off like a rocket. You certainly got here on your own ample merit. There's just one thing I've always wondered."

"What's that?" The sandwich dispatched, she licked her fingers.

"What happened after the verdict?" He shrugged sheepishly. "I remember going to the Inns, and then...."

Her cheeks flushed. "You don't know?"

"It's funny, or sad, or maybe just merciful, how many victory celebrations I have no memory of. Did I do something stupid—jump up on the bar to play an air guitar solo, maybe? Would you be kind enough to fill in the gaps?"

The Chief leaned back in her enormous chair, looking relieved. "To think all these years I worried about you dining out on the story of that evening."

"You're implying I may not have been the only one who acted like an idiot? I'm crushed," he said, only half-jokingly. "That you could think me capable of gossiping about a nice young DA who maybe got a little tipsy after a split verdict. Anyway, you've never acted like a fool in your life."

"You really don't remember," she said, shaking her head. "What a load off my mind."

She couldn't expect him to be content with that for an answer. "Now you have to tell me," he insisted.

"I beg your pardon. I'm the Chief Justice."

"Oh, right. No, I beg yours. Well, then, I'll just have to track down witnesses."

"You wouldn't, Quirke. Would you? All right, I suppose it doesn't matter anymore. The fact is I—I *was* rather tipsy and I—I made a pass at you."

His amusement gave way to an ineffable sadness at the long-ago carouse. He remembered how he used to feel being hit on, when he had not gotten too drunk to remember: hopeful, reckless, annoyed at feeling compelled to put on the brakes, if the other party was attractive; awkward, uncomfortable, anxious to make an escape if she wasn't.

"What did I do?" he asked quietly.

She gave a half-smile. "Ask yourself what you'd do if it happened today. It's probably what you did then."

Before he could reply, there was a knock at the door, immediately followed by the entry of Ward Freitag, the court's Clerk-Administrator, cradling fresh copies of a thick memo.

"Chief, Quirke, glad to have caught you both. Here's a little light reading for you. I understand the plan is to conference this at 5:30." He handed each of them a copy of the memo.

"Yes," she said. "That's less than an hour from now. Justice Quirke, thanks for the *banh mi*. It's been delightful seeing you, but I'd better focus on this. See you back here again very soon."

Chapter Eighteen

5:15 p.m., Thursday, February 25

The third floor felt like a tomb compared with the fourth. It was past five, but upstairs plenty of people were still around, and not only because of the execution; the court's other work continued. Anya stood tentatively in the hall, trying to think of a good line for Quirke's attorney. She began to walk toward the judge's office when her quarry emerged from his own.

"Hi!" he said. "Looking for someone?"

"You, I think," she said. "Mike, right?"

"Yeah, Mike Frentz. And you're—"

"Anya Holmquist. Clerking for Justice Rackrent."

"Of course. What can I help you with?"

She'd known others of his type. He was tall, inelegantly wiry, well-scrubbed, fresh-smelling (unlike Rusty); probably a gym rat. His face was too long, his ears too large, his eyes too small to be considered handsome; he'd go out of his way to engage with any halfway cute girl who happened to come by looking for assistance. Helpfulness was a lifelong habit with him; he'd probably been an Eagle Scout. "Well, I'm assuming you're here because of Dormund?"

"Yeah. Are you tracking, too?"

"Yes, and it's my first execution. I thought you might be able to tell me what to expect. I'd ask my judge, but it's her first, too."

"Sure, yeah. Well, I should say up front, I've only done one before, with Justice Hetford. If you're looking for a real old hand, you might want to talk with—"

"I just want somebody who's familiar with the protocol and...and can spare a little time to educate me."

"Of course, I'm happy to pass along what I know. Come on in." He extended a hand toward his office and motioned her toward the solitary guest chair. A legal pad and several old books lay open on the hulking linoleum-topped metal desk; a partly evaporated mug of coffee, evidently from this morning, was the only amenity. A diploma from the University of Virginia Law School and a photo of Mike and a man in a black robe standing next to a marble column in what looked to be another courthouse hung on the otherwise bare walls.

"Is that you?" she asked, pointing at the picture.

"Yep, me and Judge Molyneux of the Eleventh Circuit. That was right out of school. I worked on a few capital cases there, but it's quite different, as you might imagine, on the federal side. Plus, we were known to have something of a rocket docket. Unlike this place."

"I guess our counterparts in the Ninth are going to be keeping a vigil tonight, too, after our court denies Dormund's petition."

Mike smiled. "So, you're sure that's how it's going to go?"

Her eyes widened. "Even I could tell there was nothing to that petition. Unless you know something I don't?"

"No, I suspect you're right. My boss isn't too hopeful."

Anya feigned greater surprise than she felt. "You mean he's voting to grant?"

Mike nodded. "I guess he still isn't over losing when Dormund was here last. In his view, Dormund's stated a prima facie case of actual innocence, and we should issue a stay and an order to show cause and fix the mistake we made last time. Just between you and me, it's kind of exhilarating. That would never have happened with my old boss."

"Justice Hetford?"

"Yes. He was...pretty conservative."

"I've heard my judge talk admiringly of him. He was here for only a few years, wasn't he?"

"He was here three years and left right after the last general election. No connection; he wasn't on the ballot. I was lucky Justice Quirke hired me; I kinda like working here and wanted to stay on." He grinned.

She tried to return his smile. "And have you and Justice Hetford stayed in touch? What's he doing now?"

"You don't know?" When she shook her head, he gave a short, incredulous laugh. "Nobody around here talked about anything else for a while, but it was before your time, I guess. He married Quirke's wife—ex-wife, that is—and became the general counsel of—"

Quirke appeared in the doorway just as Anya was struggling to sort through the incongruously sensational relationships Mike was describing. His face was drawn; he seemed somehow older, smaller, than when he'd hosted the lunch with the annuals.

"I made my pitch," he said. "But I didn't prevail, and Dormund's headed for federal court. I asked to be noted on the order."

"That's too bad, Judge. You've met Anya?"

"Yes," he said, nodding at her. "Good idea to see what an execution night's like before the death penalty's abolished." He shrugged. "Well, comrades, our work here's done for the time being. Care to get some dinner with me? You, too, of course, Anya, if you don't have other plans. We'll be back in plenty of time; we don't assemble until a quarter to midnight or thereabouts."

At Anya's uncertain look, Mike explained. "What Justice Quirke's referring to is the court's execution protocol. Each justice and his or her staff attorney, and Ward Freitag all gather in the Chief's chambers a little before the execution's set to happen. There's an open speaker-phone line to the death chamber. The warden asks if anything's pending here, and Ward tells him no. Then the prison carries out its protocol. Why does the court gather when it doesn't officially act in any way? Well, that's the court's protocol."

"None of what Mike's saying is secret," Quirke said, "but I doubt many regular citizens know. If they did, they might give us a little more credit."

The question left her lips before she could check it. "For what?"

Quirke smiled sadly. "For having the willingness to sit with the consequences of our decisions. It's as close to witnessing the execution as a court can come. If you listen really closely, Anya, you'll hear Dormund draw his last breath."

"I think the Judge is exaggerating slightly, but you'll see," Mike said. "You'll be there with Justice Rackrent. The Judge and I'll be there, too."

Anya nodded. She had to stifle a wild urge to tell him he was mistaken.

"Do you need to confer with your judge, or shall we leave now and hopefully beat the dinner crowd?" Quirke asked.

Her heart began to race; she tried to slow and deepen her breath. "What time is it?" she asked. There was something of crucial importance to do before setting this evening's events in motion.

Mike looked at his phone. "I have ten to six."

"I need to run upstairs and get something," she said. "My purse."

"Sure, of course. We'll be here," Mike said.

She nodded and vanished into the stair as Mike's gaze followed her.

"I didn't know you two were friends," Quirke said.

"I wouldn't say we are. She just came down and introduced herself and wanted to know what's going to happen later on tonight. She seems like a nice sort of person."

"I don't think she likes me," Quirke said. "Of course, I've gotten over being surprised when that happens."

Chapter Nineteen

2:45 p.m., Thursday, February 25

"I can't thank you enough, Sadie. When will he be home, do you think?"

Ever since the election, it had been as if Justice Hetford had undergone a personality transplant. Where before not a word passed his lips that wasn't marinated in sarcasm or rebarbative insult, now his constant humble, friendly sincerity, and his perpetual gratitude for Conal's forgiveness, made Sadie feel unworthy for once having hated him. And his flourishing, obviously mutually devoted marriage with Eleanor only threw into high relief the cracks in her own relationship with Conal. She paused, reminding herself her attitude toward Conal was no concern of anyone's but her own. "I wish I could tell you, Judge—"

"Really, I wish you'd call me Allan. I'm hopeful we can all be friends, despite what I did."

"Sorry—Allan—of course we're friends. Old habits die hard with us handmaidens of justice, that's all. You know—or maybe you don't— there's an execution tonight. The court's going to be up late, so you might be able to get hold of him at the office. Or I can pass along a message; I'll be dropping by later with Ruairí for a quick visit."

"Now that you mention it, I remember reading about the execution. Dormund, isn't it? I remember your memo on his last petition; very well written indeed. Well, my sympathies to both of you. Execution duty can be rather disruptive to domestic tranquility. Say, I'll bet Quirke could use a little diversion on a grim night like this; I think I'll drop by the court myself. Just for a few minutes, of course; his time's too valuable to be frittered away on casual visitors. But there's a little matter on which I'd very much like to get his advice."

Sadie was immediately curious, but did not like to pry. "Then maybe we'll see you there, Ruairí and I."

"That would, of course, be delightful. We must get together again soon, the four—or even the five—of us. Eleanor's quite smitten with Ruairí."

After ending the call, she realized Conal would doubtless appreciate a warning if Allan Hetford was thinking of turning up at his door. She called first his cell phone and then, getting only his voicemail, tried the office. It was only just turning three, so the dedicated Margie in all likelihood would still be at her desk.

"Supreme Court, Justice Quirke's chambers," the assistant answered.

"Hello, Margie, it's Sadie."

"Hi, Sadie, how nice to hear from you. How are you? And how's the baby?"

"Both well, thanks. I hope the Judge isn't planning to keep you there all night."

"No, no—he was kind enough to say he didn't need me. Ward put a floater on duty in case anyone needs clerical support."

"That's good. I was hoping to talk with the Judge before he goes to conference, or to dinner, or whatever's planned for the evening."

"I'm sorry, Sadie, he went out for a walk. They have a long night ahead, and he wanted some fresh air. Did you try his cell? Never mind—I see he left it on his desk."

"If you don't mind, tell him Justice Hetford might be stopping by to visit sometime tonight. And I'll be coming over...so he can say good night to Ruairí."

"Oh, I'd so like to see you both, but I'm due home in an hour."

"We'll see you another time—soon, I'm sure. Till then, Margie."

"Good night, Sadie."

"Wait, I—can you put me through to his voicemail? I'd like to leave a message myself, spare you the trouble."

"It's no trouble, but of course I'll transfer you. Anyway, do come up and say hello whenever Justice Latimore can spare you for a few minutes; I miss seeing you. Adair and Mike are wonderful, of course, but—well, see you one of these days."

"Sure, Margie. Good night."

After a pause, the Judge's outgoing recording invited her to leave a message.

She spoke with no prologue, from mid-thought. "I think I'll bring Ruairí by for a few minutes tonight. He misses you." She bit her lip and hoped her sigh didn't come across on the recording. "I know it's weird, but part of me wishes I were on execution duty tonight. Like old times." This was all sounding too cryptically elegiac; she tried to lighten her tone. "This afternoon Allan Hetford called and said he may stop by your office for a visit; there's something he wants to consult you about. Whatever might that be, I wonder? I know you've been...a bit out of sorts lately. I'm sure you can tell I've been...feeling the same way. There's something we need to talk about. So, I'll see you? Later. I'm—"

The voicemail system cut her off. Should she call back and finish the message? No, she was talking without saying anything.

※

As soon as she set foot in the loft, Sadie sensed Roísín was holding a secret. The younger woman was uncharacteristically taciturn, although her eyes tracked Sadie wherever she went. She wore a knowing look as she played with Ruairí—another unwonted act for her, at least on those nights when she was supposed to rush off to class; she seemed to be waiting for some reaction from Sadie. Her very presence, usually a comfort, was tonight almost a provocation.

At last Sadie felt forced to confront her. "Roísín, did you know Father Liam's gone on a leave of absence?" The way Roísín pursed her lips told her this revelation didn't come as a complete surprise. Before she could answer, all of Sadie's anger, fear, and frustration erupted. "You had something to do with this, didn't you? You went to Father Bridges. You must have known what he'd do."

Roísín put Ruairí into his high chair and turned to Sadie. "If any of your professed interest in the Church was real, you'd understand why. Look, I'd prefer to stay out of this, but it's hard to watch how you treat my uncle. I can't be a part of deceiving him. He adores you, you know—"

"Stop it. Stop. You've been great, coming here, taking care of Ruairí, but just stop. Please. I don't need your help to feel guilty; believe me, I've got it down on my own. Not that I owe you an explanation, but long before I met Liam I knew it wasn't meant to be with Conal. I learned I'm not strong enough, after all."

"Strong enough for what?"

She cast her gaze downward, shaking her head. "I don't like to say anything against him. He's a great man."

Roísín gave a bitter little laugh. "Now I believe you don't love him. But what are you getting at?"

"I know he loves Ruairí more than anything, but I can't be with a man who'd endanger a child." Sadie wiped her eyes. "Do you know why you're here? You're here because I can't trust him to stay sober around Ruairí."

Roísín closed the cupboard door too violently, and Ruairí began to cry. "That's ridiculous. I haven't seen him take a single solitary drink since I've been—"

"Of course you haven't; he knows I'd leave him." Sadie lifted Ruairí from his chair and hugged him, but her agitated attentions only increased his distress. "When he's been drunk," she said, raising her voice over the baby's fussing, "all I can think of is what I went through as a child. I know it's cruel to drag this out. It's unfair. But because there's no telling when he'll do it again, I can't help it."

When Ruarí had calmed down, she turned again toward Roísín. "I've decided to tell him it's over. Please tell me you haven't already said something?"

Roísín shook her head. "I haven't. I swear."

"Promise me you'll let me tell him myself."

She nodded.

"I want to get on the other side of this as soon as I can. I'm going to see him tonight at the court after dinner; I'll take Ruarí with me, of course. Don't let me make you late to school."

As Roísín lifted her messenger bag over her shoulder and kissed Ruairí's head, Sadie added, "I'm so sorry for all this."

Chapter Twenty

6:30 p.m., Thursday, February 25

With Ruairí straddling her left hip and her overstuffed all-purpose bag dragging on her right shoulder, Sadie looked forward to setting down her burdens once she reached Conal's office. By special request of the Judge, her key card still worked on the doors to the third floor, and she'd let herself into the chambers where she'd worked and fallen in love in what seemed a past life. There was much to say, but a sizable chance he'd want to have the talk elsewhere; after his disciplinary trouble, he'd come to take seriously the need to separate the personal from the professional. Still, she meant to carry out her plan to tell him she was breaking off their relationship, and Ruairí needed his good-night kiss.

Approaching along the hallway lined with staff attorney offices, one of them formerly hers and all of them now dark, she saw lights and sensed a presence in Conal's office. He hadn't returned her voicemail, but had apparently returned, and while striding into his office she announced to Ruairí, in singsong tones, "Let's go say hi to Daddy, shall we, sweetie?"

But it wasn't Daddy. Looking up mildly from the sofa, where he was leafing through a copy of *Judicature*, true to his word, was Allan Hetford. He quickly stood and approached her, smiling, his arms opened as if welcoming her to his own home.

"Sadie, hello. How good to see you and the little guy. Looking more like his father every day." Ruairí grinned wetly at the recognition. "Justice Corcoran let me in," he went on. "I hope you don't mind."

"Of course not, Allan; nor will Conal, I'm sure. I left him a message you might be stopping by. He's not here, then?"

"Doesn't look like it. He and whatever lucky staff attorney drew execution duty must have gone out for a bite to eat."

"I'm sorry you made the trip for nothing," she said.

"Oh, I'm perfectly willing to wait," he replied.

She wondered what could be so important as to incline Hetford to cool his heels indefinitely in Conal's empty chambers. Perhaps it was merely nostalgia for the court. Or maybe he was seeking advice on how to handle Eleanor, although he had always been much better at that than Conal.

She realized it must seem as though her manners had deserted her, and tried to correct the impression. "So how have you and Eleanor been lately?"

"Very well, thanks. We're just back from Singapore and Hong Kong."

"Sounds exciting. Business?"

"Partly. Eleanor did loads of shopping. Don't tell my wife, but sometimes, Sadie, I miss this place. Not that the business world isn't stimulating, but nowhere else is the work so marvelously varied and gratifying as here."

She nodded. "I miss it, too."

He patted her shoulder. "Of course, you would. And I miss my former colleagues. In retrospect, and after heading up the legal department at Marvelocity for a year, I'm certain there's no finer group of people to share a mission with than the justices of this court. Of course, I was too full of myself to know it when I was among them."

She failed to stifle a laugh. "I wish I'd known you better then, because I somehow got the sense you weren't a big fan of Conal's."

Hetford winced. "Somehow, someday, I'll prove to you that despite the awful things I did in the past, I'm worthy of your trust now."

"I have no doubt you are," she said. "Actually there is something you can do, if you don't mind."

"Name it."

"I need to run down to my office and...and pick up a book. Would you like to babysit for about five minutes?"

He gave a quick gasp. From his reaction she supposed he couldn't have changed that much after all. "It's no big deal," she said, hurriedly. "I'll take him with me—"

Hetford blushed, shaking his head. "No, no, I'd be delighted to spend some time with Ruairí. Why, Eleanor and I were just saying, the other day, how adorable he is. Damn, I—sorry, excuse me, that won't happen again, I promise—but if I'd known Ruairí and I were going to have a play date tonight I'd have stopped and picked up some toys on the way and—"

Sadie laughed. He really did seem enthusiastic about having a little time with the baby. "Yourself is all the entertainment he needs. Oh, just one warning: For some reason, he's terrified of itsy-bitsy s-p-i-d-e-r—"

"Aha. Got it. And who wouldn't be; those old nursery rhymes can be pretty dark stuff. No s-p-i-d-e-r-s on my watch, I can assure you."

"Perfect. I'll just literally run down, get my book, and come right back."

"Take your time, my dear."

"Thanks." She put the child into Hetford's arms. Ruairí stared solemnly at his father's former nemesis, who bloomed pink at the unaccustomed sensation of holding a warm, slightly moist, squirming baby. She'd never seen such a look of sweetness in Hetford; suddenly she understood what Eleanor must see in him.

"Hmm," he said, a little uncertainly. "He's a lot...denser than I expected."

Sadie laughed. "Yes, there's muscle and bone inside that chubby little exterior, you know. I'll be right back, then," she said, turning toward the door. "Ruairí, be a good boy."

The baby lifted a hand, opening and closing it to wish her bye-bye, then returned his attention to the tall man, who was like yet unlike his daddy and now was holding him securely in his arms, looking back at him intently.

Chapter Twenty-One

6:57 p.m., Thursday, February 25

"Thanks again for picking up the check," said Mike as they left the Burmese restaurant and started toward the state building. "But I'm going to pay you my share; I insist. I'll get some cash; my ATM's right across the street."

"If you feel you must," Anya said. "I'm happy to treat." But Mike was already jogging toward the corner.

Quirke stood dully looking after his staff attorney, relieved that his dinner with Anya was drawing to a close. She'd conversed with marginally more animation and less hostility than at the only other meal they'd shared, but he doubted he'd soon seek the pleasure of her company again. There was something irremediably humorless about her.

"I should be getting back to work," he said. "Shall we go in?" There seemed little point in hanging out on the sidewalk in front of the state building; Mike was obviously capable of finding his way back to chambers by himself.

"I thought I'd get a little fresh air while I can; we're going to be here for a few more hours, aren't we?"

"Yes," Quirke replied. "Only a few, if we're lucky and nobody files anything. I suppose it is nice to take the air when the traffic isn't so bad." Now that the evening commute was over, a freshness, hinting of the ocean beach a few miles to the west, had replaced the exhaust fumes that were the daytime signature fragrance of the Civic Center. Too bad it had grown too dark to see anything of the neighborhood. Anya gave a rare smile; but for the unhealthy leanness of her face, she would almost be pretty.

A hand suddenly gripping his elbow from behind made Quirke start and turn around. "Con, I've been looking for you."

Unshaven, sweaty, and shifting from one foot to another, his shirttails half out of his pants, Tad stared at him with a telltale exhilaration, looking jaundiced under the spotlights shining down from the eave of the building. His eyes were dilated and bloodshot; he licked his lips and moved from Quirke's left side to his right and back again.

"Excuse me, Anya," Quirke said, stepping away from her. He planned to cut this conversation as short as possible, and it was certainly not one he wanted an annual to overhear. "What do you want?" he whispered. "I have a feeling you didn't do what we talked about."

"I made a mistake, okay?" Tad said. "At least, I'm sure I'll think so tomorrow. Right now I'm just kind of fucked up. But when I saw you standing there, well, I figured you saw me, and I didn't want you to think I don't know I made a mistake. I'm sorry. Day zero."

"Relapses happen, Tad. Don't beat yourself up. The important thing is what you do starting now. In particular, you could start by getting rid of the stuff, like you told me you would."

"Not here, man!" Tad grabbed Quirke's arm again. "That's the federal building across the street. You know the FBI has offices in there. They could be looking through their telescopes at us right now. No, I gotta wait till really late—after midnight, or later. Or—or you could—"

"I told you I can't. And that's final."

Quirke cast a glance over his shoulder at Anya. She was still waiting, staring at him talking with Tad.

"This isn't a good time," Quirke added. "I have to go back to work."

Tad stamped a cowboy boot on the sidewalk. "Man, it's never a good time with you, is it? Ain't anyone twelfth-stepped you when you needed it?"

Guilt overswept Quirke. Of course, he'd been the beneficiary of twelfth-stepping, the best kind, from Bobby on multiple occasions. When he'd had the idle thought a little glass of bourbon couldn't hurt him, Bobby had been only a phone call away. Bobby had always given Quirke what he needed in the moment, talking him through the craving, dragging him to a meeting—when had he last seen the inside of a meeting, anyway?—or pointing him toward a helpful passage in the Big Book. Bobby would make time for a fellow addict.

"I'm sorry. I know I haven't been there for you like I should be," Quirke said. "We should sit down and have a chat."

"Yeah, that would be terrific. I'm not in the sit-down mood right this minute, though."

"I can see that. We could...take a walk, I suppose. Look, let me tell my colleague over there—"

"You work with the skinny chick, huh?"

"Sort of. I'll tell her to go back to the office without me. Just a sec, don't go anywhere." Quirke turned toward Anya, but she'd moved; she was behind him now, walking toward the curb.

"Anya," said Quirke, approaching her. "Don't wait for me; I'm going for a—"

As hard as he later tried to sort out what happened, the sequence of the next events remained murky. There was simultaneously a hard bump from behind, pushing him forward, and a large man, whose face he never saw, walking quickly away. Other footsteps, light ones, ran after him. Now he was so close to the street that when the van stopped and the door opened a millisecond later, he was within reach of the grabbing hands inside. Hands were also pulling on him from outside: Tad's. A pop, then pain, tearing pain, in his left shoulder. Grunts: his own. Shouts of at least two men. "If he won't let go, he's coming with us." A gunshot. Gasps, his and the others'. Darkness: cloth over his eyes. Men beside, on top of, him, subduing his struggles. Van door slamming. Cries of pain: Tad's. Hard acceleration. Plastic rings tightening down on his wrists; he knew what zip ties felt like. Tad crying out again. Then a breathing mask over his face and nothing more for a while.

Mike considered it lucky the Golden Donut Shop on the corner of Lamden, next to the ATM, still had holes at this hour. He bought the lot, half-price, and knew some of the attorneys and judges at the death vigil would thank him. As he crossed back to the state building, he saw that his boss and Anya had gone—up to chambers, no doubt, and he planned to get right back to work himself. As he was getting out his keycard to make his after-hours entrance, he heard a big noise from somewhere around the corner on Foltz Street. Then the building alarm began to sound.

Ninety-nine alarms out of a hundred were meaningless, and so he took his time heading to the elevator, but already there were people, colleagues he recognized, starting to emerge at the bottom of the staircases and walking through the door leading to Civic Center Plaza.

"Mike!" A Corcoran staff attorney, Morty Glaub, waved from across the lobby, and Mike jogged toward him. "Come on," Morty said, a little breathlessly, "the highway patrol's taking us to a secure location. Judges, attorneys, judicial assistants, everybody."

"Why? I heard a big boom; what just happened?"

"Nobody's really sure, but we have to get out. The execution's still on, as far as anybody knows. We're going to reassemble—they haven't actually told us where."

"Is Justice Quirke with you guys?"

"If he's in the building, he's gotta be. Come on, we have to get out of here."

Mike frowned. All his notes and papers on the Dormund case were upstairs, on his desk, but he wasn't about to miss his ride to the secure location. As Morty headed for the stairs to the basement, which gave onto the parking level, Mike followed.

Chapter Twenty-Two

7:00 p.m., Thursday, February 25

Sadie headed down the still, dark hallway toward the stair. She fished her phone out of the bag that was still pulling at her shoulder, and checked the time. Seven exactly. With Allan determined to wait for Conal, there was little or no chance of a serious talk with him tonight. Even if he hadn't returned by the time she got back to the third floor, she'd have to take Ruairí home, or else between the bath and remaining evening rituals he'd be up well past his bedtime.

In the stairwell someone, presumably an occupant of an office on the third floor, had left a volume of the F.2d reporter on the metal railing. She decided to ignore it for the time being and proceeded down the stairs to her office on the floor below, in Justice Latimore's chambers. Everything was even darker there than on the third floor, since no official business was being conducted at the Court of Appeal on this night.

Once away from Allan and the baby, in the quiet Latimore chambers in the Court of Appeal, she felt her tenuous self-control slipping. She thanked God no one was around to witness her agitation; she could let tears fall freely on the briefs, treatises, and photocopied cases littering her desk, knowing that when she returned to work in the morning only faint ripples in the dried paper would betray the evening's emotion. But if it happened that she did have the chance to speak to Conal tonight, and to end their relationship, tomorrow would be different in unpredictable ways. Would he leave the loft voluntarily? Or would he drink himself into a transport of fury and do and say things he'd regret, things that would make it impossible for her to let him see Ruairí? Would Roísín be too angry to stay on? Would Conal tell of his unhappiness to his old friend Justice Latimore, and would he, in turn, fire her for her cruelty? She sat, head in her hands, for long minutes.

Above all else, she needed to talk with Liam. Unless Father Bridges had taken away Liam's phone—were any pastors that medieval nowadays?—his being on a leave of absence wouldn't preclude him from talking to her, if he wanted to. She was still angry at him for cutting off communication, and fully intended to tell him so; she would also tell him of the coming change in her situation and that she loved him, whatever he might choose to do. Taking her phone in her trembling hands, she tapped his number.

"I hear you came looking for me." His phone manner of bypassing pleasantries—a hillbilly thing?—had a way of always thrilling her.

"You heard right. I planned to tell you how furious I am with you. But...are you still in Sant' Urbano?"

"Do you really think I'd leave town without telling you?"

"It's just that Father Bridges said you were on a leave, and he was looking at me like some of the Goetic demons I've conjured. I remembered what you said about how they—I mean the Church—treats priests who stray—"

"Makes me sound like an old hound dog," he laughed.

"Anyway, I didn't know if they'd handcuffed you and taken you away in the dead of night as if this were some cheesy intervention, or what. I hope you're okay?"

"Okay? Yeah, I'm okay. I'm annoyed myself—not at you, of course, but at Bridges's presumption that I'll submit to being treated for what they want to think is my emotional disorder, immaturity, sex addiction, or whatever the fuck they want to call it. Sadie, I've thought it over."

"And?" she asked, barely audibly.

"And I've realized Bridges is right about one thing. I do have a fit problem. I just don't think I need fixing."

"I don't, either." She was prepared to tell him or anyone who asked that he was perfect as he was.

"That's gratifying, but will you still think so when I'm an unemployed ex-priest?"

"You'll get tired of being unemployed. Maybe you can finally get that outdoor job you've always wanted."

He laughed. "You're sure it's not the glamour of the Roman collar that caught your eye? I'd hate for you to be disappointed in me."

"Yes, I'm sure. But, Liam, I'm going to solve my own fit problem. That was one of the things I called to say. I'm going to tell him it's over. I'm at my office right now. He's supposed to be working tonight, and I went to his chambers, thinking I'd see him when he got back from dinner. I was too early, and then a friend of his showed up. I'm not sure when I'll have the chance to do it, but...but I'm going to do it."

"Darlin', I know it takes courage to do what you plan to do, and I'll be thinking of you, praying for you. Call me anytime. Sadie, I love you."

"I love you, too," she said. The visible world seemed to dissolve, shimmering, into a bright unity that erased all of the distance and the barriers between them, promising that all the difficulties would be overcome. She felt his strong arms enfolding her, protecting her. Never again, she felt, would the past haunt her or contemplation of the unknown future dishearten her.

She would make one more call, to let Roísín know she would soon be on her way home, and then go back upstairs and retrieve Ruairí from Allan. The call took but a moment, and then she shouldered her bag, turned out the lights, and headed toward the stairwell. She was thinking she'd pop into the library and return the loose volume of F.2d on her way back to Conal's office.

Climbing the steps and drawing closer, she could see something was different about it; it was a book, yet not a book.

Chapter Twenty-Three

7:12 p.m., Thursday, February 25

The restless charm in the child's blue eyes reminded Hetford of his father; his auburn ringlets were his mother's. It was just as Eleanor said: Ruairí was a really cute baby. Alas, his attention span was no better than what one might expect of an eight-month-old; he quickly tired of sitting on Hetford's lap and having a *Judicature* article read to him about the decline in the number of civil trials, and he showed no patience at all for a statistics-laden study on the impact of mandatory minimum sentencing. Before the child grew excessively fretful, Hetford hit on the idea of giving him a horseback ride. Accordingly, he sat Ruairí on his knees, lifted his little fists, and began to bounce him vigorously while singing, in a western twang, a song from an old Gene Autry movie: "I'm back in the saddle again / Out where a friend is a friend / Where the longhorn cattle feed on the lonely jimson weed / Back in the saddle again.' " Ruairí burbled approvingly. "Ah, we like that, do we? Another verse, then. 'Ridin' the range once more / Totin' my old forty-four / Where you sleep out every night and the only law is right.' " The lad squealed, apparently applauding the antinomian sentiment. " 'Back in the saddle again.' Well, my young friend, what shall we do next?"

Before Ruairí could voice an opinion, a gigantic crash rocked the state building. Hetford fell off the sofa onto the carpeted floor; Ruairí, lying beside him, was too stunned to cry out. Hetford scrambled onto his knees, scooped up the baby, and held him close against his chest.

"All is well, all is well," he murmured. "I've got you. No worries, Uncle Allan's got you." He kissed the top of the baby's head. A sob in the child's throat dissolved, and he exhaled. What in God's name had just happened? It felt like an earthquake, almost. Holding Ruairí, he stepped out of the office.

Justice Wiggins and one of her attorneys were standing in the hallway, shaking their heads, looking as confused as he felt.

"What happened?" Wiggins asked. "I tried calling the Chief; couldn't reach her. It felt like a bomb went off just now. Allan, what are you doing here?"

"Hello, Carol. I've been waiting for Quirke; you haven't seen him?"

"Babysitting now? Yet another career change?"

"Sadie brought the lad by to see his papa and went downstairs for a minute. She—"

The building alarm began to sound, loudly and annoyingly, in triplet bursts. Then the alarm stopped and a voice, one of the security guards or perhaps a highway patrol officer, came over the speaker system. "Attention! Attention! All personnel are to exit the building. Follow normal evacuation procedures. Attention, attention! Leave calmly and immediately." The triplet bursts resumed and showed no sign of stopping.

"I guess they mean business," said Justice Wiggins. "Emily," she said to her attorney, "let's get out of here. I wouldn't wait around if I were you, Allan."

"I'm sure Sadie will be back any second now for the baby. I think I'd better—"

Just then one of the double doors to the Wiggins-Quirke wing of the third floor flew open and a tall, well-knit man, a highway patrol officer Hetford recognized as a member of the Judicial Protection Detail, ran toward them. "We're going to need everyone to evacuate immediately," he said as he arrived at their side. "That blast may have been deliberate, and there may be more. The bomb squad's going to have to search the whole building. Justice Wiggins, the court is assembling on the Lamden side for transport to a secure location."

"Staff, too?" said Wiggins, glancing at her nervous-looking attorney.

"Yes, of course. All non-court personnel are evacuating per the standard protocol, to Civic Center Plaza," the officer said, looking at Hetford.

Wiggins frowned. "Allan Hetford was a justice up until about a year ago. Plus, that's Justice Quirke's child he's got there. Allan's the sitter. Isn't there some way he can get preferential—"

"Not the sitter exactly," Hetford interjected. "But the child's mother's on the premises somewhere. She went to the second floor a few minutes ago to retrieve something from her office."

"Then she'll undoubtedly be evacuating to the plaza herself," said the officer. "I'm sorry, but I have to insist that everybody get out now. I don't want to sound too alarmist, but we don't know what kind of a situation we've got here. For all the times we've rolled our eyes at the word, there's a strong possibility we're dealing with a terrorist event."

"Say no more, officer," said Justice Wiggins. "We're out of here. I'm just going to go scoop up some papers on my desk and—"

"With all due respect, Judge, no, you're not. In the secure location, there'll be materials and facilities for conducting court business." The officer lightly laid a hand on the shoulders of each of the women and began walking them toward the double doors. "And, sir," he called to Hetford, "please don't force us to come back and get you. The whole unit's been recalled to duty, and each of us officers is going to be spread pretty thin tonight. Just head out to the plaza, please."

"All right," Hetford replied, following them, still holding Ruairí close in his arms.

A handful of workers from the courts and the other agencies in the state building complex gathered in the plaza; after a few minutes, most gave up the vigil and walked away. Across the street, City Hall was lit with rainbow lights. Ruairí stared, fascinated, at the scene; firetrucks and other emergency vehicles that had pulled up, skewing at various angles on Foltz Street, seemed to hold a special interest for him. Floodlights on the ladder trucks illuminated the side of the building the blast had come from, but from where he was standing Hetford could see nothing amiss. He wanted to get close in and take a look, but it seemed wrong to subject the baby to a scene of violence and chaos, even from across the street; for all he knew, it could traumatize the little fellow. Besides, the officer was right: After taking part in innumerable emergency drills at the office over the years, Sadie would know to look for them right here.

Except she didn't. Hetford stood directly opposite the main entrance to the state building and saw that, pretty quickly at this late hour, the trickle of evacuees stopped and no other persons emerged. He could also see that guards, still holding red placards, were turning away the few who sought to reenter. It was very odd that Sadie, whose first thought in an emergency would doubtless have been her baby's safety, would not have found them right away.

A few minutes more, and he and Ruairí were alone in the plaza save for the derelicts, cocooned in sleeping bags, whose residence it was. Hetford found an unoccupied bench and sat down, Ruairí on his lap. The baby had fallen asleep in the bracing air. Hetford adjusted his suit jacket around him for warmth and pulled out his phone, stifling a flare of unease when Quirke's voicemail picked up.

"Quirke, Allan Hetford here. Sorry to bother you; I assume you've evacuated with the rest of the court to the 'secure location,' wherever that might be, and you're busy with official duties at the moment, but I find myself in Civic Center Plaza with your little boy. Now, don't panic, papa dear, he's fine; we're simply waiting for Sadie to join us so she can take him home. I was wondering, Quirke, will you call me back with her phone number, just in case she got evacuated somewhere else and is wondering where we are? In the meantime, we'll be here. For you I suppose the show must go on in spite of this bizarre thing, whatever it is, that just happened. Anyway, please give me a call as soon as you can."

News media trucks were beginning to pull up to the building, their film crews trying to find the optimal angle. The emergency vehicles showed no signs of leaving, and Hetford could see that Foltz and Lamden Streets had been closed to traffic.

He and Ruairí had now been sitting on the plaza for twenty minutes; Sadie really should have found her way here by this time, unless she'd been forced to exit the Golden Gate side of the building for some reason and been unable to get through to the plaza. Most likely, and reasonably, she was expecting him to be able to find her in this mess. Alternate possibilities might exist, but he could not allow them into his mind.

He had to try to find her. He rose from the bench as smoothly as he could, held the sleeping Ruairí on his right arm, and slipped his left arm out of his jacket and covered the baby against the cold night air. He crossed the street and mounted the steps to the main entrance to the state building.

The only person stationed at the door was one of the private security guards. The man, who looked old enough to have retired from some other career and to be nearing the end of this one, still clutched his red placard, wearing a bewildered look. "Hello—" Hetford began.

"Can't let anybody in yet," the guard interrupted. "Sorry, sir."

"I understand that, but I need to find someone. Can you tell me where the other evacuation areas are, so I can go and look for her?"

"I don't know what you're talking about," he said. "Everybody went out into the plaza. That's the protocol. This person you're looking for—think she might have started walking over to Market Street to catch a bus or a subway or something?"

"Not without the baby. Look, can I talk to somebody who's been through the—the damaged area?"

"Negative, sir. I'm sorry. You would not believe how many officers they've got investigating the scene right now. As well as searching the rest of the building, in case there are any other bombs or whatever the hell it was. It's probably going to be all night before they tell us anything. I wouldn't count on coming in to work tomorrow morning if I were you."

"Look, there's a chance she may still be in the building. I need to let the authorities know so they can look in the right place. Give me the number for the highway patrol, Captain—what's his name?—or Lieutenant...Grimes, Lieutenant Grimes. I need to tell them where to start looking for her."

"I haven't seen either one of them tonight," the guard said. "I know Sergeant Kaperski's here, want me to tell him for you?"

Hetford's arm was beginning to tire with Ruairí's weight, and it didn't seem wise to keep the child out in the night air indefinitely on what might turn out to be a long and inefficient search. With some reservations, he nodded to the guard. "Her name's Sadie Quirke. She's a petite young woman, about thirty-five, reddish hair, dressed in...I think black. She has an office on the second floor, in Justice Latimore's chambers in the Court of Appeal. Or she may be somewhere else in the building."

"I'll tell Sergeant Kaperski. Sadie Drew, you said."

"No, no, Quirke. Sadie Quirke."

"Sorry. Now why did I say Drew? Tired already; don't know how I'm going to last through the night. Quirke. Right. I'll pass that along next time I see the Sergeant."

"Well, can't you go and find him? Time may be of the essence."

The guard stared uncomprehendingly at him. "Sorry, sir. I'm not permitted to leave my post until my break or somebody tells me it's okay."

Hetford was about to remonstrate with him, but could see it would do no good. "All right. Thank you for your help. By the way, my name's Allan Hetford. Let me give you my card." Gently transferring Ruairí from one shoulder to the other, he fished his wallet out of his back pocket, pulled out a business card, and handed it to the guard. "Please have them call me with any news about Sadie Quirke. And thanks."

Back in the plaza, the bench they'd been sitting on had been preempted by a now somnolent street person sheltering under a collection of tattered shopping bags. The time had come for him and the child to go indoors, he thought. From his front pants pocket he retrieved his phone.

"Allan darling! Where are you? I heard—"

"Dearest, I'm at the state building. I came down to see Quirke, but there's been some kind of disaster down here and...and I need you."

"I'm on my way. Where will I find you?"

"On Civic Center Plaza. Actually, the streets around the state building are closed, so look for us in front of City Hall, on the plaza side."

"Us?"

"I'll explain."

Chapter Twenty-Four

8:00 p.m., Thursday, February 25

Quirke awoke—dizzy, his head aching, an ominous burning sensation in his left rotator cuff—on the carpeted floor of the van a foot or two from some irregular bloodstains. The breathing mask was gone, but the zip-ties still bound his wrists. The van was parked inside a cavernous, warehouse-like space; its side door stood open, the harsh dome light augmenting the dim illumination in the structure around him. He did not immediately see anyone.

He felt only anger in the moment. "Fuck," he muttered. Being kidnapped was like being struck by lightning or contracting smallpox: if it happens to you once, you should be able to expect not to have to go through it again. What kind of idiot would kidnap a judge, anyway? It wasn't as if he had any money. If anything, he was now famous for being the penniless ex-husband of the socialite daughter of Marvelocity's CEO. It was Hetford who ought to be watching his back nowadays.

What he saw next made him wonder if it was ketamine they'd pumped through the mask, for the sight of Rackrent's annual, Anya, leaning into the van with an AK-47 slung over her bony shoulder had to be a hallucination.

But it wasn't. "On your feet, Judge. Let's go." She waved the barrel of the weapon at him, pulling at his jacket as a tall, lanky man in a black hoodie, from whose waistband the black grip of a semiautomatic handgun protruded, yanked at his left arm. Quirke yelled in pain and the man let go, instead taking hold of his right. They soon had him standing outside the van and were marching him, gun barrel poking his ribs—another unpleasantly familiar sensation—toward an open door in the wall just ahead, following a trail of blood spatter on the concrete floor. Neither Anya nor her crime partner spoke.

Through the door was a metal staircase, and they began to climb. Reaching the floor above, they push-pulled him through another doorway into what must once have been an office space in this industrial building. Four heavy wooden desks were pushed together in the center of the room, their corresponding chairs queued against the wall underneath a huge, many-paned window. Long metal file cabinets lined two sides of the room; ancient computer equipment was piled in a dark corner in a nest of cables. In the corner farthest from the door a vertical pipe ran from the ceiling down through the floor; tethered to it was Tad, bloodied and subdued but conscious. He shot Quirke an anxious look devoid of his usual irritated bravado.

Sitting on one of the desks, a young man—pale, wiry, in stained sweatclothes, kinky strawberry-blond hair poking out around the bandanna tied at the back of his neck—nodded and gave an arrogant smile, and the man in the black hoodie collapsed, as if exhausted, into one of the chairs arrayed against the wall. Across Rusty's lap lay a rifle like the one Anya was carrying. Still zip-tied and in pain, pretty certain there could be no explanation for her participation in this event consistent with loyal service to the court, and annoyed at the interruption to his evening, Quirke turned around and laid into her.

"Anya, what the hell is this all about? Who are these people? And are you familiar with Penal Code section 209, aggravated kidnapping, specifically the sentencing provisions? If not, you might want to take a look before this little adventure gets out of hand."

Still training her rifle on him, she would not meet his eyes. "Rusty will tell you all you need to know."

Her passivity infuriated him. "I suppose you're Rusty," he said, turning to the strawberry blond man. "As Anya may have mentioned, I'm Conal Quirke, Associate Justice of the state Supreme Court. This abduction thing seems like an exceptionally stupid idea to me but, luckily for you, I'm prepared to forget all about it after you let me and the other guy over there go."

"We know who you are, and that's not how it's going to work. So I need your Twitter handle." Rusty held Quirke's phone, looking at him expectantly. Off to the side, Quirke could see Tad staring at him, amazement mixed with incredulity on his face. Tad was probably going to find out sooner or later who Quirke was, but this was not the way he'd have chosen to self-disclose.

"I don't have one of those," Quirke said. He began to formulate an unpleasant theory regarding what Rusty was planning.

"You don't? Well, we'll pick one for you, then, because you're going to be tweeting prolifically tonight. What do you think of 'QuirkeJ'?"

"Nice," Anya said.

"And you know what you're going to be tweeting?" Rusty asked him.

"Evidently this isn't about money. If you think anyone's going to believe—"

Rusty didn't wait for Quirke to finish his objection. "No, it isn't about money. You, Conal Quirke, are going to be making an impassioned plea for the commutation of Marcus Dormund's sentence and an end to the death penalty. You know, you should be glad you get to be a part of this—it's going to be a historic moment, when the state finally gets rid of this barbaric ritual. You, just by being here, are going to make an actual difference in people's lives."

Quirke glared. "I was in the process of doing that when you kidnapped me."

"So I'll go ahead and open a Twitter account for you," said Rusty, as though he'd said nothing. "Play Store password?"

Quirke stood in the center of the disused office, the radicals' eyes on him. For the first time he noticed a third man crouched in the shadows near Tad; rugged looking, probably over six feet tall, he now stood and moved toward the others, his rifle slung over his shoulders. It seemed resistance would be unwise, but perhaps there was room for negotiation.

"I'll give you the password," Quirke said, "if you let that guy over there go. This has nothing to do with him."

Rusty laughed. "Oh yeah, like that's happening."

"Look, he knows how to keep his mouth shut. This is not a guy who's ever going to the cops. That I can guarantee."

"He's right!" Tad exclaimed. "I so won't say a word. I have terrible memory problems—you might say my memory's nonexistent."

"You can see he needs medical help," Quirke said, more calmly. "Don't multiply your problems by letting anything happen to him." Conscious at every step of the three weapons trained on him, Quirke crossed the room and squatted beside Tad.

"First, thanks for trying to stop this. I appreciate the risk you were taking and I'm sorry you got shot," he murmured.

"Last time I ever try anything that altruistic."

Grimacing, Tad was applying pressure to a wound on his arm, trying to stanch the bleeding. The blood on his hands and shirt was still dripping onto the pipe and floor, and the untreated wound made Quirke feel guilty and useless. "How are you doing?" he asked.

Tad shook his head as if to brush off the inquiry, but the greyish-white of his complexion indicated the answer would not have been encouraging. "Con, are you really...what you said? No wonder you get on my case so hard." Tad lowered his voice. "I never heard of a drug addict judge before."

"Well, now you have," Quirke said. "Look, I'm trying my best to get them to cut you loose. How much pain do you have? On a scale of one to ten?"

"Eight. Nine," he said, wincing.

"You still have the stash?"

"In my undershirt in back. Also in my socks." He lowered his voice. "These dorkwads just grabbed my phone, didn't even pat me down."

"Well, hang onto it for now."

"Con, or should I say Judge, it ain't like I have a lot of choice at the moment."

Rusty was addressing Quirke. "I suppose you don't have a Facebook account, either, eh, Conal?"

"Everybody calls me Quirke," he said, getting awkwardly to his feet. "Except my closest friends. And no, I don't. Judges don't do social media, as a rule."

"The sacrifices our public servants make," Rusty said, sneering. "Well, I don't see why not. We're going to create a platform where you can call out the evil of the death penalty and demand change. Best of all, you don't need to worry about content—I've written a shitload for you. In fact, I'm going to make this so easy, you won't need to do a thing; I'll even upload it."

Visions of the social media nightmares Hetford had engineered to gum up his retention campaign, and the fantastically distorted impressions of him many people still entertained, rose in his mind. "I'd strongly suggest you give this a little more thought," he told Rusty. "This might surprise you, but my fifteen minutes were up a while ago. The number of people who'd pay any attention right now to tweets purporting to come from me would probably number in the low tens. Hardly enough to set off a dramatic change in social attitudes or catalyze a movement to abolish the death penalty. Hey, wait—there's already a movement to abolish the death penalty. It's called the initiative process, and it's happening in the general election in a few months. You might want to consider voting, if you can spare the time. Can we go home now?"

"Conal, you don't do sarcasm very well. What do you think, we're idiots? We know all about the election. Trouble is, the voters got it wrong last time. We—you—have to make sure there are no more fuck-ups."

There is nothing you can say to a vanguardist, Quirke thought sadly. He tried pressing on a spot he hoped was more vulnerable. "And what about you, Anya? Are you really down for this? Nothing in the oath you took to become a lawyer gives you any qualms when you point that thing at me?"

She remained silent, looking at her feet in the manner of a child apprehended in some misdemeanor.

"And what's your exit strategy, have you given that any thought?" he continued. "Any plan for after this?" Still she hung her head and said nothing. "Looking forward to life underground?"

"I need that password now, Conal," Rusty cut in. Quirke saw him nod at the other man, who, with his finger on the trigger of his gun, moved closer to Tad.

There was no point in putting Tad at greater risk. "Sadie—capital S—nine-three-nine-three."

After making a note, Rusty smiled. "In a few minutes you're going to be trending. And you can be damn sure the guy who holds the cards is going to be following you."

"If you're referring to the Governor, I doubt he'll be receptive. He's not a huge fan of mine." Hetford, in a confessional moment, had told Quirke his initial aim in trying to torpedo Quirke's re-election chances, and thus open up a seat on the court, had been to impress Governor Stan Darven—Quirke's political polar opposite—and score points toward the attainment of his higher ambitions. According to Hetford, Darven had expressed glee at the prospect of Quirke losing. "This little conspiracy isn't going to get very far, I'm afraid," Quirke added. "You really ought to abort it before things get out of hand."

"At this point I'm going to ask you to keep it down, Conal; I need to concentrate. If that's too much for you, we can stuff a rag in it."

Tad yelled, outrage in his voice. "Show some respect, you fucking little douchebag. That's a Supreme Court justice you're talking to." The third man wasted no time in giving him a hard backhand to the cheek. Blood sprayed from his mouth. Quirke started toward him, but stopped when the man grabbed the barrel of his gun.

"I'm tired of listening to his shit," Rusty said. "Put him in the other room." The third man nodded and untethered Tad from the pole, then pulled him, stumbling, away toward a darkened passageway beyond the file cabinets. "As for you, Conal, if I have to tell you again to shut up, you're going to be joining him."

This wasn't going very well, Quirke thought, even for a kidnapping. He had to form some kind of rapport with these young idiots, no matter how distasteful the prospect.

"So, Rusty," he said, "how long have you been a death penalty activist? I mean, of all the many societal issues crying out for—"

"Tie him up and gag him, Dane," Rusty said. The hoodied man who'd brought him upstairs with Anya stood up for the first time since they'd come in and approached Quirke, undoing the bandanna on his head.

"Wait, I'm sorry. No need for that. I'll pipe down." Quirke knew he'd have to work carefully to ingratiate himself with these hotheads, and it was critical not to be silenced. "Sorry."

Clearly unenthusiastic about further restraining Quirke, Dane looked to his leader. But Rusty was too busy uploading content to Quirke's brand-new Twitter feed to give orders, and Dane sidled off to the cluster of tables to sit down again.

"May I ask what I'm saying, at least?" Quirke asked, half expecting the butt of a gun to come down on the back of his head. "On the feed."

"First, sit," Anya said, pointing to the bare concrete. He complied with some reluctance; she brought her phone closer and, sitting on her scrawny haunches, held it in front of him.

"A little farther away, please," Quirke said, his zip-tied hands unable to make the necessary adjustment themselves. "An old man can't see up close any longer, I'm afraid."

He waited for polite contradiction, but received none. This was going to be an exceptionally long night, even if he wasn't killed. As the feed scrolled up, he couldn't help being impressed by his own eloquence. "I wish I'd said that. Where did he get this stuff? Oh wait, I recognize that one: 'If Jesus had been killed twenty years ago, Catholic schoolchildren would be wearing little electric chairs around their necks instead of crosses.' But everybody's going to think I'm plagiarizing Lenny Bruce. 'Since governments take the right of death over their people, it is not astonishing...if the people should sometimes take the right of death over governments.' A writer like Maupassant can get away with voicing sentiments like that, a judge not so much. 'Being condemned to death is the only real distinction...the only thing that cannot be bought.' Have you ever read *The Red and the Black*, Anya?"

"Of course I have," she snapped. "I double-majored in French and political theory."

"I'm sorry, did you tell me that already?" He read aloud as the tweets proliferated. "'With every cell of my being and with every fiber of my memory I oppose the death penalty in all forms...I do not believe any civilized society should be at the service of death...I don't think it's human to become an agent of the angel of death.' Great quote. Elie Wiesel, I'm pretty sure. 'People who are well represented at trial do not get the death penalty.' Ruth Bader Ginsburg; she's wrong about that, actually; there are some facts no amount of good lawyering can overcome. 'Judicial execution can never cancel or remove the atrocity it seeks to punish; it can only add a second atrocity to the original one.' I like that. Oh, finally an attribution: Auberon Waugh. Huh. Not exactly a progressive, but that's the Catholic influence for you."

"He's starting to drive me nuts again," Rusty interjected.

"Look, could you just sort of shut up?" Anya asked. "It's better not to irritate him."

Quirke gave a mock moue. "That's a pity. We were just starting to have fun."

She shot him the most fleeting of smiles, a major victory.

"Hey, Rusty," Dane called. "You up for something to eat?"

"Yeah, I could eat. What were you thinking of?"

As the three men discussed whether one of them should go on their behalf to a takeout falafel place they'd spied in the neighborhood, Quirke hazarded further rapport building with Anya, who had withdrawn her phone as the food discussions temporarily silenced the feed, and was now standing, looking bored, a little distance away.

"I'm concerned about Tad," Quirke told her. "He was still bleeding. Mind if I go check on him?"

She looked startled, then shrugged. "I suppose not. Here, I'll help you up." She pulled on his left arm, reigniting the pain and eliciting a sharp groan. "What's that about?" she asked. It seemed to Quirke, or perhaps he only hoped, a trace of concern underlay the brusqueness.

"My shoulder. Something happened when I was pulled into the van," he replied, trying to breathe through the pain. "If you could touch me somewhere else, please. If you need to touch me."

"Just a minute," she said coldly. She went to the window and returned with one of the chairs. "Push off this."

With the aid of the chair, he succeeded in getting to his feet and headed toward the door to the room beyond, where the third man had taken Tad; she followed.

Turning to her, he said, trying to sound apologetic, "It's inconvenient for both of us having my wrists bound like this. If you undo them, I promise I won't try to overpower you or anything like that. Sound okay?"

She only shook her head and averted her eyes. He could see she was terrified of making a decision, lest it turn out to be the wrong one. Again he wondered what on earth could have led an honors graduate of Crowne Hall Law to this pass.

Chapter Twenty-Five

8:00 p.m., Thursday, February 25

Three midnight blue Toyota Highlanders followed an Electra Glide Harley with Highway Patrol insignia into the underground parking garage attached to a high-rise building on a quiet block of Jones Street near the crest of one of Sant' Urbano's most famous hills. The eighteen occupants of the SUVs debarked far more quietly than might be expected for a group of its size. In successive groups of six, they filled the elevators and ascended to the twenty-second floor of the building. There they entered the Chief Justice's apartment, where the housekeeper showed them to the spacious living room. Clean, light, modern furnishings, a glossy grand piano, and a wall of windows with a view of the Financial District greeted them, and one of the court's IT guys was already setting up a computer network and conference phone. Ward Freitag pulled stacks of memos out of enormous brief bags and distributed them to the justices as each of them found a place to sit. The Chief was on the phone in another room, receiving a status update from Judicial Protection officers still at the state building. The heavy atmosphere typical of the court's execution night protocol was already beginning to imbue the gathering in spite of its atypical start, but the confusion and uncertainty regarding what exactly had driven them out of their normal workspace was uppermost in everyone's mind.

The housekeeper wordlessly gestured to staff attorneys to occupy the upholstered straight-backed chairs, borrowed from the dining room, that had been arrayed along the wall of bookcases opposite the windows, but they seemed to prefer to hover, whispering, in small clumps behind the justices. Presently the housekeeper set a plate of sweets—sliced pound cake and cookies—on the coffee table in the center of the room, and made another trip to the kitchen for carafes of water and a pot of coffee. Mike Frentz remembered the large bag of donut holes he was carrying and took her aside to ask for a tray.

When court and staff were at last settled and restoring their blood sugar levels, Morty Glaub leaned toward Mike and said, "I guess I was wrong."

"About what?" Mike asked, looking up from his Twitter feed.

"I thought your boss was with the group, but he isn't here yet."

Mike scanned the room, confusion registering on his freckled face. "You're right. That's weird. He went inside the building a little ahead of me when we were coming back after dinner—he should have been right there when we started evacuating."

"Well, I don't think I've seen him at all tonight."

"I wonder what's up. Thanks, Morty. I'd better go and see Ward."

Mike interrupted a conversation between the Clerk-Administrator and Justice Farley, who were standing at the window looking at the glittering lights of the Financial District and the bay beyond. "Excuse me, Judge, Ward. This is going to sound stupid, but have you heard from Justice Quirke tonight?"

Justice Farley frowned momentarily, then left them to converse with Justice Kroner on the sofa. "I was about to ask you that," Ward said.

"We went to dinner around six and came back a little after seven— this was before the explosion. At least I thought he came back; I went to run an errand and left him on the sidewalk on the Golden Gate side of the building. Strangely enough, Anya Holmquist—Justice Rackrent's annual— went with us to dinner. She was with him last I saw him, and she isn't here, either, even though she said she was staying for the execution."

They each glanced at Sophia Rackrent, who was occupying a loveseat between the bookshelves and the windows with only her Plantinga for company. "Oh, boy," Ward said. "I hesitate to attribute significance to that, but..."

The implication hung in the air. "Oh, no," said Mike, shaking his head. "Uh-uh. I know the Judge has a certain reputation, but...no way."

"Of course not. Quirke's been the victim of more unwarranted gossip and slander than any man I've ever known, and I'm not going to add to it. Let's ask Justice Rackrent if she's heard from Anya; that might solve at least part of the mystery."

The self-possessed Justice Rackrent barely looked up from her book as the two men approached. Before her appointment she'd been a professor at Crowne Hall Law School specializing in antitrust law, and had maintained a pipeline to her former institution through which she drew the most promising graduates to serve as her annual clerks. At forty-five both the newest and the youngest justice at the court, Sophia Rackrent was of modest height and plump build, moving little and saying less when among her court colleagues, though rumor had it that in front of a friendly audience she could lecture animatedly for hours on vertical distributional restraints. She wore her mouse-brown hair in a smooth chignon and dressed in dowdy yet expensive pantsuits, this one the color of inky cabernet, adorned at all times with a double strand of pearls and matching earrings.

"Sorry to bother you, Judge," Ward said. "Counting heads here, I was just wondering if you've seen or heard from your clerk, Anya. I understand she drew execution duty tonight."

The judge lifted her eyebrows, surveyed the room, and shook her head. "No, I haven't. Looks like she decided not to stay on after all."

"Isn't that a little unusual—ducking out of a work obligation without at least clearing it with you?" Ward asked.

The judge shook her head. "I'm not surprised, and I wouldn't call it an obligation. Apart from performing the age-old ritual—a very worthy and fine thing in itself, of course—we really don't have anything to do tonight. The idea was for her to have the experience, not that I particularly need her here. If she decided it wasn't worth her time, so be it."

"That's entirely understandable. Still," said Ward, "under the circumstances it would have been nice to hear about her change of plans...just for the comfort of knowing she's safe."

"I would say I'll have a word with her tomorrow, but I'm afraid I'd only come off sounding like her mother," said the judge, a wry smile on her face. "Meanwhile, Ward, I'd advise you to chill out."

"I'll try, Judge." Nodding to her, Ward led Mike out of the living room. "I hate to do this," he confided, "but the Chief needs to know."

Mike felt self-conscious roaming about the Chief Justice's apartment, but he followed the Clerk-Administrator as he searched for her through the dining room, pantry, and kitchen, and was about to investigate the bedrooms that lay beyond. The weirdness of the situation was impressing itself more forcefully on him by the minute, when the Chief herself, slipping her phone into a jacket pocket, emerged from a bathroom.

"Only place in the house where I can hear myself think," she said. "What's up, Ward? You look about to tell me something you don't think I want to hear."

"We seem to be missing two," he began.

"Don't tell me," she said. "Mike looks just as anxious as you do. Does this have anything to do with Quirke?"

"You wouldn't have heard from him, by any chance? He hasn't been seen since just after dinner," Ward said.

"Where was that?" she asked.

Mike described his last sighting of his boss.

"That was the last anyone's seen of Rackrent's annual, too," Ward added. "Not that there's necessarily a connection, except they had dinner together. Sophia doesn't seem too nonplussed at being abandoned, though."

The Chief pursed her lips and thought for a moment. "Our convening tonight is pure formality, unless Dormund files something—we are open for business in that regard, aren't we, Ward?"

By custom, the court extends to a condemned prisoner on the night of his or her execution the opportunity to file litigation after the normal close of business. The address of a digital drop box is provided to counsel for the purpose. On this unusually eventful evening, Dormund's attorneys had not availed themselves of the privilege. They hadn't definitively said they wouldn't, however.

"We're set up for it. I've got the clerk's stamp right here," Ward said, patting his jacket pocket. "But no word from Dormund's lawyers so far."

"Until they send something our way, or in fact until they do and we've split on what to do with it, we don't absolutely need Quirke. I would have appreciated his letting me know if he planned not to be with us, though." She thought for a moment. "I'll just call to confirm he planned to skip. Excuse me," she added, retreating into the lavatory again.

Ward and Mike returned to the living room, Mike to industriously read briefs in the case Quirke had just assigned him and Ward to chat with several of the justices in an effort to make the time seem to go faster. Neither could put entirely out of mind the awareness that, only twenty miles away, time was likely passing very differently for Marcus Dormund.

"Quirke, your absence hasn't gone unnoticed," the Chief said when prompted to leave a message. "As I think you must know, we've assembled in our alternate location. I'm sorry you decided to break with tradition, but there've been no new filings, so with any luck your presence won't be required tonight. If it is, well, I'll be back in touch. Meanwhile, I hope you're enjoying the evening. Say hi to Sadie from me."

The scenario felt wrong, somehow. Quirke would never casually ditch the execution protocol; he'd said on multiple occasions he viewed the death vigil as part of the job, and he almost certainly would have told her if he'd intended not to join the court this evening. Conceivably there had been a family emergency; although she had little basis to think she could help, and no desire to intrude, she felt uneasy enough to phone Sadie. But she had no greater success in reaching her.

When she emerged from the loo a circle of faces—Ward, Mike,

Justices Farley and Wiggins, and Lieutenant Kincaid of the Judicial Protection detail—greeted her in states ranging from concerned to shocked to agitated. Only Eloise, the housekeeper, looked as calm as ever as she held out the landline phone. "Governor Darven for you, ma'am."

"There've been developments," Ward interjected.

"Has he commuted Dormund's sentence?" the Chief asked hopefully.

"Nothing like that, unfortunately. We're getting indications as to where Quirke is, though. Or, rather, what he's up to."

The Chief took the phone. "Governor? What can I do for you?"

"I understand you're missing an associate justice tonight. I frankly would have thought that, after what Quirke went through last year, he'd be avoiding social media like the plague."

"He does," said the Chief.

"Check hashtag QuirkeJ and tell me if you still think so."

Mike handed her his iPhone. There, next to a thumbnail photo of Quirke, was a tweet. She read it aloud. " 'Illegitimate use of state power must end; State, be not a murderer tonight. Abolish the death penalty now.' Governor, it's insane to think Justice Quirke put this out. Anybody can open a Twitter account with the handle 'QuirkeJ.' What's that tiny URL at the end there?"

Mike cleared his throat. "Actually, it's the court's home page."

Ward spoke up. "Here's the latest tweet. 'Breaking with tradition is what I do best.' Does that mean anything in particular to you?"

The Chief looked a little ill. To Ward she said, "I want to see all the tweets posted to this account so far. I haven't been able to reach Justice Quirke tonight, but evidently he got my voicemail." Then she spoke into the landline phone again. "You know, Governor, between the bombing at the state building and now Justice Quirke's...unavailability, this has been a challenging evening for the court. Could you see your way to granting Dormund a temporary reprieve—just until we figure out what's going on?"

"Cheer up, Chief. The night'll be over before you know it."

She handed the phone back to Eloise. "No dice on the reprieve," she told her colleagues.

Ward ended a call of his own and turned to her. "Chief, I'm told Dormund filed a petition in federal district court twenty minutes ago. It's assigned to Judge Van Minck."

"New claims or old?"

"I've asked his attorneys to drop us a copy, so we'll see. They've requested a stay, of course."

"Sounds like we're going to be here a while," said the Chief, "so, everyone, I hope you can make yourselves comfortable."

Chapter Twenty-Six

8:20 p.m., Thursday, February 25

Hetford trudged across the plaza with Ruairí in his arms, carefully lifting his feet over the treacherous little unevennesses in the pavement. At the corner he crossed to the sidewalk in front of City Hall. He asked himself continuously whether he could do anything more to find Sadie. Ruairí still slept, but who knew what he might do when he awakened in a strange house without Mommy? They'd have to use the babysitting cover story to soothe him; but did an eight-month-old understand such things? Waiting for Eleanor to pick them up, he thanked God she was in the City and not at Gene's down in Hemsbridge, which would have meant a forty-minute drive, at least.

While he was thus abstracted in thought, her Mercedes Maybach rolled to a stop in the street in front of him. She leaned over to pop the door for him, her eyes widening at the sight of the sleeping infant.

Sliding into the passenger seat, he kissed her and said, "Well, darling, we've gotten a chance to babysit sooner than anticipated."

"How on earth—?" she whispered.

"Let's go home and I'll tell you. I wish I'd thought to ask you to bring a car seat. It's not strictly legal to carry a baby on one's lap, you know, so let's try not to draw undue attention. Of course, all the police in town are probably across the street, trying to sort out the bombing."

She pulled out and turned left, and then right onto Van Vliet. Street noise was inaudible inside the opulent car. "So it really was a bomb? All I heard was there was an explosion of some kind. The media's strangely unhelpful tonight."

"In any other disaster, most of the witnesses are only too eager to tweet everything they know, and more besides. The court's just the opposite, of course; the default approach is to keep things under wraps. And there weren't many non-court people on hand to be aware of it. But I'm afraid it felt a lot like a bomb."

"Couldn't have been a very big one, fortunately."

"No, or they'd still be digging us out. Makes one wonder if it was only a diversion."

"A diversion from what?"

He shrugged. "Politics in Sant' Urbano is unpredictable. I'm afraid to guess."

They rode in silence up to the Heights and, as Eleanor remotely opened the gate to the house and continued down into the underground garage, Ruairí shifted in Hetford's arms.

"I think he's waking up," Hetford whispered. "Let's hope he's one of the more stoic sort of baby."

In the kitchen their housekeeper, the mother of three grown children and grandmother of four, Mrs. Resendiz, was now accorded her due as a genius of childrearing and an indispensable presence. Her face lit up as she inspected the infant, who, fully alert, regarded her silently but with a trembling lip, as though trying very hard not to cry. "*Es un bellisimo bebé. Un niñito guapo,*" she cooed. Part of Hetford wondered why, seeing him hold the child, she didn't seize the little guy for his own protection; why she instead smiled knowingly at Eleanor. Had Eleanor confided her dreams of maternity?

"Mrs. Resendiz, he's going to be hungry and he'll need a diaper change, if he doesn't already," said Hetford. "I know we don't have the right things on hand, and I can't even claim to know what they are, but can you get hold of them? Right away? *Me comprendes?*"

"*Sí, por supuesto.* I go to borrow some next door. Mr. and Mrs. Levenger have a little baby, too." She moved toward the door that led from the kitchen down to the sidewalk connecting the adjacent houses, then stopped and turned to him. "How long he stay?"

"Till tomorrow," Hetford said. A night's worth of supplies would surely be ample. Sadie would know to come over as soon as she could get free of whatever tangle or complication she might have gotten caught up in, or in any event Quirke would undoubtedly come by after the execution. But why hadn't Quirke returned his call? And what could have happened to Sadie?

Mrs. Resendiz nodded and was soon off on her errand. At her departure it seemed to dawn on Ruairí that the only adult in the place who was reasonably qualified to take charge of him had disappeared. He screwed up his face and began to voice an existential protest.

Still valiantly holding the baby in the face of his dismaying wails, Hetford found himself instinctively doing what he'd seen mothers do in similar circumstances, bouncing gently on the balls of his feet and swaying rhythmically at the knees, his palm rubbing circles meanwhile on the child's back to comfort him. "There, there, Ruairí," he cooed over the baby's screams. "Remember, you're a Quirke. Your people are the most courageous of Celts, the most fearsome of Fenians, and your own father stared death in the eye."

At this, the baby broke off crying and laughed uproariously.

"Allan, you're brilliant. How did you do that?" Eleanor crowded close. Ruairí glared at her, distrust apparent on his still-blotchy cheeks and brow.

Hetford began to do a walking version of the mommy bounce, Ruairí on his shoulder looking skeptically at Eleanor, who brought up the rear as they made the circuit of the kitchen.

As they passed the Sub-Zero for the third time, Ruairí whimpered softly, laid his head on Hetford's shoulder, inserted his thumb into his mouth, and sucked pensively. A painful jumble of sympathetic feelings gripped Hetford. "I hope Mrs. Resendiz gets back soon," he said hoarsely, "or we may simply have to forage through the cabinets and see what we can find. I understand *au courant* parents make their own baby food these days. We could give the blender a higher purpose than daiquiris."

Hetford knew he was going soft. At the office today, he'd exercised forbearance with a fintech vendor to one of Marvelocity's subsidiaries, when he probably should have sued for fraud instead. At the symphony board meeting over the lunch hour, he'd voted to give the music director another year's extension on his contract to see if his proposed new-new approach to programming would goose ticket sales, even though he knew as much about the sunk cost fallacy as the next man. Literally, around his increasingly ample middle, he was going soft. And now he was becoming incapable of objective thinking where this blue-eyed, curly-headed little offspring of the man he'd once thought he hated was concerned.

He supposed that was only fitting. In the fatal moment when Hetford's psychoanalyst had said, so offhandedly, "You claim to despise this Quirke, but you speak of him more tenderly than you do of your lover, his wife," he understood why he'd risked everything to try to ruin Quirke. Why he'd planted negative blog posts and news articles, including outright falsehoods, in an effort to put Quirke in a bad light and cost him re-election to the court. True, Quirke was self-destructive enough to have compromised his own cause unaided, but had Hetford not conspired with Quirke's chief of staff in a variety of malicious mischief, even hacking into a government computer system in a manner intended to implicate Quirke's kooky magical associates and by extension Quirke, his re-election would have been a foregone conclusion. As it was, he barely kept his seat. The Chief, canny woman, had figured out what Hetford had done, and in her seemingly divine mercy had let him quit without exposing him. And Quirke, in an equally divine gesture, had forgiven him. Shame, fear, gratitude, and confusion had driven Hetford to a shrink to try to understand why he'd behaved so recklessly, so inexplicably; the suicide of his partner in crime against Quirke had only made achieving understanding the more urgent. And the truth, as he'd finally realized, was that he was half—more than half—in love with Quirke, and had tried to destroy what he could not possess.

To Hetford's amazement, his now-acknowledged feelings for Quirke in no way excluded his love for Eleanor. To the contrary, the better he understood his own inexpressible attraction to Quirke, the more alluring she became, the safer he felt in opening himself to her, the more responsive she in turn grew, and the richer and more solid their relationship felt to him. Not that he'd spoken directly to her of his passion for her ex-husband; as a topic of discussion it remained bundled inside the secret cocoon of his therapist's office. "Do you remain silent because you fear she too retains a passion for him—that your confession would reignite hers?" Dr. Kurzweil had asked last Tuesday. Hetford feared the answer might be yes.

One day, not long after his psychodynamic epiphany, he began to feel an irresistible need to atone. And not merely to make up for his sins, for that, in truth, was impossible, but to turn himself into a good man where formerly he'd been merely an accomplished one. He'd apparently succeeded: More than one friend and colleague had said he seemed lately like a different person. From their attitude toward him, expressed in various little ways, he could tell he was a far more lovable one. It was then, in short, that he began to go soft.

Lately he'd begun to experience a really alarming escalation of this softening. At moments—initially only at the onset of sleep or upon waking, but more recently at unpredictable points throughout the day— whenever he would let go of all internal resistance, he felt as if he were dissolving completely. Still, even as he as such was ceasing to be, somehow his ego remained intact enough that he would feel himself flooded with love or something indistinguishable from it: love undifferentiated and undirected, cosmic and godlike; or love of an object, anything or anyone at hand, whether beautiful, mundane, or ugly. This very evening, the feeling had come over him while he was speaking with Sadie. As she'd lifted the baby into his arms, the preciousness of their unique lives had hit him for an instant that seemed to last and last, coming on simultaneously with a painful sadness centered in his upper left chest. These feelings would pass only when he forced himself to think of, say, the Robinson-Patman Act or the Uniform Commercial Code. He was beginning to worry for his sanity.

And now he was hovering as Mrs. Resendiz, back from her supply expedition to the Levengers, was showing Eleanor how to mix formula and heat a bottle. When it was ready, Mrs. R deposited the baby in Eleanor's arms. Ruairí took the bottle like a pro, like it was serious business, as Eleanor beamed, amazed. Afterward, Mrs. R gathered the baby and a bag of borrowed supplies, and led them to the bathroom off the kitchen. There, at her direction, Hetford folded a thick towel and spread it on the commodious countertop, and Mrs. R initiated them into the mysteries of a proper diaper change.

"He's uncut," Eleanor was whispering into his ear.

"I noticed," Hetford whispered back. What inferences could one draw from this remarkable fact? Didn't most fathers want their sons to look like them?

"The tabs on the sides—not too tight, not too loose," Mrs. R cautioned.

"Aha," Hetford said. Eleanor nodded, following along with the avidity she normally reserved for previews of the next season's designer fashions.

Hygienic tasks completed, Mrs. R encouraged Eleanor to carry Ruairí back to the kitchen. "Now we see if he take some *cereal de arroz*," she said. But Ruairí squirmed in Eleanor's arms and reached toward Hetford.

As Eleanor's countenance wilted, Mrs. Resendiz laughed. "He think you look like his papa, Mr. Hetford."

He could feel himself blushing. "Oh, I don't know about that, Mrs. R. I've just known him a little longer than Eleanor has."

Eleanor shook her head, a trace of envy visible on her face. "No, Allan, he's certainly more attached to you. You have almost as good a way with him as Mrs. R. Just think how it would be with our own little one. Can't you just imagine..."

But the fantasy of their own parenthood that Eleanor was about to invite him to entertain had to wait, as Mrs. R had already led him to the breakfast nook and put a small bowl of white mush and a baby spoon in his hand.

Chapter Twenty-Seven

10:00 p.m., Thursday, February 25

The place where Tad was now manacled to floor-to-ceiling metal shelving had evidently been a storeroom in the building's industrial incarnation. Even in the dim light Quirke could see it was still the repository of obsolete office equipment, along with flip charts, unmoored dry erase boards, and other once-trendy management training tools, plus a half-deflated life-sized female sex toy whose droopiness gave her a distinctly buzz-killing air. He squatted beside Tad as Anya stood watch.

"At least you have someone to talk to," he said, nodding at the doll. "How are you doing?" At Tad's uncharacteristically silent shrug, Quirke's worry increased. Blood from the backhanding Tad received had crusted on his face and his arm seemed to have stopped bleeding, but he looked far from well. "Anya," he said, "this man needs some water. Would you—"

By the time he turned to look at her, she had already gone to fetch it. "Help me up if you can," he whispered to Tad, who lent his shoulder. On his feet again, he picked his way over the miscellany littering the floor, looking for anything potentially useful to an escape effort, although the lack of illumination and Anya's imminent return kept him from making a thorough search. At the opposite end of the room, weak light from outdoors glowed through a shoulder-high foot-wide window, braced open to admit the cool night air. Thinking the temperature too chilly for a wounded man, he considered shutting it, but then thought vaguely the better of it.

"No offense, dude," said Tad, "but this is the last time I ever try and save your neck from a bunch of lefty wack jobs."

"I told you to get a new sponsor. Look, I have a feeling—don't ask me why—if you can hold out a little longer, it's going to be all right."

"So what's your plan? Can you get the Governor to abolish the death penalty, like they want?"

"Not gonna happen. But I think I can get the wack jobs, or some of them anyway, to see reason."

"Good luck with that. Meanwhile, Con, Judge, I gotta have something for the pain. The big dude clocked me something fierce. And my arm—hey, I just realized, I never took a bullet for a guy before. Don't you owe me something? This ain't for recreation, man. You know if they took me to the hospital right now, I'd get some kind of opiate, legit."

"I get it. You have a genuine need. I'm not trying to stop you."

"Well, can you reach in my shirt and—oh yeah, you're still zip-tied. Fuck."

"Wait, I might be able to—"

"Bitch'll be back any minute, so—"

Hobbled as he was, Quirke managed to undo the top two buttons on Tad's shirt and reached down between the scapulae of his bony back where, just above the belt line, a large baggie of psychotropic chemicals rested.

"God bless you and your descendants forever," Tad breathed. "That little vial, there—two of those, please."

"Give me a second here," Quirke said, the need to administer the drug quickly, before Anya returned, warring with his fear of dropping the capsules from his still tied hands. "You sure you know what these are? And how much you need?"

"Oh, yeah. Believe me, I'm a walking PDR."

The operation completed, Tad relaxed against the uncomfortable-looking shelves and smiled for the first time.

"You know, Con, a lot of sponsors would call bullshit on me, even though I'm covered in blood here and I got a bullet hole in my arm. And you an actual judge, like, the last person I'd expect to give a guy the benefit of the doubt. You must be a really good judge. Know how I know that? You got compassion for the weak."

"It comes from being weak myself," Quirke said.

"And you don't need to worry about nothing. I'll never, ever tell anybody about this."

Quirke gave a mirthless laugh. "About me furnishing you narcotics, you mean?"

"Mum's the word." He made a zipping gesture across his mouth.

"Listen to me, please. If a cop or a prosecutor or anyone in authority asks, tell them exactly what I did. Don't omit, don't embroider, don't evade. Lying only makes this kind of trouble worse. I speak from experience."

"Sure, whatever you say, Con—wink, wink."

Quirke looked up to see Anya, her arms crossed in front of her, staring coolly at the two of them.

"What have you got there, Judge?" she asked.

He exchanged glances with Tad. As resolutely as he'd previously resisted Tad's entreaties to take custody of the stash, doing so seemed the wisest course now. If the radicals were to start using the drugs, the already unpredictable dynamic of their situation would become even more unstable, and as the higher status captive he thought he stood a better chance of limiting access. "Give me the rest of it," he commanded. Tad pulled two smaller baggies out of his socks and stuffed them in Quirke's jacket pocket. "If you must know, I'm confiscating contraband from this man. It'll be disposed of properly as soon as circumstances permit."

She considered his explanation, then handed each of them a Camelbak water bottle. "He needs his face washed," she told Quirke.

"You'll have to cut the ties," he replied.

She looked startled.

"The zip-ties," he said.

"Oh," she said dully. "Just a minute." She left them alone again momentarily, returning with a pair of scissors, which she promptly used to slice through the ties and a quarter inch of skin on Quirke's right wrist.

"That was stupid. I'm really sorry." Her eyes widened at the sight of red welling out of her captive.

"Don't worry about it." He held his wrist and sucked the blood away, flinching at the shoulder pain the movement activated. "Do you have a towel or anything like that?"

She looked around helplessly. "We didn't think of cleaning supplies."

Grimacing, he undid his tie, unbuttoned his shirt, and pulled his undershirt over his head to stand half-dressed in the chilly air. Then he sprinkled water from the Camelbak onto the undershirt and began to dab at Tad's face. "My apologies for the less than sterile washcloth."

"Ooh, this is exciting. Your undershirt smells yummy, Con. I mean Judge. And you have an even nicer body than I thought."

It was all Quirke could do not to laugh. "Would you kindly contain yourself? It's hard enough to maintain a minimal level of human dignity under these circumstances without you mocking me."

"Who's mocking? I mean it sincerely. Doesn't he have a nice body?" Tad looked to Anya for concurrence. "She's not denying it. Look, she's trying not to smile." In fact, her head was level with her shoulder blades and her eyes kept traveling between his pectorals and her feet, but Tad was right: her frown was too intense, too studied to be anything but an effort to appear indifferent.

"Speechlessness isn't necessarily agreement," Quirke said. "Give me your arm." Quirke began gingerly to blot off the bloodstains around the wound on Tad's forearm. Glancing at Anya, he could not miss the blush spreading over her face. She said nothing, but continued to watch him. With luck, perhaps he could play on this sympathy or attraction or whatever it was she was feeling.

As Quirke was completing his cleanup efforts, his undershirt now a dripping pink mess in his hands, Anya spoke up. "Rusty wants you both in the other room. You go there, and I'll cut him loose."

" 'Him' is Tad."

"Okay...Tad. Just...go to Rusty, okay?"

"Sure." He leveraged himself up with a hand on the shelving, wincing. How long he'd be able to hold out against the shoulder pain without availing himself of whatever Tad had just taken he didn't know. Although possession of the quantities of illicit substances of which he'd just relieved Tad was probably worth more years in prison than he had left on the planet, he felt oddly secure with the stuff in his pocket. Trying not to cry out at the pain, he put his shirt and jacket back on, draping his tie around his neck. Tad followed him into the center of the big office space.

There, Rusty was grinning exultantly. "You should see some of these reply tweets! 'Quirke you old commie, they should impeach your ass.' 'Quirke, I can't believe I voted for you.' 'It's a free country, say what you want, but resign first.' 'Once a socialist, always a socialist.' So is that right? *Are* you a socialist?"

"Does it matter now?" Quirke asked.

"Well, if people are taking all this shit at face value, we're even better positioned than I thought.   It's not so implausible that you'd endorse our program."

"I haven't endorsed your program, though."

"You're about to. I want a little clip to go with this." He aimed the phone's camera at his captive.

Quirke held a hand in front of his face. "Please don't." It didn't seem worth dying over, but keeping his job would become exponentially more complicated if the public were to hear him call for the abolition of the death penalty out of his own mouth. And he was still inclined to think he'd find a way to outmaneuver his captors. "It would violate the Geneva Conventions, you know. Even the SLA gave Patty Hearst that."

Rusty lowered the phone and frowned, considering whether this was true and, if so, whether the fact outweighed his political goals. Then he shook his head. "This isn't wartime, so I can't see how the Geneva

Conventions have anything to do with it." He again pointed the phone camera at Quirke and clicked. "Raise your head, Conal, look up. I want you recognizable. I want you to tell the Governor—tell the world—the death penalty's discriminatory, unfair, and immoral. And it needs to be abolished and all the existing death sentences commuted. Oh, and tell 'em you're saying this of your own free will. Say it. Start with your name." When Quirke remained silent, Rusty reached down his side and raised the barrel of his weapon. Behind him, Anya stood, thin arms crossed over her flat chest, looking stonily at him.

"My name is Conal Quirke."

"Who are you?"

"Associate Justice of the state Supreme Court."

"Do you have a message for the viewers?" Rusty wore a triumphal look.

Quirke paused, searching out Anya's eyes. "You're my witness here."

"Shut up," said Rusty, stopping the clip. "Cut out the bullshit, Conal. We're going to do this in one more take or somebody's going to be in even more pain." Pointing the phone at him yet again, he asked, impatiently, "What's your name?"

"Conal Quirke. Associate Justice of the state Supreme Court."

"Thank you. What day is this?"

"The twenty-fifth of February—the night set for the execution of Marcus Dormund in the state prison at San Maurizio."

"What do you want to say about that?"

He wished he'd had time to rehearse; successfully acting the part of someone who needs to look as though he's speaking voluntarily but wants it to be obvious to the most casual observer he's only talking under duress was an accomplishment likely beyond his meager college-theater-level talents. Particularly as, deep down, he wholeheartedly shared his captors' view that the death penalty needed to go, and planned to vote for abolition in the election in a few months' time.

"Say what you just told me," said Rusty.

You said it, not me, Quirke thought.

Rusty grew more insistent. "What do you want to say to the viewers?"

"I want them to know the death penalty is evil, immoral, discriminatory, and should be abolished."

"Didn't you also say it's unfair?"

"Unfair?"

To say the death penalty is unfair would be to condemn the process, to undermine the very foundation of the system in which he'd labored all his judicial life. He could readily enough acknowledge that the death penalty was a gross waste of societal resources and a complete failure as a deterrent, that it served only to teach citizens the misguided lesson that killing is a solution to social problems; but could he stand here and imply the courts were actually getting it wrong as often as not? People out there might believe it, coming from him, and lose confidence in the judiciary. Then again, there was that AK-47 hanging off Rusty's shoulder.

"Unfairly administered?"

"Yes, I did," said Quirke. He looked as penetratingly as he could into the recording lens, thinking, *Chief, don't believe a word of it! I just want to live to see another petition conference.* "The unfairness permeates the system."

"And it's supposed to be a deterrent, right? So is it?"

"Nobody's ever produced any convincing evidence of that."

"You ever voted to uphold a death sentence?"

"Many times."

"Ever regret it?"

"I've done what I thought the law required me to do."

"I didn't ask you that, I asked if you ever regretted what you did."

Rusty, standing a few feet from him, glared expectantly. He didn't need a teleprompter to know what Rusty wanted him to say.

"I've come to regret it."

"Why?"

Quirke drew a long breath and sighed. "I remember the first death penalty case I authored at the court. The trial wasn't perfect, but the defendant couldn't point to any egregious error. He almost certainly did the crime, and other bad stuff besides. At the time, I thought that was enough; the law was clear and left us with no option but to affirm. But I still think of his case, wondering..."

"Wondering what?"

"Why he got death for a little convenience store robbery murder when some double and triple homicides I've seen didn't. Well, I know—or I think I know. Geographic disparities exist, county by county."

"And racial and economic discrimination."

"I wouldn't try to dispute that."

"So how does that make you regret your decision?"

Quirke fell silent again. It was hard to steer a course between the banal lie and the idiosyncratic truth. "At an impressionable age, I studied philosophy. It made me want to live in a rational world. The criminal law tries, but its raw material—people—will never quite cooperate."

Rusty stood there waiting for him to continue, his camera blandly recording.

"Innocent people, besides the victims, are bound to be executed at some point."

Rusty probably wanted him to say *have* been executed, but fuck it, he had already said enough to create a social media firestorm, his shoulder was killing him, and this dialogue was giving him a headache. Quirke turned and walked away, toward the far end of the space. Fishing around in his pocket, his fingers closed around a baggie with a handful of little tablets in it—the same thing, he thought, that Tad had taken. He popped two, washing them down with a gulp from the Camelbak.

After a too-brief moment of peace Rusty was at his side. "Not bad for your first. Don't worry, you'll get better at this as we go. But, so, she never said you were a lefty, or seen as a lefty, or however you want to spin it."

Would Rusty never shut up about his politics? "You see yourselves as so far to the left of me I'm indistinguishable to you from every other judge. Others look at me from 180 degrees the other direction. People will think what they please."

"You mean to say your politics were never radical?" Rusty persisted.

"Before I became a judge I did a little work for the Benfields, father and son. You know, the former governors? About as middle of the road as it gets. This is a matter of public record. Obviously, I haven't done politics in many years. Why people have the idea I'm a Trotskyite or whatever they think I am, I can't tell you." He took a deep breath. "Unless it's my family background they're picking up on."

"Whoa, say that again?" said Rusty, clicking the video camera on the phone again.

"I've never told anyone this, but I come from a long line of revolutionaries." Quirke smiled. "Personally, I've never been into overthrowing governments."

"Oh, really? Let's see, you must have been born in the sixties, were your parents SDS? Weathermen?"

"No, not Weathermen. This was in another country. My birthplace."

Suddenly each of his captors, and Tad as well, were staring at him, unsure, it seemed, whether he was telling the truth or merely a weird and pointless joke. "My parents were IRA—Irish Republican Army—the Official IRA, initially, and then when the Officials gave up armed struggle, they joined the Provos. Or so I was told. I didn't hear it from them; they were sent to prison when I was a tiny kid and died before I had a chance to get to know them."

"I'm sorry," Anya said.

"Did they get caught planting bombs?" Rusty was now hanging on his every word.

"Not exactly. They were convicted of robbing banks in the U.K., in the service of fundraising for what I suppose you could call their terrorist activities. My aunt and uncle, my mother's sister and her husband—proper bourgeois, the furthest thing from revolutionaries you could imagine—raised me here in the States to be law-abiding."

"Long line, you said? So—"

"And my small-r republican grandparents and great-grandparents took the losing side in the Irish civil war back in the '20s. And long before that, we were Fenians—my nickname in college was 'Fenian Scum.' "

"So you're not an American?"

"I am American. And Irish. Dual national."

"Cool," said Rusty. "And you're all right with what your parents did?"

A tangle of feelings—loss, shame, anger, and others more obscure—stopped Quirke's tongue momentarily. He struggled to bear in mind that Rusty's callow attitude sprang from a perspective as limited as his life experience. He knew Rusty was fishing for an endorsement of his own revolutionary activity, and providing it might somehow better his situation, and Tad's. But he couldn't say what Rusty wanted to hear.

"I won't deny I dream of a united Ireland; it's in my blood. But if you'd grown up as I did, having family affected as they were and still are, you wouldn't entertain such a romantic notion of political violence. And now that I have a son of my own I can't even begin to imagine doing what they did."

Frowning, Rusty busied himself with Quirke's phone but did not reply.

Anya had seldom seen Rusty at such a loss for words, but then they'd never anticipated the Judge would turn out to be anything other than a pampered member of the elite. Beneath the bougie American exterior lay a man from a different culture, a European, with first-hand knowledge of the struggle against imperialism and colonialism. He was also obviously kind and caring—he'd so gently washed his friend's wounds—and he had a son—and hints of the courage of his revolutionary forebears now seemed to shine through his judiciously neutral demeanor. He'd borne this whole ordeal with no small degree of grace and patience, all things considered. And there was something to Tad's assessment of his physical attractiveness. Strangely, it had never before occurred to her how gorgeous were his crinkly blue eyes, how thick and silky his wavy salt-and-pepper hair would feel to her exploring fingertips, how perfect was the shape of his pale torso with that light growth of still-dark hair across his chest, and how willingly she'd tolerate the scrape of those Van Dyke whiskers on her chin for a taste of his lips. She hadn't expected to want his approval, hadn't given a damn about his judgment on their politics or their revolutionary enterprise; now she found herself wanting him to see her as a woman, or at least as something other than a lowly judicial clerk, radical operative, or—worst of all—mere adjunct to the guys.

In that moment, her submission to Rusty evaporated into the fantasy world from which it had emerged. She rejoiced at her liberation until she realized that in order to fully grasp it she would have to stand up to him.

And he was still holding an AK-47.

Chapter Twenty-Eight

11:30 p.m., Thursday, February 25

On the settee in the sitting room off their bedroom, Eleanor and Hetford sat on either side of the energetic scion of Quirke, who was raptly engaging in failure analysis of a pile of obsolete electronic devices Hetford had found in various drawers around the house. The television was tuned to SpongeBob SquarePants cartoons, which neither Hetford nor Eleanor had ever seen before, but which they each unexpectedly found rather clever. Periodically Eleanor would get up to take or make a call or to text a friend. On her return from one such interlude, Hetford squeezed her hand and smiled. "In a year or so, dearest, if we're lucky, we can be spending every night this way."

"You're really enjoying yourself, aren't you?" she said, a measure of incredulity in her voice. "I thought it might take more to persuade you."

"Persuade me of what? That it's time we became parents?"

"Not even that—just to try spending a little time with a child. I thought it would be almost impossible to convince you to actually have a baby. But you seem quite committed to the idea."

"Do you mean you're having second thoughts?" His voice grew quieter.

"No, no. I want a baby—desperately. Your baby, Allan. But—home every night? I know myself well enough to know I need intellectual stimulation: the ballet, dinner with friends, the occasional restaurant or gallery opening. We are who we are, darling. You can't expect all that to go away."

"Of course not. Besides, those are highly educational activities that any child might want to take advantage of in a city like Sant' Urbano. But there'll be nights like this when he—or she—will prefer to sit at home and destroy old cell phones. And when we'll be too tired to do anything but watch."

Eleanor looked at him, half-smiling. She reached across the settee, over Ruairí's head, and drew her husband's face toward hers, as the child experimented with buttons. One long kiss later, Hetford murmured, "I made an appointment for us with the Oceanica Fertility Center."

She gasped and kissed him again. "Oh my God," she whispered, "we're going to have a baby."

Hetford had stretched out for a nap on the chaise lounge in the master bedroom with Ruairí lying prone on his belly, the onset of the little snore he'd been making lately proof he'd fallen asleep. Eleanor lay in the bed adjacent, going through her Tivo with the volume muted, when the baby gave a little wail, balled his fists, and settled into a distressed cry. Allan looked about, confused, and sat forward, holding fast to the child.

"What is it? Are you all right?" she cried. "You're looking so flushed, both of you. I'm calling Mrs. R." Before Hetford could discourage her, the housekeeper had been summoned and was hovering over the two, thermometer in hand.

"I'm perfectly all right, just hot," he insisted. "The little chap throws off a lot of heat when he sleeps. No need to bring out that thing."

Eleanor loomed over him, pressing the back of her hand against his damp forehead. "But you feel awfully warm, darling. Much warmer than normal. Let Mrs. R take your temperature."

After token grumbling, he submitted, while in the en suite bathroom Eleanor washed her hands. When she emerged, Mrs. Resendiz displayed the digital readout.

"Ninety-eight *punto* five."

Hetford nodded. "I told you, dearest."

"That's wonderful, but we should take the baby's temperature, just to be certain. I'm sure Sadie would want us to."

"But is this the right device?" he wondered. "Will he be able to keep it under his tongue?"

Mrs. Resendiz rummaged through the Levengers' diaper bag and presently produced a packet with a happy infant pictured on it containing what looked like stickers. "This is like what my grandchildren use. It sticks under the arm."

"Amazing," said Hetford. "Is it reliable?"

"*Así así.* It will tell if he has a high fever, certainly."

Taking the opportunity to perform a diaper change, Mrs. R deployed the sticker. Within a few minutes she interpreted it as showing nothing amiss.

"Now I feel silly," said Eleanor, "making a fuss for nothing."

"Nonsense, darling. This just shows the vigilance of your maternal instincts. Mrs. R, thank you, and do get your rest—pleasant dreams." As the housekeeper shuffled back to her quarters, Hetford scooped the baby from the chaise and deposited him next to Eleanor.

"Excuse me just a moment," he said.

She registered alarm. "Where are you going?"

He pointed to the bathroom. "Back in a minute."

"But what if—are you sure he's not sick? What would we do if he did have a fever? Do you think he looks well? He seems...more subdued than before. I wish we knew what's normal for him." She looked at him pleadingly, as though he might agree to forswear micturation until the baby went away.

"He's probably subdued because it's the middle of the night in his world; the best thing for him is to go back to sleep." Hetford suddenly understood her panic. "Dearest, you're not afraid of him, are you?"

She began by dismissing the accusation. "Afraid of Quirke Junior? Certainly not. There's nothing about him we can't handle between us."

"Kids are little disease vectors, of course. We're bound to catch one bug after another when our baby comes along. I know you're—"

"Oh, Allan, go ahead and say it: I'm the biggest germophobe in the world. You know what a horrible nursemaid I am—I admit, I moved back to Daddy's when you caught norovirus last year. But it's not that I'm an unfeeling monster—you do know that, don't you?—it's just that I'm terrified of being sick and helpless. Does that disqualify me from being a mother?"

"Darling, I understand. I used to feel the same way, but now when those thoughts come along, I think of my college roommate, who became an Ebola specialist at the Centers for Disease Control. And if we're going to start talking about unfeeling monsters, you know, quite a few people have described me in those terms. And you'll never be helpless as long as I'm around." He leaned in to kiss her, then swooped away with a resounding sneeze. Ruairí laughed.

"So sorry. Purely coincidental," said Hetford. "I'm as healthy as I could possibly be."

Chapter Twenty-Nine

12:01 a.m., Friday, February 26

An hour after self-medicating, following a brief initial period of nausea, not only was Quirke's shoulder no longer screaming at him, but life in general felt exponentially happier despite the indeterminacy of their situation and the worrisome presence of the AK-47s still in various hands around the room. With the small part of his mind not absorbed in contemplating the exquisite pointlessness of everything, he wondered what pain reliever could do so much so beautifully. It reminded him of his drug of choice, minus the quick IV onset.

"Tad," he asked, "what was that capsule thing you took?"

"Demerol. One of my favorite drugs of all time. I'm feeling no pain, as they say. And how are you doing? You really went to the head of the class there, Judge. I mean, when you relapse, you fuckin' relapse."

"What do you mean, the oxycodone? I took them after knee surgery once; they ought to do the job."

"Those aren't oxys. They look kinda like 'em, but they're not."

"Well, what are they?" But Quirke didn't need to ask; this bliss he was feeling gave him the answer.

"Fake oxys, is what they are; there's been a lot of 'em floating around. They're mainly heroin and fentanyl, with maybe a little oxycodone. Very popular lately. But I'll stick with my Demmies. It's not like there's a hella difference between prescription drugs and street drugs, but prescription drugs seem more, I don't know, genteel."

It was a matter of no more than mild interest, not even worth mentioning to Tad, that the last time he used heroin he would have died but for the Costante Police's timely jab of naloxone. And fentanyl, as everyone knew, was even more potent than heroin. On that earlier occasion, like this one, he'd been restrained of his liberty, but his captors were deliberately trying to kill him. This time his death was at most an indirect aim of his captors, and it still seemed reasonable to entertain hope of his eventual liberation, unless he'd just unwittingly taken a fatal overdose.

Tad's voice and prodding elbow woke him after a cruelly short interval of oblivion. "No time for nodding, Con," he was saying, "the guy over there's asking you a question."

Rusty's face was reddening with the effort of repeating himself. "I said, what does this tweet mean? 'Dormund's execution has been stayed while the district court considers his latest petition.' I thought the litigation was all over. Tonight was the night, she said."

"Wait a minute, I—" Anya retorted.

"Shut it, I want to hear what he has to say." Rusty dismounted the desk in the center of the room and strode toward the rank of chairs on which Tad and Quirke were sitting. "So, Conal, what the hell's going on with this case?"

Quirke struggled briefly to keep his eyes open, then yielded to the irresistible narcotic influence and let them fall shut. "Last-minute litigation is nothing unusual," he murmured. "The stay is to give the district court time to decide." He yawned and lay down across four of the lined-up chairs.

"How much time?" Rusty demanded, kicking Quirke lightly in the ribs with a greasy Doc Marten.

Quirke, shrugging, struggled to sit up. This man's obsession with the pending execution was becoming both tedious and bizarre. "As much as they need. How should I know?"

"What? How can they do that?" Rusty expostulated.

"I thought you *wanted* to end the death penalty," Quirke said. "So chill, buddy: it's happening, one federal judge at a time. Look," he added, "they understand the state needs an answer. Comity is a big thing with our federal counterparts. They'll rule as soon as they can. Of course, then the loser will take it up to the circuit."

"I told you all this," Anya said.

"*You* said all the claims had been decided. That there was nothing more for Dormund to argue. That the execution was going to go down unless we took action. That's why we picked tonight. That's why the judge is here and there's a hole in the effing state building. So she was wrong, Conal? Is that right? She made a fucking stupid call."

"For Chrissakes, man, don't put me in the middle. You're harshing my high." He lay down across the chairs and shut his eyes again. *What kind of hole in the effing state building?* he wondered vaguely.

Even the renewal of Rusty's rant now failed to penetrate Quirke's narcotic haze. After a few minutes of loudly impugning everything about Anya, from her hair to her legal ability, he stopped and looked as if for the first time at Quirke.

"And what the hell's going on here? If I didn't know better, I could swear he's on something."

Tad, though no soberer than Quirke, rose to his sponsor's defense.

"May I remind you the Judge and I got completely fucking banged up while you were snatching us? I mean somebody here, I ain't naming no names, put a hole in my arm, and the Judge did something awful to his shoulder; there was a really big, scary, loud pop when the dude in black threw him in the van. You can't blame a guy for self-medicating. It's not like you even offered us an aspirin or anything."

Rusty spoke in an unwontedly cold, quiet voice. "I want to know where the fuck you got the drugs."

"Well, I ain't telling you. However, I will share if you ask nicely."

Quirke, who was not, after all, quite asleep, laughed. "Now that's an idea. After all, with the stay in place nothing's going to happen for a while. You may as well relax."

Rusty considered the suggestion. "Well, what've you got?"

"For you," said Tad, "I might suggest some pane. When was the last time you had yourself a nice trip?"

A smile spread over Rusty's face. "Dane—you hear that? Tad's sharing."

Anya shook her head anxiously. "I don't—do you really think—"

"Not for you; I wouldn't know how to figure out the right dose for somebody who weighs forty pounds. You can be the sitter. So, what's in that bag? You really got some pane?"

"Wait a minute," said Quirke. After no small effort, he succeeded in sitting up. "First, the guns go out of sight." He pointed to the staircase some thirty feet away. "For safety. Anya can hide them."

Rusty considered this condition, then nodded. Anya began collecting and removing the weapons, making several trips out to the stairway.

"That's better," Quirke said. "Enjoy your trip."

"Everybody takes some," said Rusty. "Except her. Come on, you go first, Tad."

Tad tore off a square of blotter paper and stared reverently at it. "God bless you, Fred, wherever you are." He placed the square on his tongue, tore off one more, and handed it to Quirke.

In Quirke's mind, the thought of somehow palming the hit and merely pretending to get high(er), in order to get Rusty off his back, warred with the narcotized impulse to simply go with the flow. On the one hand, LSD was unquestionably illegal, he didn't want to multiply the sins he'd eventually have to answer for, and how it would interact with the fake oxys he was already on he could not predict. On the other, he hadn't dropped acid since college, and he remembered it fondly. He very much doubted that in his present state he had either the coordination to deceive Rusty or the strength to take him on, so in the end he put the paper in his mouth and hoped for the best.

Dane found appropriately trippy ambient trance music on YouTube and they settled down to wait for the drug to kick in. Only Anya kept moving, walking ceaselessly the perimeter of the room as if on patrol.

An hour in, as Quirke was minutely studying the amazing pinkish-bluish rays that were beginning to emanate from the fluorescent overhead lighting, wafting faster and slower in time with the music, Rusty announced, "I need to call her."

"Who are we talking about, Hayley?" Dane asked.

"Who else, dude? Got her number?"

The ever-competent Dane was indeed able to supply the number, but in less time than it took to place the call, Hayley told Rusty never to make such an idiotic mistake again. It seemed the consensus among radicals, somehow overlooked by Rusty, was that placing cell phone calls to each other during operations was something to be avoided. The rebuke effected a change in Rusty's mood, and not one for the better. Soon, however, he had a much better idea.

"I think I can speed this whole process up," he said, pushing buttons on Quirke's phone.

"Who are you calling now?" Anya demanded.

"Somebody I should have called a long time ago."

In view of the enforced inactivity under the federal stay, Justice Wiggins decided to try to salvage some of the night and left the Chief's apartment about 11:30 for a room in the Wentworth Hotel in the nearby theater district. "I'm a light sleeper and my phone will be at my ear, so call me if you need me," she instructed the Chief and Ward. Justice Farley and his staff soon followed her lead in decamping to their own respective residences, located within a ten-minute drive of the Chief's, and Justice Rackrent made herself comfortable on the sofa in the Chief's study. Mike Frentz, who had hung around out of a nearly unbearable and, so far, ungratified curiosity to learn something of his boss's fate, and the staffs of the Chief and Justices Corcoran and Kroner got up a bridge game in the kitchen. After accepting a sweater from Eloise, the Chief dispensed the housekeeper from further service for the night.

Shivering despite the extra layer, she turned to Ward, who was standing at the windows in the living room surveying the cityscape. "Maybe we're a little too attached to our traditions at times," she said quietly, "and it's not like I mind everyone gathering here at my place, but somehow this isn't the way an execution vigil ought to go down. All the focus and solemnity is gone. It feels more like a dull New Year's Eve party."

Ward smiled ruefully. "It would have been more fun with Quirke around."

She nodded. "Why do I always worry about that man? He has somebody else to do that now."

In the Chief's pocket, an electronic chime sounded. Her eyes widened; for the first time all evening, Ward detected a glimmer of happiness on her face. She pulled out her phone. "Quirke! Where are you?"

After a pause, a woolly-sounding voice asked, "Who's this? Are you the Chief?"

She blanched. "Yes. And who are you?"

She heard a muffled crowing or exultation at the other end. Then the caller began to address her monotonously, as if reading a bus schedule. "Our names are unimportant. We are activists who...who demand an end to this barbaric racist, classist punishment. It has outgrown its usefulness, if it ever had any. It can't be...be administered fairly, and it must stop."

"I see. Is Justice Quirke there? I'd like to speak with him."

"Well, suppose he is here?"

"Put him on, please." Receiving no response, she spoke a little more sharply. "You're using his phone. If he's there, put him on it."

For an interval, the Chief heard only a muffled discussion between the caller and an irate female whose voice sounded faintly familiar. Although the Chief strained to take in every sound, she detected no evidence of Quirke's presence on the other end. At last her interlocutor spoke again.

"He's definitely here. However, he—uh...he's unavailable at the moment."

"Why?"

"He...uh, he's in the bathroom."

"I'll wait," the Chief said.

Further incomprehensible muted discussion; then: "What about our message?"

"What about it?" The Chief had long since mastered her emotional responses toward members of the public, but this exchange was taxing that control to the limit.

"We demand that you...that the death penalty be abolished. Marcus Dormund must not be executed."

Reminding herself that, as stupid as the man on the other end seemed to be, there was nevertheless a strong possibility he had some sort of leverage over her friend and colleague, the Chief spoke gently. "I hear what you're saying. But I must tell you this court can only act in the context of pending litigation; we simply don't have the power to repeal laws or issue new laws, just like that. Marcus Dormund has no litigation pending before us at this point. His lawyers have filed a petition in federal district court, though, so the next step is in the federal judge's hands. Also, Governor Darven has the power to exercise clemency in Dormund's case, but I should tell you he's already declined to commute his sentence. I don't know what else to say. It would make me feel a whole lot better if you'd put Justice Quirke on the line, so I can be sure he's okay. He is okay, isn't he?"

More conferring in the background, then, "Yeah—he's totally, totally okay. So you're telling me there's nothing you can do about Dormund?"

"As I just said, we have nothing pending. Now, about Justice Quirke; I need you to give him the phone so I can talk to him. Otherwise, I—"

"You know, I spoke to him a minute ago, and he...he says hi."

"I'd like to hear it from him—" The call ended.

The Chief stood, trembling, staring out the window at the city lights glowing in the night sky, tapping her phone against her palm. She looked up at Ward, who had been listening to her side of the exchange. "I want to know where this call came from. See if Lieutenant Kincaid can get anything."

"Kincaid went home for the night; Grimes is on his way here, from the state building, to spell him."

"Even better. You know, Quirke might skip an execution for a family emergency, but not to hang out with an idiot whose idea of activism is calling me to demand an end to the death penalty. We have enough now for law enforcement to start making a serious effort to find him. And I need to get hold of Sadie—I don't understand why she hasn't returned my call." She sighed. "I really don't like the feel of this, Ward, but at least it's something to do."

Chapter Thirty

1:00 a.m., Friday, February 26

At 1:00 a.m., the court remained in a kind of suspended animation at the Chief's apartment. Dormund's case was still before the federal district court with a stay of execution in place. A few more staff attorneys had departed homeward, with their justices' blessings, as had Justice Kroner, whose angina was not improved by the uncertain situation. In the kitchen, the Chief made tea and consulted with Lieutenant Grimes of the Judicial Protection Detail and Detective Harry Shadlack of the Sant' Urbano Police Department, who came to pass along a potentially significant fact uncovered in the bombing investigation. Shadlack, whom the Chief knew well from her days in the District Attorney's office, had interviewed as many witnesses as he could find who'd been on or near Golden Gate Avenue in the period before the explosion, no small feat at this hour of the night. A security guard on duty in the federal building, across the street, said he'd noticed Justice Quirke standing on the sidewalk in front of the state building with an extremely thin young woman about 7:00 p.m. The judge was talking to a man whom the guard described as not looking like an attorney or another judge. The next thing he saw was a white van pulling up to the state building, obscuring his view of the judge. When the van drove away, none of the three was any longer on the sidewalk, although the guard couldn't say whether any of them gotten into the van.

"Did he hear anything?" the Chief asked.

"He was wearing headphones," said Shadlack. "And he couldn't see a license plate."

"I don't know what to make of the other man, but let's suppose Justice Quirke's been with Anya Holmquist this evening," said the Chief after a moment. "Suppose they both left the building in that white van. Where might that take us, do you think, Lieutenant?"

Grimes nodded. "We can work off of that assumption."

The Chief left the two investigators in the kitchen and found Ward Freitag in the living room, dozing open-mouthed on the sofa. She touched his arm. "Ward. Sorry to disturb you, but I need a home address and phone number for Anya Holmquist."

The look of bewilderment passed quickly from his face as pulled out his phone and found the court personnel data file in his Dropbox. "3837 Sanchez Street." He read out the phone number. "Someone going to pay her a visit at this hour?"

"Sophia may not care, but I'm curious what was more important to Anya than the execution tonight," the Chief said.

※

Shadlack grunted. "You say this Holmquist went to fancy schools? Comes from money?"

Grimes, sitting in the passenger seat of Shadlack's Buick Regal in front of a decrepit-looking Edwardian three-flat row house on a poorly lit block of Sanchez Street, nodded. "You wouldn't know it to look at her, but yeah, according to some of her fellow staff attorneys at the court. She didn't talk about it much, but her family lives on the upper East Side of Manhattan. Seems to suffer from noblesse oblige—"

"You're gonna have to translate."

"Guilty rich."

"That explains the dump we're looking at, I guess. Well, now, that's lucky," he said, scanning the screen on his dashboard computer.

"What is?"

"Heiresses' addresses don't usually pop up in our database, but she's got roommates, and one of 'em, Dane Forrester, is on probation. Want to toss the place?"

"Let's start by ringing the doorbell," said Grimes, getting out of the car.

※

"For real?" Shadlack was becoming exasperated. The Nordic-looking trio rousted out of their beds by his imperative knocking kept shaking their heads in response to his repeated inquiries as to their identity and purpose. "There can't be half a dozen Swedes in the world who don't speak English, and somehow they're all in this room."

"Maybe they're not Swedes," said Grimes. "Maybe they're Norwegian or Icelandic or Faroese."

"*Passports*," Shadlack said, articulating the consonants heavily, as the fair-haired tourists, looking terrified, shook their heads and shifted their weight from one foot to the other. "I want to see your *passports*."

"Bay-en-bay," the tallest of the visitors, a man of about twenty-five, suddenly blurted out. "Ah-ey-ro bay-en-bay." He began digging energetically in a duffle bag on the couch, eventually pulling out a piece of paper and handing it to Shadlack.

"Seems like they read English, anyway," said Shadlack, unfolding and inspecting the document. "This is an Airbnb contract. Got this address,

3837 Sanchez, on it, all right. Between one Braden Wentworth and Onni Korhonen of Helsinki."

Hearing an approximation of his name, Korhonen nodded vigorously. The other two travelers likewise nodded and identified themselves.

"Matias Karppinen."

"Venla Jokela."

Grimes finished conducting a search on his phone and smiled at the three Finns. *"Passi,"* he said. *"Näytä minulle passi.* Sorry if I butchered your language."

Far from looking put out at any mispronunciation, they returned his smile with evident relief and pointed to the sleeping quarters at the back of the flat. Shadlack nodded, and they hastened off to retrieve their identification. Soon Grimes had confirmed each was who he or she claimed to be. "We're the police, and we need to search the premises," he said. *"Meillä on poliisi. Aiomme etsiä tämä paikka."*

"Okay," said Onni, sweeping his arm broadly to indicate consent.

The two officers split up and took different rooms. In the first room on the right side of the hallway, no more than eight feet by eleven, Shadlack saw a mismatched bed, dresser, and cane chair that might have been scavenged off the street on any random night in the city. He flopped down on his belly and shined a flashlight under the bed. "Well, well," he muttered, reaching through the dust bunnies and pulling out a black nylon-covered box, about a foot wide by three feet long.

"Hey, Ed. Here's something interesting."

Grimes appeared in the doorway, eyebrows raised.

"Gun case. Empty. Looks to fit an AK or something on that order. Not an item a probationer's supposed to have lying around the house."

"Let's see what else he has that he's not supposed to have." Grimes entered the second room on the right. Although Shadlack was clearly thinking of this as a probation search focused on Dane Forrester, Grimes had not lost sight of the fact he was supposed to be looking for any sign of where Justice Quirke might have gone. He scanned the room, which was furnished with a queen-sized bed and two dressers, for some indication that Anya normally occupied it. Several scarves had been tossed in a pile on the taller dresser, and through the open closet door he could see skirts and blouses hanging on a crowded pole. Now to confirm that the woman who lived here was Anya Holmquist. Neither the bed nor the dresser top held papers, bills, or any other identifying items, so he moved down the hallway.

He flipped on the lights in the kitchen. The place was in relatively good order, considering the age of the reported inhabitants; the cupboards held little in the way of edibles, apart from a couple of bags of brown rice and rolled oats. In the refrigerator were boxes of soy and almond milk, a bowl of apples, three bottles of sriracha sauce and, in the crisper, a wilted bunch of carrots. One laptop sat on the dining table and another on a smaller table near the door to the back stairs. On the smaller table was another item that caught his eye. He whistled.

"Harry, come on back here and bring our friends." In a moment Shadlack appeared, the three Finns just behind him.

Grimes pointed at the computers. "Do these belong to any of you?" They shook their heads in unison.

Shadlack was already powering them on. "You kids can wait out there." He gestured roughly toward the front of the house, and the Finns skittered back down the hallway. "Funny how they seem to understand English perfectly well now," he observed.

"Unlikely you'll get in," Grimes commented. "Only an idiot would leave an unencrypted computer in a group living situation."

"Well, it seems we're not dealing with the sharpest knives in the drawer. Although I thought Miss Holmquist was supposed to be some hot shit lawyer. Okay, I'm in. Want to take a look at the search history for me while I start up the other one?"

"Sure, but first tell me what those little things on the table over there look like to you."

Shadlack stared at the three tubular metallic devices. "It's been a while since my bomb squad training," he said, after a moment, "but I'd bet my retirement these are time fuses."

Chapter Thirty-One

1:25 a.m., Friday, February 26

At the end of one side of the L-shaped sofa, Justice Corcoran, wearing big noise-canceling headphones, was writing on a yellow legal pad equipped with its own clip-on lamp; apart from this device, the lights in the room were low, like those in the cabin of a red-eye flight. Next to him lay Mike Frentz, on his side, legs semi-tucked, deeply asleep; and around the sofa's corner sat Ward Freitag, taking a phone update from the team still at the state building. Searchers, he learned, had determined that only a single, radio-controlled improvised explosive device, disguised in a volume of the Federal Reports, Second Series, had been planted, in the second floor stairwell on the Foltz Street side of the building. It was not powerful enough to have done grave damage, and the device's location was luckily a place of low fire risk, but it had blown a part of the metal stairs and railing off the wall. Unfortunately, someone— presumably a court employee at that hour—had been ascending from the second to the third floor when the device detonated, and was knocked unconscious by plaster falling off the wall; she'd been found by firefighters and removed to the best trauma unit in the city. No personal effects had yet been found, but the scene investigation was just getting underway, and all hoped an identification would be made soon. After all, as someone pointed out, to be going from one floor to another in a secure stairwell, the person would have to be carrying her photo ID keycard, which was probably buried under debris and would come to light before long. Ward wondered if the victim could be the missing Rackrent annual, Anya Holmquist, although the rough description he was given—very petite, thirtyish—did not quite match her.

Indeed, the description more closely fit the other person known to be missing on this chaotic night, but as Sadie was last seen with baby Quirke—according to Quirke's niece, who had been contacted at their residence—and as a thorough search of the building and immediate area had yielded no sign of any baby—it seemed unlikely the injured woman could be Sadie.

Nearly an hour had passed since Ward had last spoken with his federal counterpart, and he decided to check in.

"I was just about to call you, Ward," Sandy Wormsleigh, the district court clerk, said. "We're done over here. Judge Van Minck just denied the petition, but he's keeping his stay in place for an hour so Dormund can file in the circuit."

"The judge certainly gave it due consideration," Ward said.

"You're telling me," she said. "I skipped dinner thinking I'd be out of here by nine. What is it now, midnight?"

"One-thirty."

"Oy. At least there won't be much traffic to the East Bay at this hour. Hey, any news on what the heck happened in the state building tonight?"

"It was a little IED in a staircase."

"No kidding. Wow. Anybody take responsibility yet?"

"Not that I'm aware of. I'd better let you go, Sandy."

"Yeah, thanks, Ward. I need to go home and get some sleep. It sure is a good thing the state's so miserable at actually executing anybody; I don't have the stamina to do this on a regular basis."

"I hear you. It would be awful if these things became routine."

"Good night, Ward."

"Night, Sandy."

He spent the next ten minutes establishing contact with the circuit clerk, who promised to call immediately with news of any filing or order.

The Chief, when Ward informed her of the status of the federal proceedings, called Quirke's number, although Quirke had not answered his own phone all evening. "Justice Quirke," she said, wondering who would be listening to her message, "I hope you're well. You may be interested to know the district court has denied Dormund's petition and he's expected to file in the circuit. The stay remains in place for an hour, or until the circuit acts. Of course, there's no way to know when that might be. I'd love for you to call me back at your convenience." She considered advising him Sadie and Ruairí were missing and unaccounted for, but something in her counseled against adding that layer of complication and anxiety for the time being.

Rusty was now in a quandary. They had planned nothing beyond issuing an ultimatum to the Chief Justice and, if it failed, executing Quirke when Dormund met his end, but the Chief had told him it was out of her hands and the Governor had already denied clemency. Dormund's attorneys had messed everything up by going to federal court. The feds, as Rusty saw it, probably didn't have enough of a stake in getting rid of the state death penalty to incline them to grant the radicals' demand, so the kind of pressure that could successfully be brought to bear on them was unclear. It didn't help that he and Dane were tripping when Yago called on the burner phone to urge them to figure something out and move forward. Rusty tried to explain the political intricacies of the situation to him, but Yago, who had previously seemed so intelligent, only grunted like a truffle-hunting boar and insisted he put Dane on the line. Dane, however, always tended to muteness when abusing substances, this time being no exception, and he wordlessly passed the burner phone on to Anya.

She was already growing bored and anxious at the static mess they were in, and had almost decided to move to her Plan B, when Yago—without waiting to hear her assessment of the situation—instructed her to call the Governor, whose name he pointedly failed to remember, and deliver the ultimatum before something happened in federal court. After all, he noted, the Court of Appeals was known as the most liberal in the country, or the most often reversed by the United States Supreme Court, which amounted to the same thing. Who was to say the circuit wouldn't put a stop to the whole execution itself? That would be a disaster for the operation. The clarity of their message and the beauty of this opportunity would be lost, maybe never to return, and a whole new set of problems would arise.

Anya was unsure how the conclusion followed; after all, wasn't stopping Dormund's execution the whole point of this thing? As the Judge had said earlier that evening, abolition was happening one federal judge at a time. Apparently what Yago meant was that Quirke's presence would at that point become superfluous, and getting rid of him without jeopardizing everyone's welfare was a challenge he doubted any of them was up to. Still, if all efforts failed and the prisoner were killed, so too would Quirke be killed, Yago said. But the message had to be clear; did she understand? She did.

"You will now do as I have told you to do and then lose this phone," he said. She was certain she heard Hayley's voice, uttering apolitical enticements, in the background just before the call ended.

She stood in the center of the disused office space for some moments holding the phone, unable to move, apart from an uncontrollable trembling. Yago evidently expected her to call the Governor's office, get through to the man himself, and accomplish what none of them had yet been able to do: obtain his agreement to spare Dormund and the other 810 people on death row in exchange for the judge's life. Merely to articulate the problem was to see its absurdity. As she agonized, trying and failing to visualize herself moving in any direction, Quirke approached her.

Although he'd taken more than one of the pills he called fake oxys and had consumed a healthy dose of LSD on top of it, only the numb, fixed look in his eyes gave him away. He must be well practiced in concealing his inner state, a skill he'd probably acquired on the bench.

"Anya," he said. She waited as he seemed to be inwardly rehearsing and rejecting a series of conversational overtures before continuing. "I don't seem to be serving any purpose here, and I'd like to go home to my girlfriend. All right if I leave?"

The judge was reasonableness personified, and she wanted to grant his wish and end this whole stupid project, but Rusty's likely reaction frightened her. But then so did the consequences of not granting the judge's wish. Instead of responding she asked, "What's the best way to reach the Governor, do you know?"

"I used to have his number, when it was Benfield in office. Darven, you got me."

She stared despairingly at him. "Is there a way to disguise my voice on the phone?"

Again he paused before responding. "There are voice changer apps. Why do you want to do that?"

She gave a half-vocalized cry and turned away; he laid his hand on her arm and said, "It's a little late to be asking, but why am I here?"

"Haven't you figured it out?" she yelled.

"Maybe I have," he whispered, "but why don't you tell me."

"You and Dormund have something in common, did you know that? Either you both live or you both die tonight." His cold blue eyes held hers. Why was he smiling? He must be completely wasted. She pulled her arm away.

Quirke's low voice penetrated to her core. "Don't do this to my son, he's only a baby." After allowing her a painful space of time for thought, he added, "Your parents will still love you if you do, but it'll be a lot easier on them if you don't."

She pushed him angrily and could see that despite her meager weight the blow had hurt his injured shoulder. "What do you know about it?" she said.

"I've done some very stupid things, but they weren't the reason why my wife and my girlfriend stopped loving me."

"Really?"

Ignoring her sarcastic tone, he carried on. "Yes. They stopped because I held out on them. In the case of my wife, thirty years of holding out. It would have starved the life out of anything on the planet."

"Judge, I'm not sure I want to know—"

"My girlfriend's exceptionally smart and figured it out much sooner. I'm just saying, Anya, a mistake isn't going to drive your parents away. All the same, if you can avoid killing a judge, you should. It'd be a pretty lame irony if you got the death penalty for trying to end the death penalty."

"I won't," she said. "Listen, shut up and listen. I'm going to get you out of here. I have a plan."

She refused to elaborate. Not wanting to annoy her enough to make her change her mind, if she really had some way of freeing him, he sidled over to keep an eye on Rusty, who was on some social media account trying to gin up interest in the QuirkeJ posts. She slipped away into the stairwell.

Chapter Thirty-Two

3:00 a.m., Friday, February 26

"Daddy?"

"Is that you, Anya? Hold on." Frederick Holmquist felt along the top of the bedside table for his glasses and left the bedroom in order not to wake Anya's mother. Once in the hallway, he continued. "It's barely six o'clock here. Is everything all right?"

"Not really," she said, talking into her cupped hand. "I need your help. I can't explain everything now, but I need to get away from a man with a gun."

"Jesus, Anya! Where are you?"

"I'm in Sant' Urbano. There's more than one of us being held here. Can you send somebody, like right now, I'm not kidding?"

"Somebody, you mean—"

"Daddy, you must know somebody in the security business, executive protection business, whatever. I mean somebody with rescue skills and all the necessary equipment. Because I'm telling you, it could get ugly really fast. There are at least three AK-47s in this place and people who seem to know how to use them."

Holmquist gasped, running his free hand through his thinning hair. "My God, honey. When you're safe you're going to have to tell me how you got yourself into this mess. Okay, I have some ideas on how to get you out. But first the basic info. How many people are being held? Including you?"

"Two. Three, I mean, three." *Me, the Judge, and Dane*, she thought.

"As near as you can say, where are you? Can you tell me the address, and what kind of building? And how many people are holding the three of you?"

"It's an empty office or, I guess you'd say, light industrial building near the bay in the southeastern part of the city. Glendinning Way, I think, is the street. I don't know the cross street, but it's right by a 76 gas station."

"What color's the building?"

"Grayish-green, I think. We're on the second floor, in a big open-plan space."

"Are you restrained?"

"They let us take off the zip-ties after a few hours. But the leader's a fucking lunatic; he could put them back on us any time. Please get someone out here as quickly as you can, or I don't know what's going to happen."

"Just one more question, Anya: If you're able to call me, why didn't you call the police?"

She'd known he'd ask. "Because I trust you more than I do the Sant' Urbano police. And because there are a lot of drugs and stuff going on here, and it wouldn't be very good for my career if the cops thought I had some connection to it. Daddy, one more thing: After you get us out, I want to go back to Seven Shores. Right away."

His groan, she knew, was not a commentary on the cost of the eating disorder rehab facility, which, although steep, was as nothing for him. Rather, it was one of fear, since, the last time she was admitted to Seven Shores, the doctors told her parents she was perhaps a week from starving to death.

"What do you weigh?" he demanded.

"Seventy-one yesterday. I've eaten once today. I tried to eat more, but—and there's nothing here."

"I understand, sweetie."

"I feel like, if I'd been stronger, I might have been able to fight off the guys who—who took us. I really don't want to die, Daddy."

"When you hang up, I'm going to make two calls. One to an associate of mine who I'll just say is sort of a fixer out there; I'm sure he'll have an idea how to extract you and your party. The other to Seven Shores. Now, I take it you managed to get out of their sight somehow to make this call. I don't want to put you in even more danger. Is it safe for me to text you when I firm up the plan?"

"I think so."

"Then expect a text from me sometime in the next hour with the details of what's going to happen. Okay, Anya?"

"Thank you, Daddy. I love you. I want to go home."

"I love you, too. Now let me go and get things moving."

In the dark of the hallway in his upper East Side apartment, Holmquist shook his head. Anya had always been a little mad, unpredictable, untrustworthy in spite of the profession she'd ultimately chosen. As a child she'd never developed a sense of self-preservation; it seemed he and Metta had spent most of the first six years of Anya's life running into traffic after her. She'd been a child of fierce hatreds and consuming loves; then, at adolescence, after another girl's forgettable slight, she'd become obsessed with her weight, regulating her food intake so severely and exercising so compulsively she'd come several times close to death. He and Metta had argued with her for hours over her decision to move across the country to go to law school, and come close to forbidding it; to let her plunge into that sort of academic pressure cooker seemed utterly reckless, but either she'd started to outgrow her eating disorder or imposing the external pressure somehow counterbalanced some of her implacable internal stresses. Things had gone remarkably well until she'd graduated; then the old demon seemed to return, and in every Skype call they could see her wasting away. She'd been singularly uninformative about her personal life, but then perhaps her job with the judge left little time for one. At any rate, in a matter of hours she would be with them—or at least near them, at Seven Shores, getting well. First things first: Holmquist lost no time going to his study to try to get hold of the one man he knew in the Sant' Urbano area who, he hoped, could liberate his troubled daughter and the two others.

Chapter Thirty-Three

3:15 a.m., Friday, February 26

KNBC Radio @knbcradio #statebuildingbombing Death at state building? Seeking confirmation of reported fatality as police and fire department investigate.

"Shit," said Rusty, pocketing Quirke's phone hastily.

He jumped off the desk he'd been standing on and began to zigzag around the space, punctuating his mutterings with curses and further scatological references. It was supposed to be an act of political vandalism, not bodily harm. Anya had told them she'd found the perfect spot for the bomb, in a place where nobody ever went after hours. She set it up and told them it was cool. Could she not do anything right?

Physical movement, instead of releasing tension, seemed to wind him up more. At last he had to discharge his anxiety, and began to run around the room, yelling, "Hey. Hey, Anya, Conal. Dane. You see what they're saying? That somebody died at the state building?"

She drew a sharp breath. "How?"

"How do you think?" he said, stopping inches from her face. "Looks like the placement wasn't so smart."

"I don't understand," she said. "I've never seen anyone in that stairwell. Are you sure?"

"Hashtag state building bomb. That puts a little different slant on this operation. It's maximum exposure now; I don't even have to ask Conal to know that."

Anya's eyes glittered with tears and anger, as though the injustice had been done to her, but she said nothing. They could hear Dane, who had been standing alone under the windows for a long time, begin to moan. As they turned to look at him, he bent suddenly, vomited a little on the floor in front of him, clamped a hand over his mouth, and ran to the stairwell. Then they heard more retching, followed by appalling sobs.

Quirke had heard Rusty's announcement, as something vaguely absurd, as if on a radio or TV. He began to turn over in his mind the idea of someone dying in his workplace, possibly someone he knew or saw every day. The state building was six stories in height, a city block wide and half a block deep, veined with hallways and elevators and terrazzo stairs, its interior space cut up into offices grand and modest and, of course, the courtroom, the nerve center of it all. Though death by one means or another often brought parties before the court, the building itself was an orderly haven, a fortress of justice, a monastery of the law, a place where ordinarily the worst injury that could befall you was bruised feelings on account of a pointed dissent. Now the place was proved to be as perilous as any other.

It occurred to him now that he'd felt no psychic trace of Sadie tonight. If she was thinking of him, the drugs were blunting his mind too much for him to perceive it. And perhaps she wasn't thinking of him. He needed to find out the truth.

Rusty was marching around the space with such angry vigor, repeatedly thrusting his fists away from him, that Quirke found it difficult to get his attention despite repeatedly calling to him. To Anya, he finally said, "Can you get him to stop for a minute?" But she did not meet his eye and merely shrugged.

Dane emerged, white and shaky, from the stairwell and approached the desks in the center of the room. His silence, as he leaned against them, finally drew Rusty's attention.

"Wasn't supposed to happen," Dane said quietly. "It was only supposed to be a diversion, till we got the judge away. What a fucking catastrophe."

Rusty shook his head. "Dude, you can't blame yourself. It's Anya's fault, she's the one who said it was a safe place to put the thing. And just remember, everybody in that building's part of the system, complicit some way or another."

Dane shook his head. "What if it wasn't a judge or a lawyer? What if it was a cleaner, a security guard, somebody like that? I didn't want that kind of blood on my hands."

"My blood would be okay, though?" Quirke spoke up incredulously.

"It's not wrong to save 800 lives by sacrificing one," Rusty retorted. "Your IRA mom and dad knew that." He pointed the phone camera at Quirke again. "Stand up, we're going to talk about this. You believe it's not wrong to save 800 lives by sacrificing one, and you're going to say it. Or I'm going to blow your fucking head off, and I really mean it this time."

"You don't want me to say something insensitive like that right now," Quirke said, as Dane walked away in disgust. "It's not going to do your cause any good."

"How would you fucking know? Okay, Conal, three-two-one: Is it wrong—? Is it wrong?" He clutched the curved magazine of his weapon with his other hand.

"It's not—*fuck this*," Quirke muttered under his breath, "—it's not wrong to save 800 lives by sacrificing one." A click signaled the end of the clip. "Death to the fascist insect," he concluded.

The simplistic utilitarian rationale annoyed the philosopher in him, the reference to his parents enraged him, and he knew the loved ones of the bombing victim, if they were ever to hear his little speech, would suffer and hate him. But he hadn't yet given up hope of changing Rusty's mind. Quirke moderated his voice almost as well as he habitually did on the bench when the more obtuse attorneys spoke. "I get that you have no particular fondness for the rule of law or faith in the courts. Still, your argument only works if it works. But this is just not going to accomplish anything. I told you the Governor couldn't give a flying fuck about me. He'd happily put one of his cronies in my seat. Your best bet is working to get the abolition initiative to pass. Ring doorbells, make phone calls...do the safe, boring retail politics. It was polling even, last I checked; you can't claim a big slice of the public's not ready to listen to you on this." Rusty continued to stare insolently at him, while Anya and Dane wouldn't meet his eye. "Unless your real goal is a grand failure," Quirke continued. "Maybe you're just trying to impress somebody—your political higher-ups, or a pretty girl. But are you, even you, really capable of that kind of venality?"

Rusty snorted. "Conal, your naiveté is showing. Do you really think the powers that be are going to let that initiative pass? Every time something like this gets close, there's a mass shooting or something like that that makes people think only the death penalty can keep them safe. If it doesn't happen on its own, the government or the police or the prison guards can engineer it. We're a necessary corrective to that kind of power."

"Conspiracy theorists tend to be impervious to facts. I can't make you hold a rational world view, and apparently the LSD isn't helping much. Whatever. But I need my phone for a second."

"What for?"

"I have to see if my girlfriend is all right," he said.

"Why wouldn't she be?" Rusty asked.

"I just need to hear her voice," Quirke said.

"I'll tell you if she called. What's her number?" Rusty began to scroll through the call log on Quirke's phone.

"It's 515-611-6667."

After a moment, Rusty said, "No calls."

"Or 515-821-0438."

"No. Nothing."

This too made Quirke despair. There had been a time when she'd leave messages, sweet or erotic or adoring, whenever they were forced to spend an evening apart. Everything had changed in a year and a half.

Suddenly, from the stairwell came a gun blast. In the room where he was standing, Quirke counted only the four of them—himself, Anya, Rusty and Tad. The third man had gone to get falafel hours earlier and, he now realized, never returned.

"Oh God," said Tad.

Alone, Quirke ran to the stairwell, skidding to a halt just outside the circumference of the blood spatter and brain-gobbets on the walls and floor surrounding Dane. He thought he saw a movement and screamed "Call 911!" But then, forcing himself to look more closely, he could see Dane had lost the top of his head and seemed not to be breathing. The boy's face was wet, as if he'd been crying when he put the barrel of the gun in his mouth. "Call 911!" Quirke yelled again.

He tried to persuade himself it could be shock and not callousness that rooted Anya and Rusty to the spot where they were standing, that Dane had been their comrade and friend and they must be overwhelmed to the point of paralysis at his unanticipated, brutal loss. But they only looked at him blankly, defensively, as if expecting him to reprimand them, or to make it go away.

"I gotta think, I gotta think," Rusty blurted out after a moment. "What have you got in those pockets, Conal? You got any crystal?"

Quirke could understand self-medicating in the circumstances. He'd have preferred that Rusty indulge in a downer rather than an upper, but he wasn't in a position to argue. He looked inquiringly at Tad, who nodded. Rusty strode over to Quirke, took the baggie, and pawed through it for his drug of choice.

"That powder there," said Tad. "I crushed it earlier today—sorry, Con."

"Doesn't matter now," Quirke said.

Rusty snatched the small baggie containing the methamphetamine and threw the larger baggie containing the rest of the stash back to Quirke, who caught it, his shoulder protesting a little despite the fake oxys, and pocketed it without thinking. On one of the desks, Rusty dumped a thimble-sized pile of powder and with a credit card pushed it into two lines.

"Anya, give me a dollar," he said. She drew a bill from her pocket, rolled it, and passed it to him. He put the end of the rolled-up bill against the table and snorted both lines. Time would tell, Quirke thought, whether the dose would clear his head or bring on unmanageable paranoia.

※

The meth influence brought a cold intensity into the already strained atmosphere. Rusty paced, his heels striking the floor hard, sweat stains spreading over his shirt. They could hear him muttering to himself, hypothetical planning statements—"We drive to the valley, and then we...No, we go back to the house and pick up the...And you call Yago, and...I mean I call, and..."—giving way to semi-coherent grievances and flares of anger. Two of his comrades had now departed, one by stealth and one by self-murder, and the remaining comrade was too weak to be relied on in any crisis; he seemed to be winding himself into a panic. When he'd become oblivious to Anya and his captives, she pulled Quirke into the storage room.

"It's set," she whispered.

"What's set?"

"I told you I'd get us out."

The sentence cut through the LSD and narcotics well enough, but he could not see quite what she meant. "Okay, how?"

"Sometime very soon, an associate of my father's is going to be here. He'll know how."

"You know this because..."

"He texted me a minute ago. They're on the way. Why don't you believe me?"

"I do believe you. Look, I'm not as sharp as I might be at the moment, but this could be a risky operation. How do you plan to stay alive?"

She looked blankly at him.

"Your father's associate might thank you to get the gun away from Rusty. Think you can?"

She considered, then shook her head. "He won't let me get that close to him right now. But if he simmers down—"

"Fine, so keep an eye on him. I'm going to give Tad the good news."

"Wait a minute, I didn't mean to...I'm talking about getting you and me out of here."

It was hard for anger to penetrate the drug fog, but he couldn't overlook the omission. "You're taking him, too, or I'm going to wait here for the cops."

"No, please don't say that. Don't try to be a hero. You know, you're not exactly pure yourself, Judge. If you talk to the police about what happened tonight, I'll have to talk to them about your little stash. What are you doing walking around with a street pharmacy in your pockets, anyway? If you have any intention of serving out your term, please just do what I say."

He had no way to argue with her advice. For the first time since he'd popped a pill that night, the potential consequences bore down on him with real weight, and he fingered the drugs in his pocket irresolutely. Still, the next sound he heard drove from his mind the vague thought of losing the stuff.

"Anya!" Rusty's voice had a new quality, one that reminded him of nothing so much as the Jack Nicholson character in the final reel of *The Shining*: cagey, desperate and unhinged.

Anya looked uncertainly at Quirke.

"Go see what he wants," said Quirke.

She returned to the large open space, where Rusty was standing. Under the cold fluorescent lighting his face wore an oily greenish sheen and a malicious grin. "You're getting too cozy with Conal. I want you where I can see you from now on." Head drooping, she shuffled mechanically to his side.

"What do you mean, cozy?" Quirke demanded. He shot Anya a look, trying to signal he planned to provoke Rusty; he prayed she'd seize any opportunity to grab the gun Rusty had left on the desk.

"I mean cozy. You know, overly friendly. Intimate."

"I don't like your insinuations. I'm confident Anya will confirm that I've never—"

"Shut it. I don't mean sexually intimate. Ha! You can have her, if you don't mind getting lacerated by her hipbones while you're fucking." She colored to the roots of her hair and looked away. "No, I heard the two of you whispering. A conspirator knows a conspiracy when he sees one. What the fuck were you talking with her about?"

Quirke swallowed, then began to bait him in earnest. "You know, you might have succeeded with her if you'd paid her a little more intelligent attention, treated her with a little respect. She's not some bimbo."

Rusty hooted. "I hate to break it to you, old man, but that's the way power exchange relationships work. She wants it, she needs it, and I know how to give it to her."

"You can call it that if you want, but—"

"But what?"

Quirke stepped closer and faced him from less than an arm's length away. Pressing into Rusty's personal space, he maneuvered him a foot or two farther from the desk. "I don't know either of you very well, but it's obvious to me that however strong it might once have been, your hold on her's broken now. I could have gotten her to make love to me—to *really want to*—a few minutes ago, just like that." He snapped his fingers under Rusty's nose. "A totally open relationship, maybe that's where you think it's going. Or where you want it to go. But you're no longer in charge. Of that, I can assure you." He'd now come nearly chest to chest with Rusty, and the gun was, for the moment, out of his reach.

"What a pile of bullshit. Anya—"

When he turned to enlist her support, he found himself staring into the barrel of the AK-47. "Stay where you are," she commanded. "Judge, the zip-ties are in his pockets."

Chapter Thirty-Four

3:30 a.m., Friday, February 26

The warm weight on him, and his unaccustomed position—half-sitting, half-lying on the chaise lounge next to the bed in which Eleanor lay asleep—awakened Hetford, and the digital alarm clock on the bedside table confirmed the time. The weight, named Ruairí Quirke, shifted, seeking a softer place on Hetford's belly, and, having found it, sank back into slumber. Hetford too began to drift off again until the lateness of the hour forced itself into his awareness. If it was after three, why hadn't Sadie or Quirke come for the child, or at least called? Since Quirke might still be tied up at the court, Sadie's absence was the more worrisome. He was certain she'd have been in contact by now were it humanly possible, and he suddenly felt called upon to take action.

He slung his feet off the side of the chaise and struggled, his abdominal muscles working harder than they had in months, to sit upright without waking the baby. Briefly he considered putting Ruairí down on the bed next to Eleanor but, given that all evening he'd barely tolerated being parted from Hetford, even for the time it took to answer the call of nature, he put the sleeping baby over his shoulder instead. Slipping his phone in his pajama pocket, he left the bedroom.

By the time they reached the kitchen, Ruairí was whimpering, and Hetford wondered if he ought to have left well enough alone. "Or maybe," he whispered, "you're feeling a bit peckish? I could stand a little something myself." A can of Enfamil and a brace of clean bottles, thanks to Mrs. Resendiz, still stood on the counter and, with one hand supporting the baby on his left shoulder, he measured, mixed and heated the formula with the other. Ruairí was now awake, quietly supervising the preparation, and took the bottle as soon as Hetford set him on his lap and proffered it to him.

Hetford, meanwhile, turned his phone over and over in one hand, wondering what to do. Another call to the Quirke residence went unanswered, as did a further call to Quirke's phone. On Twitter, a search for "state building bomb" had brought up a heart-stopping tweet posted a couple of hours earlier: "Body found in state building." "My God," he groaned. He simply had to find someone to talk to. In his contacts was a number he hadn't used in over a year. It was insanely late to be calling, but it seemed only one person could help him now.

Two rings later a familiar voice answered. "Allan, how good—and unexpected—it is to hear from you. What's up?"

"My apologies for calling at this hour, Chief. How are you?"

"Well enough, but I wish this night would end. And you?"

"Frankly, concerned. I understand a body's been found."

"If you saw that on Twitter, it's a bit of an exaggeration. An injured and unconscious, but decidedly living, person was pulled out around midnight and taken to General Hospital. I understand the situation is serious but not life-threatening. Why?"

"Has the person been identified?"

"If so, no one's told me."

"I'm afraid it may be Sadie Quirke."

"Norrell, you mean. Sadie Norrell. They never actually got married. What makes you think so?"

"Damn it, I got her name wrong; I hope that hasn't caused confusion. Because she placed her child in my care just before the explosion and hasn't come for him. I have the little Quirke here on my lap as we speak, at our house in town. He's fine, but if Quirke's handy, I'd like to talk with him."

"Holy God, Allan. You didn't know?"

"Chief, please don't keep me in suspense. I'm on the point of a heart attack."

"I'm sorry. It's been quite a night here. Quirke, as a matter of fact, never turned up for execution duty. He's been tweeting anti-death penalty propaganda all night long."

"What?" Ruairí looked up as Hetford spluttered.

"Just look up 'QuirkeJ' and you'll see. Oh boy, here's the one I've been waiting for: 'From this day forward, I no longer shall tinker with the machinery of death.' "

"As in Blackmun's dissent in *Callins v. Collins*?"

"He mostly hasn't been bothering with attributions, but yes. Besides the aphorisms, there were several video posts to similar effect. It's definitely Quirke, but...Also, I got a call earlier from some joker on his phone, who thought I could somehow wave a magic wand and get rid of the death penalty on my own initiative. Of course, we're assuming these tweets either aren't authentic or else aren't voluntary on Quirke's part, but we just don't know anything yet. Interestingly, a minority of the court—who, I won't name—think it's for real, that Quirke's actually gone off the deep end and chose this weird way to try to abolish capital punishment all by himself."

"Quirke's many things, but lawless isn't one of them."

"I'm with you, but for whatever reason I haven't been able to get hold of him."

"Have you consulted Lieutenant Grimes? He managed to find Quirke the last time he went missing. Chief, what you've just told me only worries me more, but back to the matter of most immediate concern. Can you find out if—if it's Sadie they found?"

"I'm going to do that right away. I'll follow up with you."

"Thanks. Oh, and I take it the execution hasn't happened yet?"

"There's a federal stay in place. No idea if or when it's going to be lifted. The Attorney General usually keeps us posted on what's going on in federal court, but I guess they're a little too busy tonight to stay in contact. They had to evacuate, too, of course."

"Well, I won't hold you up any longer. I appreciate your keeping me looped in."

"And I can't thank you enough for calling, Allan. You know, I miss seeing you. A year ago, I'd never have imagined myself saying this, but Ruairí's lucky to have you as his caregiver. I'm sure Quirke and Sadie will be in complete agreement. Say hi to Eleanor for me."

Just after the Chief ended the call, Ruairí dropped his now-empty bottle. As Mrs. Resendiz had taught him, Hetford put him over his shoulder again and gently pounded his back. Ruairí rewarded him with an emphatic and resonant burp.

Eleanor, rubbing her eyes, joined them in the kitchen, her vivid hibiscus-patterned silk caftan lending a brightness that didn't quite reach her tired-looking features. "Oh dear, you should have used a towel, darling—now you've got spit-up on your pajamas."

He shrugged and kissed the baby's head, fatigue suddenly pressing on him. "The Chief says hello."

She massaged his shoulders as Ruairí watched, captivated. "Did you get hold of Quirke?"

Hetford frowned. "I don't want to alarm you, dearest, but it seems something's happened to him. And to Sadie." He related the substance of the Chief's news. "All we can do is wait and hope."

She nodded. "I'm just thanking God it wasn't you who got blown up. Well, I've got to see these allegedly subversive tweets."

He handed her his phone, trying to sound casual. "I'd bet a subsidiary or two that he's managed to fall into the wrong hands again." As Eleanor scrolled through the Twitter feed, their housekeeper, in bathrobe and slippers and carrying an armful of colorful clothing odds and ends, entered the kitchen.

"Mrs. R!" he exclaimed. "What are you doing up? I hope we didn't wake you."

"No, no," she said. "I just want to help with the baby, but I see you know what to do now. May I make you tea? Or something to eat? French toast, maybe; I know you like it, Mr. Hetford." Without waiting for an answer, she set the clothing on the banquette seat in the breakfast nook and got to work.

"And this stuff?" he asked, picking up a T-shirt from the pile. It seemed like a good time to trade his soiled pajama top for a clean one. "Are you saving it for anything?"

"What is it called? Castoffs—from my son. Some to give away, some for rags. Sorry, I put it where it belongs."

"Not to worry," he said, picking through the items. "I may be able to use something here."

"Allan, you wouldn't," said Eleanor, looking up from her phone with an admonitory glance.

"Oh, no, not for you, Mr. Hetford," said Mrs. Resendiz, shaking her head.

"Mrs. R, would you hold Ruairí for a moment?" When she'd obliged, he began to search in earnest. "How's this?"

He held up an orchid-colored tank top with a cartoon rainbow pony and the legend "Friendship Is Magic" emblazoned across it. Ruairí broke into a smile. In a moment Hetford, retreating to the half-bath adjoining, had donned the top and emerged to model it.

"I suppose this is a thing in the infant-toddler set?" he said. "Ruairí seems to recognize it."

"My Little Pony," said Mrs. R. "Little girls love it. Little boys, too, some of them. You know, these days is much more relaxed about such things. My son tell me that some men call themselves 'bronies,' watch the cartoon, and wear these shirts. But he tell me it's a little too gay for him." Her hand flew to her mouth. "I'm sorry, I shouldn't say that."

"Not to worry, Mrs. R," said Hetford. "It's not my typical style, but I like the sentiment." He smoothed the wrinkles out of the top, which fit more snugly than most of the clothes he was accustomed to wearing.

"You're getting a tummy, Allan," Eleanor observed.

A year before, he'd have run, in high dudgeon, straight to the gym at such a comment. The size of his waist was somehow a matter of far less moment now, but he knew Eleanor had a strong preference in this regard. "I suppose I should do something about it," he murmured. "As soon as things settle down around here again."

Chapter Thirty-Five

4:30 a.m., Friday, February 26

The three men froze momentarily as Anya's toothpick arms began to tremble with the exertion of holding up the AK-47. Then Rusty laughed. "Child, leave that to the grownups; it weighs more than you do."

"That's so tired," she said. "Get down on the floor."

He sneered. "Like you could make me."

Using his good shoulder, Quirke yanked Rusty's head toward him and, as he'd once seen a woman do to her assailant in a self-defense video, shot a leg out to sweep Rusty's feet out from under him. After Rusty hit the floor, he followed up, in a non-regulation move, by sitting on him.

"Con, you da man. Let me help." Tad approached from the sidelines to squat beside them, and reached into Rusty's hoodie pockets. "Here's your phone." Handing the device to Quirke, he continued rummaging, finally fishing out a handful of zip-ties.

Quirke accepted his phone, inwardly rejoicing that his career as a star of propaganda videos was over. Anya was now standing over the three men, looking so exhausted she might drop the gun. "Let's switch," he suggested, sliding off Rusty. Tad took Quirke's place on the small of Rusty's back as Anya handed the rifle to Quirke and knelt to fasten the ties around his wrist.

"Loop one around his belt, if he's wearing one, or his belt loops," Quirke suggested. "Then run the other end through it, like a waist chain." They now had him reasonably immobilized. Still holding the weapon in case of any stupid moves on Rusty's part, Quirke stepped back to check his voicemail.

The Chief had called an hour earlier. "Quirke, I hope you're holding up all right. All our thoughts are with you. You might like to know that Lieutenant Grimes and Detective Shadlack of the Sant' Urbano PD are investigating Anya Holmquist and her associates. They've already uncovered some interesting information. I wouldn't doubt they'll be knocking on her door before long. As for me, I'm hoping to see your face around here again very soon. Stay safe and take care."

A half hour later, Hetford, of all people, had left a message. As Quirke listened to it, his frown of impatience gave way to shock. "Quirke, hoping you're all right. Eleanor and I are very concerned about you. I'm sorry to be the bearer of bad news, but you need to know that Sadie was hurt in the blast at the state building tonight. There were some early reports of a fatality, but thank God that's not the case. She's got some rather serious injuries, though, and they took her to General Hospital. Best trauma center in town, I'm sure you're aware. And I have—Eleanor and I have Ruairí here with us. I'll explain it later; just know he's safe, and we and Mrs. Resendiz are making sure he's well cared for. So do make your way over to the hospital as soon as you can; Sadie's going to want you. Keeping you always in my thoughts, my friend."

By the end of the message, Quirke was shaking with rage. It wasn't enough these idiots had grabbed him and his innocent sponsee off the street and put them through this torturous night with their absurd political demands, that they'd made him their ventriloquist's dummy for the world's entertainment and set him up for God only knew how much trouble with the CJB just to hang onto his job. No, they had to blow up the state building and Sadie with it and, worst of all, made him seem to publicly endorse their having sacrificed her, invoking his misguided radical parents in the process. Not even the narcotics he shouldn't have been indulging in all night could stop him from breaking Rusty's face now. He'd happily do his time for it and throw himself on the CJB's mercy.

Rusty was now sitting sulkily on one of the bunched-together desks in the center of the room with his hands bound behind him, Anya standing awkwardly nearby trying to look in charge. Quirke considered simply bringing the barrel of the AK down on Rusty's head, but he didn't know how sensitive the thing was and whether he might in the process accidentally cause it to fire and hurt someone. Consequently, he strode up to Rusty and, with his good arm, clocked him as hard as he could.

The red spurt that rose to arc over his knuckles rejoiced him deeply. Rusty cried out in surprise and bent at the waist, groaning. "What the fuck? He fucking broke my nose, that fucker." Mesmerized, Anya and Tad stood watching the blood drip onto the floor. No one moved or spoke for some seconds.

Then the room was overrun with ninjas. Black-clad men moving too fast to be counted, their leather booties whispering across the bare concrete floor, were dragging Anya, Tad and Rusty—all too surprised to make a sound—toward the stairs, as though to a party Quirke was not invited to. Ten seconds after the ninjas materialized they, and the others, vanished backward down the stairway—but not before tossing a brace of little canisters in Quirke's direction and unleashing the brightest flashes and loudest bangs he'd ever felt or could imagine this side of the apocalypse.

Chapter Thirty-Six

5:00 a.m., Friday, February 26

Blind and deaf, Quirke lay overwhelmed on the floor, regretting the loss of his senses. Once, he tried getting onto all fours, hoping to crawl toward the staircase, but the flashbang concussion had obliterated his balance, and he swayed uncontrollably before collapsing onto his side. Complicated ratiocination was beyond him, but he understood the ninjas and their stun grenades had somehow been part of Anya's escape plan. Their taking Rusty instead of him was an understandable mistake, given he was the one holding an AK-47 when they sneaked in, and Rusty was zip-tied. On the bright side, Tad was free.

Time passed as Quirke lay on the cold floor, still missing significant parts of his sensorium. Under other circumstances, those not involving the presence on the scene of a deceased gunshot victim and his own fingerprints on a weapon capable of having inflicted the fatal wound, he might have stayed to assist with the investigation. Tonight, however, prudence seemed to dictate leaving the interpretation of the evidence to the professionals, who presumably could be trusted to recognize a suicide as clear-cut as poor Dane's. As well, he was still perhaps a little under the influence of various controlled substances, and a second 11550 arrest would probably put him at least three standard deviations above the mean for judges. Above all, he needed to get to General Hospital to see Sadie, but then again she might not look with favor on him showing up at her bedside in his present state.

"Oh, fuck," he said. Or at any rate he felt his vocal cords vibrating, his lips moving, and air being expelled from his mouth; he still couldn't hear a thing.

He realized his hearing had started to return when he caught the voices rising on the open stairway from the level below. Although he couldn't distinguish words, from the tone of their conversation the two men, who could only be law enforcement officers, were commenting on their observations as they worked their way up the building. They were now in the garage area where he had come to earlier that night; soon they would be in the room where he was unsteadily standing. *Should I stay or should I go?* he wondered; then his hand happened upon the drugs in his pocket and his heart flew into his throat. There was only one way out, and he had to take it now. He jogged to the storage room, barely avoiding falling over in his still wobbly state, and thrust one leg, then the other, out the window, thinking *Like parkour.*

He'd actually seen people—people much younger and fitter than he, of course—jump out of second story windows without injury. The trick was to push off smartly, land on your feet, immediately flex your legs to absorb the shock, and extend your arms like an Olympic gymnast for balance. He managed the first two parts, but—still woozy from the flashbangs—upon contacting the ground he plunged forward with the full inertial force of his 142 pounds onto his right shoulder, the formerly uninjured one. At least he'd fallen onto a patch of grass instead of the sidewalk. He allowed himself but a moment to celebrate his landing before gathering himself up and moving on, lest the police inside the building from which he'd just self-defenestrated notice his presence and attempt to make contact.

Trying to ignore the searing pain in his shoulders and an ominous new strain in his right knee, he found himself limping alongside a body of water—the bay, judging by the lights on the shore opposite, rather than the ocean. This was nowhere near Aquatic Park, at the northern end of Sant' Urbano, he knew; he must therefore be somewhere in the southeastern quadrant of the city. Fortuitously enough, so was General Hospital. Consultation with Google Maps revealed he was no more than a mile from the hospital, although with two major highways slashing the direct route, he would have to find some sort of conveyance to get there.

Sweating with pain, he swallowed one more fake oxy, belatedly realizing the inevitably ensuing drowsiness might not help him make the Uber driver understand where he needed to go. As he waited in this lightly traveled and, truth be told, rather dodgy area, he told himself this night, and in particular the substances he'd taken, was a one-off. He would take no more fake oxys today. He would get himself to the hospital, sober up, and, after seeing Sadie, have his shoulders looked at. Or should he sober up first and then go to the hospital? If he delayed going to her, she'd have reason to be displeased with him. Then again, in recent months she'd been displeased with any deviation from sobriety, and with a lot of other things he usually understood only after the fact. Maybe it would go better if he waited; she was so unpredictable lately.

The Uber driver, in a red Prius, pulled up next to a streetlight and beeped, rousing him from his musings. Sticking his head out of the window, the driver, a youngish man wearing a Giants cap, frowned as Quirke approached the car.

"Thanks for stopping," said Quirke, leaning into the window. "I'm going to General Hospital."

The driver shook his head. "Not with me you're not. I mean, sorry, dude, but you'd get blood all over the seats."

"What are you talking about? I'm not—okay, I see what you mean," said Quirke, taking another look at his clothes, which bore enough genetic material to keep a DNA analyst busy for days.

"Look, the bus stop's at the end of the block. See over there?" he asked, pointing. "That bus goes to the hospital. Law says Muni drivers have to carry anybody who gets aboard. It's your best bet, trust me. Good luck." He reversed and drove off without ceremony. Only after the Prius was out of sight did Quirke realize that the bloodstains all over him might have conveyed the same mistaken impression of his character and motives that the ninjas had apparently acquired.

He trudged to the stop, marked by a graffiti-splashed shelter illuminated with garish fluorescent lighting, and sat on the treadlike seats, designed to thwart anyone hoping to lie down for a nap. Dawn was breaking; the LED clock mounted in the shelter read 7:22, and the next bus was estimated to arrive in 27 minutes. He let his head fall back against the shelter's glass wall. How did anybody in this part of town ever get to work on time? He knew he should call someone, Roísín or maybe Hetford, but was reluctant to awaken them this early in the day, and even now he doubted he could hear well enough to easily carry on a phone conversation. He was desperately tired under the influence of the fake oxys, but he feared that if he allowed himself to nod out, he'd fall so deeply asleep the arrival of the bus would fail to awaken him.

A few minutes into his wait, a young woman in black leggings and an oversized plaid shirt and hoodie stepped into the shelter and dropped her backpack onto the ground. Out came her phone, and for a moment they coexisted in neutral silence while she scrolled through a feed. Then, glancing in his direction at the moment a twinge in his shoulder happened to cause him to groan, she took a closer look at him. Without a word, she swung her pack onto her shoulder again and, with 24 minutes remaining until the bus, strode off. Two minutes later, several teenagers holding spray-cans hopped out of a yellow Celica and began tagging the shelter; when Quirke glanced in their direction, trying to appear more neighborly than reproachful, the crew eyed him, ceased their decorative efforts, and piled into their idling ride.

Alone again, his thoughts kept revolving between Sadie—what had

Allan meant by "rather serious injuries"? And how did Ruairí come to be with him and Eleanor?—and his own ethical situation in the wake of the evening's propaganda efforts.   Now and then he remembered to be thankful Rusty hadn't had time to kill him.   If Rusty and Anya were now safely away, they'd likely have an interest in keeping mum about certain details of the night's events, including, he hoped, the battery he'd inflicted on Rusty's face and the drugs he'd supplied them.   And, realizing what it would mean to conceal that information from the CJB, he felt sick. He'd always thought of himself as an honest man, whatever his other flaws.   During his last disciplinary trouble, after being caught drunkenly making love to Sadie in his chambers and, later, smoking marijuana at a party among her friends, candor had rescued his reputation, had enabled him to negotiate the penalty down to a public admonishment and retain enough respect among the electorate to keep his seat on the court.   But tonight he'd willfully gotten high and beat up a man.   Although Rusty richly deserved what he got, Quirke regretted hitting him with his hands tied behind his back; that was unfair.   Worst of all, he could have thrown the drugs in the bay as soon as he escaped from captivity, but— inexplicably—there they were, still in his pocket.   Not so inexplicably, really: He was a drug addict, after all.   He'd claimed it at meetings, to his sponsor and sponsee, and to Sadie, but because he'd never reached the point of physical dependence on narcotics he'd somehow not fully believed it himself.   But only the insanity of addiction could have persuaded him that he, a Supreme Court justice, the father of an infant child, should walk around with a stash that could send him to prison for years and years.   And he was now scheming to keep the truth from coming to light.   It was no mystery why a sensible person like Sadie would refuse to marry him.   He wasn't even sure he wanted to spend the rest of his life with himself.

He stood and looked around for a trash can—the city's solution to the problem of overflowing garbage containers was to remove them from places where they might be used, so naturally none was near the bus stop—but just then the bus pulled up and he boarded.

Somehow, despite the deplorable state of his sobriety, he managed to locate the correct fare on his person and insert it into the fare box. As the bus zinged along its wires down the street, he slid into a seat. Some dozen other passengers, a randomly assembled jury of his peers, silently sized him up and, announcing their verdicts only to themselves, returned their gaze to their phones or shut their eyes again. At the very back of the bus a man—mumbling, shouting occasional accusations at no one in particular—wrangled three large black plastic garbage bags filled with unseen angular objects toward the rear door. He appeared to be wearing nothing below the waist, but his hands were protected by muddy suede gardening gloves. At least until the man exited at Texas Street, Quirke felt modestly pleased to be, by any measure, not the most disheveled or deranged guy on the bus.

Chapter Thirty-Seven

4:00 a.m., Friday, February 26

Around 4:00 a.m., the provisional slumber of the Hetford household's inhabitants was interrupted by happy news. The Chief called to say the evacuated bombing victim had been definitively identified as Sadie; her shoulder bag, containing her identification, had fallen down the stairs in the blast and been hidden under rubble until investigators sifting through the wreckage located it. After thanking the Chief and leaving a voicemail for Quirke, Hetford decided he would bring the baby to the hospital, although it was unclear whether Sadie had regained consciousness.

"I can't help but think his being there will do both of them some good," he told Eleanor. "Of course, I'll bring him back here straightaway if I'm wrong."

"I'm coming with you," Eleanor said, yawning. "You're not used to getting around with a baby all by yourself. And..."

"Go ahead, say it." Hetford smiled. "You aren't too eager to say goodbye to him, either."

"You're right. Allan, you're not going like that, are you?"

Evidently she was referring to his My Little Pony top. He supposed it was a bit twee, and maybe he was getting a little too soft in the middle to be parading about in a muscle shirt, but he rather liked the sentiment printed on it. Accordingly, to appease her, he put a fresh pink oxford cloth shirt over the tank, leaving it unbuttoned, and an unstructured charcoal tweed jacket over that. There, he thought, examining himself in the full-length mirror in his closet: arguably a fashion-forward look, and in any event it suited him.

With the help of the excellent and resourceful Mrs. Resendiz, the Maybach was made street legal with an infant car seat, a bottle and diapers were packed, and the three set off for General Hospital.

Sadie had been moved to a private room, and although visiting was not normally permitted in the predawn hours, the nurses made allowance for her loved ones' presence this one time, considering they'd all spent most of the night wondering if she were alive. The Chief had also alerted Quirke's niece, Roísín, who came prepared to take over the care of Ruairí. Roísín, in turn, against her better judgment but in recognition of romantic reality, had contacted Father Liam Greengold. Being, of all of them, the one geographically closest to the hospital, he arrived first. Dressed as he was in clerical black and Roman collar, hospital staff posed no resistance when he told them he was there to see a parishioner. At Sadie's side when she awakened, he was the first to speak with her. That is, he listened and wrote responses on notebook paper, as her eardrums had ruptured in the blast. She asked about Ruairí, and he happily assured her Ruairí was safe.

He continued to stand over her bed, holding her hand, as a nurse told them Sadie would eventually get her hearing back. More worrisome was the blast lung injury she'd suffered, the full extent of which they had yet to learn. And she had a concussion from falling debris—though luckily no sign of a bleed—as well as assorted scrapes and punctures and a broken ankle. She might drift, often, in and out of sleep for a while; this was good for her recovery and should be encouraged. She had, in fact, just fallen back to sleep when Eleanor, Hetford, and Ruairí arrived. The child readily enough let Roísín take him, and promptly fell asleep over her shoulder as she located a relatively comfortable chair in the hallway just outside the room in which to wait.

"Eleanor, if you don't mind, I'd like to stay and talk to Sadie next time she wakes up, just to tell her how we took care of the baby for her. I think it might ease her mind a little," Hetford told his wife. "Go home, dearest. You must be exhausted, although you're as radiant as ever."

Eleanor, looking up at him, her arms around his waist, blinked slowly in her fatigue and kissed him. "You're an angel. A lying angel, but an angel nonetheless. You're right, I am exhausted. It's been an amazing but rather draining night. Is this what we have to look forward to? You can't wait, can you?"

He grinned. "It was fun. I don't know how I'll manage without a baby until we make our own."

If he wasn't mistaken, she shivered. "But how will you get home?" she asked.

"Don't worry about that; if nothing else, I'll Uber."

"Are you sure? I know you don't like anyone driving your car, but I could send Emily down here with it."

"Well, I suppose if you can spare her for a while, that might be—"

"I'll tell her to come by the house on her way into the office, and she can bring your Tesla down here. She's usually in by 7:30, so you can expect her here by 8:00."

"Perfect. Thank you, darling." Somehow he found the thought of Eleanor as a mother rather stirring. He slid an arm along her supremely taut left buttock and kissed her neck.

She seemed a little nonplussed at his public display of affection, and gently moved his hand. "Then I'll see you later. I love you, Allan. In spite of that shirt," she added, rubbing the rainbow pony. Another kiss, and he was alone in the hallway.

Hospital staff took no note of him or the rainbow pony as they flowed around him, attending to their patients. Feeling at loose ends following an interval of a few watchful minutes, he approached the bedside. As far as Hetford could see, the priest was simply standing at her side, holding her hand and studying her badly bruised face—much as Quirke would have been doing had he been present. But why was a priest here in the first place? He'd always understood she was a pagan, a witch or something like that. He decided to introduce himself. "Excuse me, Father. Allan Hetford, friend of the family," he said, quietly so as not to wake her. "I was fortunate enough to have been on hand in the state building tonight when Sadie needed someone to look after Ruairí for a few minutes. It was just then that she had the bad luck to meet up with this calamity...so when no one could tell me what had happened to her, my wife and I brought Ruairí home with us. What a relief it was to learn she was safe."

The priest turned toward him with a look that mixed shock and something like exhilaration; his unoccupied hand shook Hetford's. "Liam Greengold. Good to meet you, Allan. How kind of you and your wife to keep the baby safe. You'd like to speak with Sadie?"

"Yes, just to let her know how much we loved taking care of Ruairí and what a stoic little guy he is. I'll wait out there—" He gestured toward the outer area where Roísín was sitting.

"No, please stay, the chair's all yours, unless you find it more comfortable out there."

It occurred to Hetford that Father Liam might want a witness or chaperone, then dismissed the cynical thought. "Well, then I will, thank you," he said, settling himself in the only armchair in the room. He took out his phone, glancing in the direction of the bed every few minutes to see if Sadie had awakened. Before long, however, sleep deprivation caught up with him and he began to doze, surfacing whenever a nurse entered the room to perform a procedure and drifting back to sleep as soon as it was done. Each time Hetford opened his eyes, the priest was still at Sadie's side, with her hand still in his, although over time—and who could blame him?—he bent forward, adjusting his weight so that his forearms eventually came to rest on the bed, his head practically lying on the pillow next to hers. Finally, a little before 8:00, Eleanor's assistant gently woke Hetford to hand over the keys to his car, along with a slip of paper on which she'd written its location in the hospital parking garage, and a large takeout cup of fragrant coffee. He supposed it was time to get a little work done, and brought out his phone.

Already a dozen emails from various of Marvelocity's European subsidiaries had hit his inbox, most involving thorny questions about a participation exemption under Swiss tax law. He was in the process of triaging them when Roísín, cradling the sleeping Ruairí in the hallway, spoke up in tones of amazement.

"Uncle Conal! Where were you all night? Did you get my voice mail? How did you—"

Hetford was on his feet and in the hallway in an instant. There was Quirke, all right, looking like he'd survived an explosion of his own. Dust and dirt and what looked like bloodstains streaked a torn business suit that must have been unexceptionable the day before; his eyes, black-rimmed and empty, scanned the area, appearing not to comprehend what they were seeing. Swaying a little, he approached the door to Sadie's room.

"Quirke!" said Hetford, touching his elbow. "Thank God you're here. She caught a few nasty injuries, but seems to be doing all right now, sleeping intermittently. And there's Roísín, with Ruairí." He tried gently to turn Quirke toward his niece and son, but Quirke seemed rooted to the spot, too much in shock to allow himself to be guided. He stared at Sadie, at her battered face, at the bandages, tubes and monitors, and at the priest who still stood quietly beside her, holding her hand.

"Lover, if thou wilt, depart," he muttered. Then, as if noticing Hetford for the first time, he looked at him, softly pleading. "I can't do this. Get me out of here, will you?"

"But, Quirke, she'll wake up soon, and—"

"It's the end if she sees me like this. Look at me," he said, and Hetford could see there was something flat and wasted about his eyes. "I'm completely fucked up. 'Friendship is magic,' yes. So work it, my friend. But for God's sake, don't touch me," he cried as Hetford put an arm around him. "Wrecked both my shoulders tonight." Hetford hastily took his arm away, only then noticing that Quirke's jacket pockets were crammed with baggies containing what looked like pills, syringes, and other controlled substances. He now understood what Quirke wanted, even if he had not a clue how he came to be in this state.

"I'm taking you home," he said. "We'll just slowly, inconspicuously walk from here to my car, okay? Lean on me if you want." Hetford stopped and looked into Sadie's room. She seemed still asleep, and the priest still faced her bed. He decided Liam hadn't noticed Quirke's arrival, and thought it better not to draw attention to his predicament by mentioning it. But Roísín had to be told something.

"I'm afraid the ordeal has been too much for Justice Quirke," he said. "He's been rather badly injured himself, as you can see. Since Sadie's asleep at the moment, we might as well go home and clean up. We'll be back as soon as possible, of course." Hetford wheeled away from her, catching up with Quirke as he shuffled down the hallway.

But Quirke's ordeal was not yet over. Approaching from the other end of the corridor were the Chief Justice, Lieutenant Grimes, and a tall man with a Sant' Urbano police badge on his suit jacket. Hetford's heart skipped once and began to hammer relentlessly. Quirke had halted and was swaying again, looking like he might collapse. It would take the officers—and the shrewd Chief, for that matter—mere seconds to realize Quirke was under the influence. They'd be eager to question him about his apparent kidnapping and the strange tweets of earlier in the evening, but he was in no shape to withstand interrogation at present.

"Behind me," Hetford whispered urgently to Quirke. "Glue yourself to me. Keep walking." He was glad for the several inches in stature and breadth he had over Quirke. He led the way, moving steadily, nodding smartly as they met up with the Chief's party, and continued down the corridor.

The Chief stopped and stared. Hetford had maneuvered himself between Quirke and the others and was moving backward along the hallway, keeping an eye on the Chief. "Allan!" she exclaimed. "Is that Quirke with you?"

He paused in his tracks, grabbing a handful of Quirke's jacket to stop him. "Hello, Chief; good to see you, Lieutenant Grimes. Yes, Justice Quirke came directly here as soon as he got my voice mail, but he can't stay just now. Of course, we'll be back soon to visit Sadie. You'll be very happy to know the doctors think she's going to be okay."

"We need to talk with him," the Sant' Urbano detective said.

"Of course. Actually, I'm representing him. Give me a call later today and we'll discuss it. The Chief has my number."

"Allan—?" she said.

He waved at them and pushed Quirke forward. Soon they made good their escape, reaching the bank of elevators that descended to the parking levels.

Quirke, leaning heavily against the mirrored wall as they rode down, laughed despite himself. "Did you just appoint yourself my lawyer?"

"Apparently I did," said Hetford, inwardly shuddering. Although he'd briefly presided over a felony trial calendar as a superior court judge, the only criminal defense experience he could claim was a temporary appearance on behalf of a Fortune 500 client in a Department of Justice antitrust investigation as a junior associate in his Big Law days. "Don't worry, I know some real defense lawyers I can sub in for—"

"Way to go, Allan," said Quirke, appreciatively.

Chapter Thirty-Eight

8:30 a.m., Friday, February 26

"*Hola*, Mrs. R." Hetford reached the housekeeper by phone as he was pulling the Tesla into its space in the garage at home. "*No, desgraciadamente, no tengo el bebé conmigo. Pero tengo el juez...El juez...Si, el Señor Quirke.* Is Mrs. Hetford around? ...Just as well," he said to Quirke, in the passenger seat, who was again nodding, whether from the exhausting impact of the night's events or from his fake oxys, who could say. "*Llego inmediatamente*, Mrs. R. *Adiós por el momento.* Well," he said, after a pause, "shall we go in? You know the way."

Quirke took a deep breath before lowering his feet to the concrete floor. There was something surreal in taking refuge here, his former home, from which Eleanor had, scarcely a year and a half earlier, unceremoniously thrown him out. Hetford had gotten out of the car and was waiting for him, the look on his face so solicitous it made Quirke feel even more disoriented. *Snap out of it*, he told himself. But though the immediate effects of the LSD and narcotics were fast wearing off, they had left a depressing psychic residue. And the pain in his shoulders had come back, flaring whenever he lifted so much as a hand.

He entered the elevator, closely followed by Hetford, and tried to prepare himself by visualizing the foyer into which he would soon pass. He found it easy to call to mind photographic details of the windows, furnishings, and marble floor, yet when he did step into the house, he felt an entirely different atmosphere than what he remembered. Light, peace, an absence of recriminations; formerly the tomb of his hopes, the old house was now a sanctuary. He wondered why Hetford had brought him here, rather than to the loft, but was glad of it.

As they were starting up the stairs, Mrs. Resendiz, about to venture out on a grocery shopping expedition, greeted them. In the shock on her face, Quirke saw a reflection of how dreadful he must look. Her arms flew to encircle him, and retreated just as quickly when he grimaced. "It's not you, Mrs. R—it's a shoulder injury," he assured her.

"When I get back, I will make you chicken soup," she said. "You need to eat, Judge. You have become so thin."

"Don't go to any trouble," he began.

"Excellent idea, Mrs. R," Hetford interjected. "The judge has had a terrible night, and we'll take care of him for a while. You can shower upstairs, Quirke—I'll find something for you to wear—and sleep, if you feel like it."

"I have to get back to the hospital as soon as I'm fit," he said.

Without thinking, he headed to the master bedroom suite and dropped his torn, bloody clothes in front of the walk-in shower he'd always used. The soap had changed—*I'm going to smell like Hetford*, he thought, scrubbing himself—and only as he turned off the water after a long hot rinse did he realize he had nothing to put on. Too tired to solve the problem, he stood in the bathroom, wrapped in a towel, looking in the mirror without seeing, until Hetford came in holding a blue kimono.

Without speaking, he dropped the towel and let Hetford drape the heavy cotton garment over him. Over his shoulders' outraged protests his hands gingerly found the sleeves and fastened the belt. Hetford was still standing behind him, and it was his face—pink, softer than he remembered—that was all Quirke could see in the mirror.

To his embarrassment, tears started coming; he sniffled like a child in front of Hetford. "I was getting high tonight while she was getting buried under a ton of concrete. I suppose I can't blame her for finding someone else. But Jesus, that was fast."

"If you mean Father Greengold—"

"*Father* Greengold?"

"He's her parish priest. He was rendering spiritual comfort."

"Is that what it's called nowadays?"

Hetford shook his head. "Quirke, I was in the room for quite a while, and it didn't seem to me they...I wouldn't say they—"

"She doesn't have a parish priest, if we're using 'have' in any but the biblical sense." Quirke laughed bitterly. "She's a priestess herself, in a magical temple. A pagan, it's fair to say. I've performed rites with her myself. But who am I to complain? 'Do what thou wilt shall be the whole of the Law.' Idiot that I am, I never understood what that meant until now."

Remarkably, sympathetic tears were rolling down Hetford's cheeks as he listened; he bowed his head and then fastened his eyes on Quirke's in the mirror. "Look, even if you're right about them, you still have a child together, a wonderful little boy," he said, trailing Quirke into the bedroom.

Quirke stood beside the bed he'd long ago shared with Eleanor, seemingly unaware he'd forgotten to pull the kimono closed before knotting the belt. He turned unself-consciously toward Hetford. "I should be anything but surprised; things have been so strained for such a long time between us. There's just something in me that...that draws women in, to a certain point, and then they can't go any farther. It was the same with Eleanor, but she stuck it out for thirty years. There's something either profoundly unloving or profoundly unlovable about me."

"When the drugs are out of your system—"

Quirke sat, then lay down, on the bed, too exhausted to reflect on the ironies of the situation, and shook his head.

"Well, if it's any consolation," said Hetford, "I love you."

A short, sad laugh escaped Quirke, but then he looked at Hetford, who stood on the other side of the bed in his rainbow pony shirt, wearing a look of misery commingled with fear and tenderness. Quirke's eyes widened, and his stomach lurched. "You're serious."

Hetford seemed to toss overboard any remaining shred of self-protectiveness, and sat down on the bed, half facing Quirke. "The thing is, I've always been crazy about you, but I realized it only lately. When we were on the bench together, your quickness, your wit, your infernal charm drove me out of my mind. In my cases, I had the idea that if I threw enough rhetoric at the result I wanted, everyone would roll over and give it to me. And I did get what I wanted, often, but usually not without a diabolically clever—and since I'm trying to be honest, legally unassailable—dissent from you. As time went on, you got deeper and deeper under my skin. I began to obsess over you. You and I had many conversations in my mind, early in the morning and late at night, and they all ended with us...actually, just as we are now, you in my bed, wearing only a kimono, if that." He paused and looked away. "I haven't been with a man since college. I thought I'd outgrown it." Turning again toward Quirke, he smiled ruefully. "Right now I'm keeping my hands to myself for all sorts of reasons, including that I doubt my advances would be welcome and, more importantly, I'm a married man. Eleanor, by the way, is the only woman I've ever really loved, and I love her deeply, and I won't gratify myself at the price of hurting her."

"Plus, she can be pretty scary," said Quirke. "I know that from experience."

Hetford gave a chuckle that was half cry. "My obsession with you led me to the worst, the only really evil, decisions I've ever made in my life. Only because you forgave me was I able to face myself and to finally understand why I'd done those horrible things. And that freed me to start over, to try to learn to be a good person. I suppose that sounds a little childish. Well, sometimes I feel like a child, lucky enough to have been born again into a sort of restored innocence. I think I'll dress like it from now on," he concluded facetiously, standing again and smoothing the magical shirt over his belly.

In this unlikely spot, in this unlikely company, Quirke at last felt safe. To his surprise, he found he could breathe deeply again. His whole body and mind had relaxed as he lay there in his former marital bed listening to Hetford's confession, which he found entirely believable. In fact, blind love seemed at least as plausible an explanation as any for the irrational zeal with which Hetford had tried to destroy him in the last election. He recalled the look on Hetford's face, during the interminable wait for the results on the afternoon following that election day, when he came to Quirke's chambers to admit his conspiracy with Quirke's ill-starred chief of staff. That odd, shyly intimate intensity in his normally hostile and distant colleague, puzzling at the time, had now dared to speak its name.

"You know I'm an alcoholic and a drug addict who's probably incapable of love," Quirke began.

"If you say so," Hetford said. "More likely you're an alcoholic and drug addict who's engaging in a bit of self-dramatization at the moment."

Hoping a touch of sadism was forgivable under the circumstances, Quirke teased, "And yet you love me."

Hetford rolled onto the wide bed and lay supine next to Quirke, his arms thrown open, staring at the ceiling. "Yes. I'll say it again, because I know I'm not likely to get another chance: I love you. I'm in love with you, Conal Quirke. It's mad, it's unwise, I've tried to stop, but there you are."

Quirke lay silent, letting the rare sense of deep ease take possession of him, until he realized Hetford was waiting for an answer. "I don't deserve your love, Allan," he said at last. "But thank you. Somehow you've made me feel that I'm not, in fact, subhuman. I would kiss you," he continued, as Hetford's face lit up, "but the pain when I move my arms is unbearable, and I can't afford to dip into that stash again."

"My God, yes," said Hetford, jumping up and vanishing temporarily into the bathroom to retrieve the drugs from the pockets of Quirke's ruined clothes. "As your attorney, I should be doing something with this stuff, shouldn't I?"

"Not as my attorney specifically," said Quirke, "but this is your house, and I can see how you might not want it around. I possessed for use, so I'm guilty six ways from Sunday, but if you possess only momentarily, in order to get rid of it, you'll probably have a defense to any criminal charges. And that's what you're going to do right now—get rid of the stash. I hope the water pressure's functioning properly."

Hetford stood mulling over this advice for a moment, then returned to the bathroom, and soon Quirke was listening to a succession of flushes, each one pricking his heart and letting the drug-covetousness leak away. By the time Hetford returned to the bedroom, he was beginning to feel cleansed.

"Of course, everything you've said to me is protected by the attorney-client privilege," said Hetford, tying up a trash bag containing the empty packaging. "Nobody's going to come around looking for the stuff, are they?"

"Nothing to worry about. It belonged to a dead guy."

Chapter Thirty-Nine

4:20 p.m., Friday, February 26

Upon his return to the hospital in the afternoon following his liberation from captivity, Quirke found Sadie alone in her room, asleep. Thus prevented from speaking with her, he took the opportunity to have his own injured shoulders looked at in the emergency department and learned, to his dismay, that he'd suffered two torn rotator cuffs. One was in a bad enough way that the attending warned him surgery and lots of physical therapy would likely be required, as she wrote him a prescription for oxycodone and a referral to an orthopedic surgeon. Quirke's initial panic at the sight of the opioids in his hand gave way over time, in the face of the pain he couldn't ignore, to a certain sense of entitlement, even as he hated the knowledge that he was back on drugs despite himself.

Allan and Eleanor wouldn't hear of his going home to the loft. They made a persuasive case that with only Róisín to look after both Quirke and Ruairí (as well as Sadie, whenever she might be deemed ready to leave the hospital), his household couldn't possibly accommodate the family's needs, whereas theirs had the staff to look after them all, and more than sufficient room.

"You're sure I won't be a distraction?" he asked Allan while Eleanor was out of the room.

"Your virtue's safe," Allan replied, with a facetious moue. Then, more seriously, "But we'll see, won't we?"

So, after token resistance, Quirke—along with Ruairí and Róisín—moved back into the house Eleanor had locked him out of some eighteen months earlier. In truth, the burden on Róisín otherwise would have been overwhelming; as it was, she felt in seventh heaven to have landed in one of the most elegant mansions in one of the most exclusive neighborhoods in the city, with others doing the cooking and cleaning.

Not everyone had the mental flexibility to easily embrace the new arrangements. Eleanor's father, Gene Scorchner—never a huge fan of Quirke's—came by one day for an early morning consult with Allan before going on to the Marvelocity offices, and did a spit-take at the sight of his son-in-law pouring coffee for his former son-in-law, as Eleanor flitted between them.

Never far from the forefront of Quirke's mind was Sadie, whose condition at General Hospital was about to be upgraded to fair. But circumstances seemed to conspire to prevent his seeing her. Between shifting his basic effects to the Hetford household, spending a little time with Ruairí, and attending to his own medical needs, including arthroscopic surgery on his right shoulder, several days passed before he managed to appear at the hospital at a time when she was awake and not occupied with some medical procedure of her own. On that occasion, she seemed guarded and a little cold; he wanted to put it down to the effects of her concussion. His next several visits proved no more satisfying. On the last of them Allan, for reasons unclear, insisted on accompanying him, and they found Sadie with Liam. This time, however, he was dressed not in clerical black but in civilian clothes, and yet again circumstances prevented Quirke from having a serious conversation with her. Mystifyingly, when she was discharged from the hospital a day or two later, she moved not into his room in the main Hetford residence but into the carriage house behind the main house. All Eleanor could say by way of explanation was that he should talk with Sadie, but every time he tried to talk with her, she pleaded the excuse of a headache.

The Chief had insisted Quirke rest for a few days before attempting a return to work. On the morning when he finally felt able to dress himself, more or less (a necktie was still too torturous to think of), he walked to the office and was met with a small cake-and-coffee celebration in chambers. Mike, Adair, John and Margie were genuinely delighted to see him; Freddie, however, was uncharacteristically reticent in his presence, scarcely able to look him in the eye, and excused himself, ostensibly to get back to work on a memo, at the earliest decent moment.

"What's up with him?" Quirke whispered to John.

"No idea," John responded. "I'll find out."

"Close the door," Freddie said when John knocked and poked his head in. "I'm ready to explode with all this stress."

Freddie had previously navigated, more or less successfully, the border between the personal and professional relationships with Quirke that his friendship with Sadie necessarily entailed, but now, as he explained to John, he could barely stand being in the same room with the Judge.

"He's about to get dumped so hard, I'm really afraid for him," he said. "You have to promise not to say a word."

John could only frown and nod.

Quirke had not the leisure to dwell on the sudden and inexplicable shift in Freddie's attitude, for just after the celebration ended, as he sat down at his desk to sort through the piles of memos that had accumulated in the week since his last appearance there, his phone rang and Margie informed him Justice Hetford was on the line.

"Sorry to interrupt. I'm sure you have a lot to catch up on, but I'm calling as your attorney. Do you remember running into Lieutenant Grimes and Detective Shadlack at the hospital?"

"Dimly. I was pretty strung out."

"Yes, you were. They're still interested in talking with you about that night."

Quirke thought for a moment. "Well, of course, I'll tell them what I can. What I can remember."

"I understand you were the best defense lawyer of your day—"

"You can skip the flattery."

"—And so it's your call whether you'd like someone there with you. Someone who, unlike me, knows what to do when his client's being interrogated. Say the word, and I'll get you the best defense lawyer of our day."

"I'll think about it. But it might look a little weird for me to lawyer up."

"True. We mustn't forget you're the victim. Will you be able to meet with them today at 3:00?"

Quirke checked his Outlook calendar, which showed an empty afternoon.

"That'll work. Would you ask them to come by my chambers? Unless they need me to show up at the Hall of Justice or—"

"No, no. I'm sure your chambers will suit them just fine. Good luck, Conal. I'll be thinking of you. Call me when it's over."

At precisely 3:00, Margie showed Grimes and Shadlack, in plainclothes, to the sitting area in Quirke's chambers. Grimes, naturally, was well familiar with the place from his court responsibilities, while Shadlack seemed to be one of the sort of men who move in and fully occupy any space in which they find themselves. They sat down without prompting, leading Quirke to suspect the interview would not be as brief as he hoped.

Shadlack's smile gleamed. "It's good to see you again, Your Honor. You may not remember me, but I testified in your courtroom a few times, back when you were in superior court."

"I certainly do remember. The O'Dell case."

"You bet."

"That was the only familial DNA case I ever tried. And it had its challenging gang aspects, too. Boy, I'd love to sit and reminisce about my days on the trial bench, but—"

Shadlack nodded. "Of course, Your Honor, we know you have more pressing obligations—and I can't thank you enough for taking time this afternoon to talk with us—so we'll focus on the matter at hand. We'd just like to get a better sense of what happened on the night of the Dormund execution—that wasn't. Looks like the feds'll be granting him relief; guy's gonna outlive me. But what we know—or think we know—is that you were returning to the court from dinner—this was before the explosion, obviously—and you were on the Golden Gate side of the state building."

Quirke nodded. They must have spoken to Mike, at least. Who else had talked?

"And then you weren't. So why don't you tell us, if you don't mind, what happened at that point."

"Yes, of course. I was with one of my attorneys, Mike Frentz, and one of Justice Rackrent's annuals, Anya Holmquist. Mike went off to run an errand—he was using the ATM across the street, I think—and I happened to see someone I knew, so we struck up a conversation."

Shadlack interrupted. "Do you recall who this person was, Your Honor?"

"Guy named Tad Laker."

He made a note. "How do you know Mr. Laker, if you don't mind my asking, Judge?"

"We met at a twelve-step group." Quirke paused, but neither officer pursued it. "Anya, as I recall, was standing on the sidewalk a few feet away, not involved in the conversation. Then everything seemed to happen at once: a man pushing, shoving me; a van pulling up and the door opening; somebody pulling me in and Tad trying to pull me out. There was a gunshot. Tad got hit, and they pulled him into the van as well. And then took off."

Grimes nodded. "Did Anya get into the van?"

Quirke shook his head. "I don't think so, but..."

The officers waited as he sorted through his confused impressions. "No, she didn't, at least not before they got the ties around my wrists and put the mask over my nose and mouth. There was some kind of sedative gas in a tank. It wasn't long before I was out, and if they circled back and picked her up while I was unconscious, I wouldn't know."

"When and where did you wake up?"

"It was in a cargo loading bay of an industrial building out in the

Dogpatch neighborhood. Or so I later learned. How much later that was, I don't know; not more than an hour, probably. At that point, Anya was there."

"What was she doing?" Grimes asked.

So far, they were asking the questions he hoped they'd ask. "As a matter of fact, she was pointing a semi-automatic rifle at me."

Shadlack nodded. "So it was you and Tad, who's wounded—"

"And I'd torn my rotator cuff in the fracas."

"—Versus this Anya. What's she like?"

Quirke thought for a moment. "Until then, I'd thought of her as a fairly typical annual—I mean a newly minted attorney here at the court for only one year. A reasonably intelligent but argumentative and rather self-impressed young woman. She looked quite anorexic. She was in a relationship with one of the other guys there."

"Tell us about him."

"She called him Rusty; I never learned his real name. Red-haired, as you'd expect, a little taller than I am, lanky. Also armed. A volatile and condescending guy, not a lawyer, judging by the things he said. He's the one who created the fake Twitter account for me and started tweeting the anti-death penalty quotations. He also made me talk."

"Made you, meaning—"

"Pointed his semi-auto at me and told me what to say. Filmed and posted it."

"That accounts for the...unusual content of the videos."

"Are they still up? I hadn't thought to check, but I certainly don't want people to see them and think...I mean, people are going to have unwarranted concerns about whether I can be fair."

"Don't worry, Judge. I think those were taken down. Okay, now—and I'm sorry to bring up this unpleasantness, but—you probably know we found a body."

Quirke lowered his head, closing his eyes against the returning image of Dane, minus the top of his head, lying in the stairwell. "That was horrible. The poor kid shot himself."

"That would fit the physical evidence. Did you see him do it?"

"No, just the aftermath."

"What was happening right before that?"

"We'd learned about the casualty in the state building. Which turned out to be my—my son's mother, Sadie. At the time the news was reporting it as a fatality." Quirke's anger began to rise again, now that all the facts were known. "Dane, the suicide, had built the bomb and was feeling terrible guilt. It was only meant to be a diversion, and the thought that he'd caused someone's death was too much for him."

"Ironic, isn't it?" Grimes asked. "What were they going to do with you, after all?"

"Yes, I pointed that out, and then Rusty threatened to kill me again and filmed the one where I said it's not wrong to save 800 lives by taking one. Dane couldn't handle it, went into the stairwell with his weapon, and shot himself. I ran to him to see if he was alive. Well, you saw him, I assume."

"You ran to him. So you weren't restrained throughout some of this ordeal."

"If you looked at the videos, you saw I wasn't."

"When did they unbind you?"

"Earlier, I'd persuaded Anya to free my wrists so I could take care of Tad—he was pretty bloody, so I used my undershirt to clean him off."

"We found it. Thanks for clearing that up. And so, after Dane shot himself, what happened?"

"Anya was remarkably cool, but Rusty was freaking out."

"Another thing we noticed at the scene," said Shadlack, "was some residue that gave a positive presumptive result for methamphetamine or MDMA."

Quirke swallowed and felt sweat start to bead on his forehead. "Rusty was using meth at one point."

"You'd recognize meth, is that right, Judge?"

"I think so. In any event, something was said about meth; that's why I—"

"So things were in quite a state at that point. By the way, what time was that, do you know?"

"Not precisely; it was a little before daybreak. They'd taken my phone, so I had no way to find out the time. But it wasn't long before..."

Shadlack laughed. "You see where we're going. Ed and I, we're thinking the Judge is some kind of Houdini, getting out of this situation. Maybe you can just tell us how you managed it."

Quirke nodded. Shadlack and Grimes looked at him, wearing neutral smiles. "Yes, so while Rusty was getting more and more cranked up, Anya pulled me aside. She quietly told me she'd arranged to get us out of there. Said an associate of her father's was on the way; she'd apparently made a phone call and somehow everything was arranged. This was when I realized she'd had it with Rusty and wanted to save herself and me. I told her she had to get Tad out of there, too. Oh, and I suppose I should mention there was another guy—I never caught his name—who was with them initially, but at some point he said he was going out to get falafel, and never came back. So I was afraid that with Rusty in the state he was in, and weapons all over the place, any rescue effort could be dangerous for everybody, so I suggested to Anya that she try to get the AK away from him. I distracted him and she grabbed it. We tied him up—he had the ties in his pocket—and I took the gun because it was heavy for her."

"That explains your prints on it," said Shadlack. "That was kind of weird, actually—we hardly ever manage to lift prints off firearms."

"I guess I'm lucky, huh? I also got my phone back and, checking my messages, I learned Sadie had been injured, that she was the victim at the state building. All I could think of was getting away to see her. Oh, and—but first, breaking his fucking nose. Which I then did."

Shadlack guffawed. "You don't say? Well, the nitwits really tried your patience that night, Your Honor; I can see why beating up the punk would seem like a priority."

"So go ahead and arrest me for battery, if you want."

"When the idiot drops by the station and files a complaint, we'll see if the DA's interested. I wouldn't let it keep me awake at night if I were you."

"I have a feeling the Commission on Judicial Behavior's going to take a less forbearing attitude. But then all of a sudden there was an army of men swarming all over, grabbing the three of them—Anya, Tad and Rusty—and tossing flashbangs at me. It was because I was still holding the AK, they thought I was the bad guy. Before I could open my eyes, they were gone."

"That explains the three little canisters we found. Must have hurt like a motherfucker, you'll pardon the expression."

"It wasn't an experience I'd be eager to repeat. And so then I...eventually I just left. I'm sorry, but calling the police was the last thing on my mind at the time. Instead, I made my way to General Hospital. That was a saga in itself. I won't bore you with it except to say, don't expect an Uber driver to pick you up if you have any appreciable quantity of bloodstains on you. I wound up getting there on Muni."

"Right," said Grimes, "and that's where we met up with you—almost. Seemed like you were in a hurry to get away."

"I was shot. Not literally, I mean. Sadie was asleep, so we couldn't talk; I was a mess, and—and Allan Hetford—"

"Justice Hetford was being quite protective of you."

"I suppose you're thinking, Lieutenant, who'd ever have thought that could happen? But we're good friends now. My son and I—and Sadie—are staying with Allan and Eleanor at their place here in the city."

Having laid the facts, or as many of them as he felt obliged to disclose, before the officers, he awaited their response, hoping he was adequately masking his anxiety. If he'd dropped so much as a pill or a pane of acid at the scene, or if they'd tracked down Anya or Rusty and heard a different version of events, his career might effectively be over. At least he knew Tad would never rat him out.

Shadlack closed his notebook. "Judge, thank you for giving us so much of your time. I should tell you we haven't been able to get hold of Ms. Holmquist; apparently she's in some kind of treatment facility in Connecticut, and her lawyers haven't let us talk to her. Rusty we're still looking for, and now that we have a name for the other guy—Laker—we'll start looking for him, too. But you've filled in most of the gaps for us. We'll let you get back to your court business." They all stood, and the two officers shook his hand and departed.

He shut the door behind them and fell onto the sofa, thinking, *My God, what have I become?* A judge shouldn't be congratulating himself on getting through a police interview without having to be Mirandized. A judge shouldn't be resorting to tactical self-incrimination in small things (simple battery) to deflect suspicion of greater things (possessing and furnishing controlled substances, God knew how many potential counts). Last time around, he'd prided himself on telling the CJB the truth, the whole truth, and nothing but the truth; this time he'd have to either adopt a darker strategy, one he wouldn't want Ruairí ever to learn of, or say goodbye not only to his judicial office but, in all likelihood, his law license, at least for a time. And having given the police a certain version of events, he was committed to providing the same one to the CJB. At the very least, he was now reduced to praying the police and the agency would never think to ask the right questions.

Now, suddenly, he knew why, while the radicals were holding him, he'd been so certain in his drug-addled mind that Sadie had stopped loving him. Innocent of conscious duplicity toward her, he had nevertheless held back the extent of his struggles with drugs and alcohol, and maintenance of the false front had exacted its cost. Was he even the same person she'd fallen in love with? In the near-week since the kidnap and explosion, he'd talked with her only once, and then but briefly; other times he'd visited she was asleep or otherwise unavailable, and the rest of his time had been consumed with his own medical treatment, caring for Ruairí, moving into Eleanor and Allan's house, and now being here, at the court, where he was beginning to wonder if he even belonged. She had never sent a message or called him, although he knew she was communicating with her doctors and others in the Hetford household. He owed her so many apologies he didn't know where to begin, and he was beginning to wonder how the fissures in their relationship could ever be repaired.

Chapter Forty

Mid-May

Over a period of two months Sadie made a nearly complete recovery from her injuries. Although she claimed she didn't hold Quirke responsible for them, the YouTube videos—once seen, impossible to unsee—nevertheless linked him in her mind with the people who had hurt her, and she made clear she preferred he call before visiting. He and Ruairí, meanwhile, stayed in the big house with Allan and Eleanor; Roísín still cared for the baby, and Allan was having the legal department at Marvelocity look into whether her immigration status would permit her to stay on and care for baby Hetford, expected to arrive the following February. The rest of the household thought Sadie was on her own excessively, but she apparently preferred her solitude.

In fact, although she sometimes longed to see Ruairí, she was never lonely. Liam came often—two or three times a day—and his towering figure could be seen, from an upper window or the morning room at the back of the big house, stepping across the driveway to the carriage house. Quirke, being so much at the office, was rarely on hand to witness Liam's comings and goings. One morning in May he was on the bench listening to oral argument when Liam took Sadie away for several hours; that afternoon, she called Quirke to ask him to come by.

He did not pause to meet with his staff in accordance with postargument custom, but obeyed her summons immediately.

She let him in. She was wearing a longish dress, pale pink and frothy, wholly unlike anything he'd ever seen on her, and when he knocked she had evidently been placing a bouquet of pink and white roses in a vase of water on the low bookshelf in the entry. Her face, brighter and healthier than he'd seen it in some time, matched her dress and the flowers. Even more startling, her hair was up in a becoming chignon, save for a single lock twisting down the back of her neck. He said the only words that came to mind: "You look stunning."

He made to embrace her; she moved slightly aside, but let him hold her hand for a moment. "That's sweet of you, Conal."

"How have you been?" He scarcely needed to ask; the answer was plain.

"Never better. And you? And Ruairí?"

"He's well. Roísín took him to the zoo today. He's trying to say 'elephant': So far he's got 'le-le.' I'm...all right, I guess. So very happy to see you; it's been far too long."

She smiled, not without a trace of sadness. "Conal, I wanted to tell you that I'm going with Liam to meet his people back east. We're leaving tomorrow. We plan to stay there for a while."

"How long is a while? I mean, Ruairí—"

"I know. That's something I can't tell you right now. I'll be in touch."

He stood there, debating inwardly. Prior attempts to broach the subject of their relationship had been deflected—sometimes offhandedly, sometimes sharply—but something told him it was either now or never, and so he came closer, pressing her—perhaps a little too emphatically— against the shelf, and she took a step back.

"I want to try again, Sadie. I know I made mistake after mistake, but I love you so—"

"Conal, don't—really, don't, please." Then, in a gentler tone: "I'm going to spend the rest of my life with him."

Hot tears blurred his vision, and though he could scarcely breathe, he managed to whisper, "Isn't there anything I can say to change your mind?"

Her lower lip trembled as she looked up at him, although her eyes glowed fiercely. "Liam and I were married this morning. Justice Latimore was supposed to tell you. We haven't announced it yet, but we're having a baby."

He fell back against the bookshelf, crumpling a little as his gut was seized by a pain he couldn't breathe through. Unable to see, unable to speak, unable to move; he was as helpless as ever he'd been in his life. How could Latimore—his old comrade on the Court of Appeal—have done this to him, marrying the woman he loved to another man? How could she, who'd never found a good enough reason to marry him, suddenly run off with a lapsed priest? And be pregnant with the priest's baby, when he so much wanted another child? A thousand protests raged and spent themselves in his mind. Finally, he forced himself upright and commanded himself to breathe, taking off his glasses to wipe his eyes with the back of his trembling hand.

When he could trust himself to speak, he said, "I wish you well, then, Sadie. Every happiness. We'll talk again about Ruairí, of course."

"Of course."

"I should tell you I'm having Allan and Eleanor appointed his guardians. In case anything happens to me. There'll be paperwork for you."

"We can talk about that. I'll send you an address when we have one. Meanwhile," she said, handing him a blank white envelope, "read this when you have a moment."

It took him a moment to understand she was dismissing him. He tried to think of a good word to substitute for the goodbye he could not voice, but nothing came, and he let himself out.

In his room, Quirke tore open the envelope Sadie had given him and began to read, the notepaper fluttering in his hands, his breath going out in hard, sharp exhalations, fear and anger and pain so bound up together within him that he could not have put a name to his emotional state.

"*Conal,*

"*By the time you read this, I will have become Liam's wife. I struggled to think of a kinder way to explain why I've chosen him as my partner in life, but in the end I didn't trust myself to tell you in person without risking a meltdown—either mine or yours. Hence this letter, which I've worked and reworked more than I did any of the calendar memos I wrote for you. Please excuse any infelicities of tone and any lack of clarity; I've tried hard to edit out all negativity and to make myself as clear as I can.*

"*When you and I first became lovers, I was your little handmaiden in chambers. Words can scarcely describe the awe and respect I felt—and still feel—for you as a jurist and a man.*" (All hope was truly gone; no lover could write words of such clueless sarcasm mixed with distant deference.) "*That you could have any interest in me was astounding. I always felt somehow beneath your notice. Three years, after all, I'd worked for you without the slightest hint you found me attractive, and the sudden change in our circumstances when your marriage ended was astonishing and, I see now, too good to be true.*" (To be rebuked like this, when she was the one who stopped loving! It was too much.)

"*I'll always think back fondly on our early days together in the loft, when Peter was around to buff off the edges of our adjustment to each other. He knows me better than anyone except Liam, and gave me the best advice when you first asked me to marry you (and many times since).*" (And what advice was that, exactly?) "*So much was happening at the beginning of our relationship, with all the craziness around your retention campaign, and my becoming pregnant, and then the horrible things my mother did to you,*"—(I nearly died for you!)—"*that there just wasn't time to spend really getting to know each other and working on our own issues. Mine as well as yours—I now realize I'd been ignoring a big part of myself that has bloomed with Liam.*

"There's no soft way to put it: when all's said and done, I can't be with an alcoholic drug addict. I'm sorry, Conal. I thought I could, but I can't. You had good intentions, you tried hard, but every time you slipped, I flashed back to what I felt as a kid growing up with Laudie and the endless parade of skeevy lowlifes that came through our trailer. Not that you're remotely like them!" (Oh, thank you for that.) *"But that one afternoon when I left you with Ruairí and came home to find you passed out on the floor with a bourbon bottle and the baby, I felt the same powerlessness and terror, and I knew it just wasn't going to work. I didn't want that for him or any other children I may one day be blessed with. I'm leaving Ruairí with you now because I'm confident that between Roísín and Allan and Eleanor—and you, of course—hopefully with Bobby's help in your sobriety—he'll be safe, and I'll come back for him after Liam and I are settled in Kentucky. I know you won't deliberately do anything to harm our child."*

Everything inside his skin went cold and shriveled. When the slip happened with Ruairí, she'd said barely a word. He knew it was wrong to drink while babysitting, but he'd made sure Ruairí was secure in the Jumperoo; if the baby had managed to overturn it, or even simply move it a few inches across the floor, he'd have collided with Quirke, who would have got much the worse end of the mishap. And he'd have awakened, he couldn't not have. It was wrong, yes, but wasn't terminating him a disproportionate reaction?

The question was beside the point. It was *her* reaction, and she had her reasons for it. But what irony: a love born in drink ended in drink.

"This letter will be incomplete if I don't try to explain the other very important reason why our relationship didn't succeed. It's not going to be easy, so please excuse the poverty of my expression. This part is more about me, the path I feel called to, and the meaning of my life (that I think I've found) than it is about you or the way we were with each other.

"Something was missing in my way of being. The sophisticated rationality of this left coast lifestyle, the superiority every Sant' Urbanite seems to feel over everybody else on the planet, the certainty that logic can solve all problems and the notion that allowing any room for something transcendent in one's life is mere foolishness—without my realizing it, my soul was grinding against these attitudes. Even the way we practiced magic seemed to suffer from the same sort of competitiveness and belief in the superiority of intellect. Yes, I know the

Tree of Life is in a sense all about wholeness and balance, but I kept feeling I was missing the point, that I'd never be able to cross the abyss and moreover didn't really want to. And when it wasn't about learning all of yoga and Enochian and Goetic magic and Qabalah all the other intellectual accomplishments of ceremonial magic, it was about spending loads of energy just differentiating ourselves from everybody weaker and dumber than us. Eventually whatever real core it had turned to dust in me, and—believe it or not— the seed planted at St. Anstrudis finally somehow germinated. I found myself drawn to—I mean drawn by—the Christian God, Jesus, and all that 'fantastical' stuff. Maybe this is simply because I'm not a genius but you really don't need to be a genius to be a perfectly adequate saint, and I want to be one of those someday. Of course, there's no room in our culture to talk about this openly, and you've mocked the idea that anyone like us could knowingly and voluntarily embrace a so-called slave religion—one that, I'll concede, has caused an immense amount of suffering along with the great joy and comfort over the centuries. But somehow I have embraced it, and now I've found my life's guide and mate along the path.

"You seem to get the point of magic, though, and I hope it continues to fulfill you. I'm sorry for all the pain I've caused; it wasn't my intention. I really want only happiness for both of us. I've found mine; may you discover and hold onto yours. —Sadie."

He threw himself on his bed, beyond tears, talk, and consolation. He'd eventually understand, even accept, being abandoned because he was an unreliable lush, but being abandoned for Jesus and a (former) priest of Jesus, especially a good-looking one who was twenty years younger and a half-foot taller, was unbearable. To be mocked by a nonexistent god is impossible, yet this avalanche of existential malice was so perfectly, sadistically, fitted to his wretchedness...could it in fact have been triggered by the One who knew him before He formed him in the womb? Or was he now going mad as well as being a hopeless inebriate? And anyway, when had *he* mocked the idea that anyone could embrace a slave religion? That was all the idea of the Order she'd brought him into; *he* was as tolerant as the day is long. She never told him about any of these spiritual revelations of hers because, despite everything they'd shared, she didn't know him, never trusted his love, never—thanks to her diabolical mother's abuse—saw herself as his equal. Or vice versa.

He was shaking too much, and was too unpredictably subject to crying fits, to safely drive himself, and so Ubered south of Market to the loft. He and Sadie had, separately, all but vacated the place since the events of February 25, and Peter Blake had returned to it on a part-time basis from his rural retreat in Sant' Amaro. He found Peter there now.

As he'd done the very first time Quirke set foot in the place, the night Eleanor kicked him out and Sadie took him in, Peter offered him tea. This time Quirke accepted, hoping it, and Peter's peculiar serenity, might help to calm him down.

"I'm glad you came by, Conal." The lithe, prematurely white-haired artist and magical adept poured green tea into small ceramic cups of his own design and passed one to Quirke across the dining table at which they'd all sat together on so many happier occasions. "She surprised both of us."

"Did you know?"

"She'd said very little to me about him. I think she was afraid I'd be angry, but it's only religionists like her new spouse who become disturbed when loved ones marry out of the faith. When she asked me to come up and witness the vows, of course, there was no mistaking—"

"So you saw the ceremony?" Quirke felt himself tensing, his jaw clenching, his hands squeezing the teacup like a murder victim's neck.

"I'm her guardian; she wanted me there. I'm sorry for your loss and disappointment, Conal, but she seems truly happy."

That, Quirke thought, was as much as to say she previously seemed falsely happy with him. Was what they had a mere illusion—simply the excitement of a forbidden romance with the married boss? Feminine satisfaction in an advantageous conquest? He refused to believe it. They'd loved each other passionately, he'd nearly died protecting her from her vicious mother and his evil former head of chambers, they'd had a son. But she was leaving their son behind to go on her wedding trip, with no firm promise to return.

"She'd better be," Quirke said. Then a realization seized him, and he couldn't restrain a bitter laugh. "I'm renouncing magic, Peter; I'll never touch it again."

"Perhaps when the associations become less painful...? You've shown a lot of promise, you know, Conal. I'm quite sure you'll become a very competent magician in time."

"To the contrary, I've already had an amazing success in a sex magic working. The aim was to get Sadie's agreement to marry and have another child. And so it came to pass; just not with me."

※

In the nursery adjacent to Quirke's room, Roísín, bent on effecting an escape from the prevailing desolation by taking Ruairí out for a stroll in his pram, kept shooting sidelong glances at her uncle. He'd repeatedly clutched the baby to his chest, kissing and murmuring to him, and the baby was beginning to raise a protest. She tried to lift him from his father's arms. "Uncle Conal, let me get him out of your hair for a bit. We usually take a walk in the park about this time of day. Best to keep him on his routines, don't you think?"

"I just need to hold him," said Quirke, resisting her, hugging his thrashing son. "He needs to learn that boys do cry."

But Ruairí began demonstrating that he'd internalized the lesson without paternal assistance, and Roísín took him away, leaving Quirke alone.

The big house was entirely still. At the window in his room, he stood looking out at the trees, their leaves an abstract expressionist pattern writhing with the early evening wind. He was beginning numbly to grasp what her leaving would mean. He no longer had a home, and one day she'd come for Ruarí. There would be no more magic and no other children. Before she came into his life, he'd maintained the appearance of rectitude and prosperity, a veneer over his emptiness and addiction. When he found her, he gained a chance of making a real life, with a fruitful and everlasting love—not to mention a reason to stay clean and sober. But he'd made the stupid, terrible mistake of taking his dreams for solid stuff, his happiness for healing; he'd failed to attend to her and to the shadow side of himself, which took over and chased out the light. This silence surrounding him would soon be all he had. And he didn't want it.

※

"Con! Dude, good to hear from you. Haven't seen you at the Wednesday 2:00 lately. How've you been?" Tad felt as ebullient as he must have sounded. He'd just picked up a 90-day chip, and his new job in men's accessories at Macy's was going swimmingly. Con—he still had a hard time thinking of him as Justice Quirke—hadn't been attending the usual meetings recently, and in his absence Tad had started to work with Con's sponsor, an old-timer named Bobby James. He hoped Con had called to arrange to meet up sometime soon.

"Not all that well, actually," Quirke replied. "Has Bobby said anything?"

"Only that he didn't want to talk out of turn. You know Bobby."

"As a matter of fact, I called you because I need something."

"Say the word, buddy. Your Honor, I should say."

There was a long exhalation, and then silence. His heavy mood came clearly across the wireless connection. Tad waited for him to speak, his unease growing.

"I find I'm in a lot of pain these days."

"The shoulders again? You still doing those exercises?"

"They didn't really help. So I thought I'd ask you."

"Ask me what?"

"For a rig and a half g. Of heroin."

Tad was speechless. Since returning to Sant' Urbano after the skinny chick's dad rescued them from the kidnap situation, he'd been clean. The dad, maybe wanting everybody who witnessed his darling daughter's radical acting-out to be in his debt, put him through a rehab program in upstate New York. It must have cost a chunk of change, but you get what you pay for and the treatment, for once, took. Even the few people still in Tad's life whom he'd known when he was using hadn't come to him wanting drugs since he showed up back in Sant' Urbano, and he felt like he might actually make it this time. But now his sponsor wanted a needle and enough junk to last a serious user a day or two. The whole judge thing aside, Con wasn't a serious user...was he?

He temporized, trying to think. "You're sure about this?"

"It's like I said, the pain is more than I can handle. I'll make it worth your taking the risk. But if you don't want to, it's fine, I'll—"

"Give me a few hours. I'll come by your place."

"Thank you. I think I gave you the address at some point—?"

"I've got it. Sit tight, my friend."

"I can't believe he had no idea it was coming." Eleanor took a bite of sole and sipped her pinot grigio. She rather liked expecting the arrival of their baby without having to abstain from her nightly glass of vino, thanks to the comprehensive services provided by the Oceanica Fertility Center. "She'd been putting about as much distance between them as possible for two people still technically living under the same roof. I mean, telling a guy to call before coming over isn't what a woman does who has any intention of marrying him. And her boyfriend, new husband, the priest, whatever, was over there night and day."

"It's easy for us to see all that; we're not blinded by love. Except for each other," said Hetford, leaning over the corner of the table to kiss his wife. "The fact is, he had no inkling, he thought he still had a chance with her, and now he's *verklempt*. Don't you find it painful just knowing how broken up he is? It practically seeps through the walls. You must go and console him."

She shook her head. "I would, but I'm afraid I'll only make him feel worse. You know I was the last woman to dump him before her."

"True, there's a risk, but I'm certain right now he needs a woman to make him feel he's still lovable. And loved." He squeezed her hand to emphasize the point.

"I don't know if I'll succeed in that. But for you, darling, I'll try."

"Thank you," said Hetford, tearing up. "It means a lot."

She laid her hand on his cheek and kissed his lips softly. She'd never have guessed, when she first met Allan Hetford—then a cynical, high-powered Supreme Court justice, the arch-rival of her then-husband Quirke—that he'd turn out to be so big-hearted, so sensitive. He had almost a woman's sense of emotional depth and nuance. Really, even after nearly two years she discovered something new and wonderful about him every day. He was going to be the best father imaginable.

She knocked on the door of Quirke's room, located on the opposite side of the house from the one she shared with Allan. Thinking she heard a response, she opened the door.

The room was dark except for a swathe of streetlight in the window and the stripe of hallway light in the doorway. It took a moment before her eyes adjusted sufficiently to make out his slight form lying prone and motionless on the bed. In an instant, based on long experience, she knew he was sober, and sat down beside him.

He acknowledged her presence without raising his head. "Eleanor."

"Hello, Quirke. Well, this is a terrible day."

A sniffle was his only reply.

"You know, it won't feel like this forever. It may seem like today will never end, but it will, and so will tomorrow, and...and eventually you'll notice things are different. I wish I could take away the pain."

"Kind of you to say."

"Roísín has a class tonight, so Allan and I will take care of Ruairí, if it's okay with you."

He rolled over and looked urgently at her. "Did Allan tell you I'm making the two of you his guardians? In case anything happens to me?"

"He did mention it...he showed me some papers. Of course, we'll do anything for Ruairí, we adore him. And I hope you know you're welcome to stay here as long as you want. We love having you both here in our house. Allan really likes you, you know, whatever he did in the past."

The lighting wasn't so dim that she failed to see a quizzical smile cross Quirke's face. "I've come to feel rather fondly towards him, too. You want to hang onto that guy."

"And I'm glad you're still a part of my life," she murmured. "We can be better friends than we ever were spouses."

He drew himself up and sat beside her. They embraced for the first time in years, since he could remember. He let her hold him, anchoring him as he sobbed, neither of them bothering about the tears he was shedding onto her blouse.

At last she sat back, her arms still around him, and laughed lightly. "Quirke, you're so thin—even thinner than when we met."

There was a sense of emotional whiplash in calling up his impressions of that night, more than thirty years before: a dope-perfumed frat party his band was playing, beer so plentiful it drenched the floor, the agreeable feeling of being the beneficiary of an eighteen-year-old coed's lust. He searched her face for a sign of that girl, and thought he found it. "So you still remember?"

"How could I forget that fateful mixer and the cute bass player with the killer blue eyes and ghastly mullet? And I certainly haven't forgotten the way Daddy groaned when I came home and told him about you."

"And the rest was history. Thank you, Eleanor. You've been good to me. I appreciate everything you and Allan have done."

"Why don't you come down and have a little something to eat? There's a nice sole tonight."

"Thanks, but I can't face it just now."

She rubbed his back, nodding.

At the doorway, she asked, "Shall I close this?"

"Please," he said.

Tad, better dressed than in previous times thanks to his employee discount at Macy's but consumed with worry, paced the sidewalk in front of the gate to the Hetford residence. Soon a tall, older black man in chinos and a windbreaker jogged up the hill toward him.

"Bobby! Thank God you're here," Tad said. "You've known him a long time, and you've got a ton of sobriety, so I thought: Bobby'll know what to do. I couldn't believe it when he asked me—"

"Did you get it for him?"

"Of course not. I'll stall—say my connection's out of town for a couple days and just hope and pray he doesn't go down to the 'Loin and try and score it himself. Unless you have a better plan?"

"Beyond showing up here, offering to take him to a meeting, and just generally being a friend, I don't know what to do. He's been out of touch lately, so I can't say I really know what's going on with him. I know he had some physical issues after his rotator surgery, so I can see him getting frustrated with the pain, but not—"

"Yeah, it just isn't Con. Do you think something else happened to...?"

"I hope to find out."

"So how do we get into this joint?" Tad rattled the gate. "I tried his cell, but he doesn't pick up. You got the code?"

"I sure don't. There's got to be a chime, or a bell, or a—I see we're being surveilled." Bobby pointed to the security camera mounted over the gate. "I'll push this one and see what happens." He tried a likely-looking button on the keypad.

A Spanish-accented voice came over the intercom. "Yes, who is there?"

"We're friends of Justice Quirke's," said Bobby, "and we understand he's staying at this address. We wanted to see him, if he's available. He's expecting one of us, and I came along for company."

"One minute, please, sir. Your name?"

"Bobby James. And Tad Laker."

They waited in silence for a few minutes, each marveling at the height of the wall surrounding the hidden mansion and the impenetrability of the foliage behind it. Wind was stirring the leaves and pushing fog-wraiths up the street, along with stray fragrances of magnolia, jasmine and salt water. There were no cars and no pedestrians to break the silence in this exclusive neighborhood.

"Too quiet for me up here," Tad said, finally. "A tsunami could wipe out Sant' Urbano, and you'd never know."

The sound of footsteps coming down the walkway from the house interrupted his observation. A tall, imposing man a few years younger than Bobby stood before them on the other side of the gate.

"What can I do for you, gentlemen?" he asked. "May I ask how you're acquainted with the Judge?"

"Bobby James, friend of the Judge. His former campaign manager, actually." He extended his hand through the gate.

"I'm sorry, Mr. James; I should have recognized your name. Like most judges or former judges, I know of you." His interlocutor shook Bobby's proffered hand. "I'm Allan Hetford."

"No worries. Call me Bobby."

"And you, sir?"

Tad shook his hand. "Tad Laker. I know the Judge from...well, he and I were kidnapped together. So, you're Allan Hetford? Man, the Judge talks about you like you're Jesus risen or something."

The man shook his head. "I'm—I'm flummoxed. Don't know what to say. Tad, good to meet you. I hope your injuries are healing well?"

"Doing great. Wish I could say the same for Con. The Judge, I mean."

They could see little of Hetford's face, backlit as he was by the house, but his expression changed perceptibly and he lowered his voice. "So you've heard?"

"Could you tell us what you're referring to, Allan?" Bobby asked.

"Excuse my rude manners, and do come in." He released the gate for them, and they followed him up the walkway to the portico surrounding the main door to the house. Under the gas lights that still flickered on either side of the door and the recessed lighting that had been added a century or so after the building was constructed, the men could now see each other.

"This has been an incredibly upsetting day, as you might imagine," Allan said, in an undertone. "Since you're both good friends of his, I assume it's all right to tell you he's not taking it well."

"What happened?" Bobby asked, his voice rising a little. "Judge spoke with Tad for a minute or two, but he didn't mention anything in particular that—"

Leaning against the door, Hetford let a groan escape him. "Let's go inside."

They followed him into his office, a spacious and comfortably appointed room just off the entrance hall, and he locked the door. He gestured to the two leather sofas flanking a fireplace that was empty on this warm spring evening. "Please sit. You're aware he's been staying here since the kidnap and bombing. Sadie, too. Do you both know her?"

Bobby nodded; Tad said, "Only from the things he's said. He's completely nuts about her."

Hetford frowned, shaking his head. "They've been living separately under this roof, with more or less separate lives. I don't know if you're aware she was seeing someone."

"Oh, my God," said Tad. "Con must have been all torn up, but I never saw it."

"We—my wife and I—saw her lover coming and going occasionally, but we weren't aware how serious it was. Well, they were married this morning. This afternoon she broke the news to Conal. It seems to have come as a complete surprise. He still hoped to work things out with her."

"Jesus Lord have mercy," Bobby murmured.

"Turns out she's having his child. I don't think it helps that he's the priest she was consulting about converting to Roman Catholicism."

Tad gave a little shriek; Hetford continued. "As you'd expect, this has knocked him for something of a loop. Did he ask you to come by tonight to provide some consolation?"

Tad shrugged. "I guess you could call it that. He wanted me to bring him...." Turning to Bobby, he asked, "Should I tell him?"

Bobby said, "Judge said he was in pain and asked for drugs."

Hetford's chest suddenly filled with an empathy indistinguishable from physical pain. That Quirke was heartsick over the loss of the woman he'd long wanted to marry, the mother of his child, was obvious, understandable. But that it had led him to want to use illicit drugs again, with all the attendant risk, was shocking. Then an even more frightening concern emerged. "What kind of drugs?" he asked. "How much?"

"He likes his bourbon whiskey, but he always used to say his drug of choice was heroin," Tad said. "And that's what he asked for. He wanted a half gram—that would probably last him at least a couple of days, since he's not a regular user—at least, not that I know of. And a needle."

Hetford dropped onto the sofa opposite them, his face in his hands. The signs were troubling that Quirke wanted something beyond pain relief. He'd been insistent lately about drawing up a guardianship for Ruairí "in case anything happens to me." He'd isolated himself, away from those who loved him and wanted to help him get through this loss; and, finally, he'd tried to acquire a means to surcease of his sorrows that, being highly illegal, risked his professional ruin if he were caught with it. Unless he knew he wouldn't be caught, because he was planning to kill himself. The brutal idea of a world without Quirke sucker-punched him just then, and suddenly Quirke's anguish and despair were his own.

He pushed down his wild fear of losing Quirke and turned to Tad. "You didn't actually—?"

"I let him think I would, but no. But I'm afraid when I show up without the shit, excuse my language, he'll just find another way to get it."

Hetford considered. "Forgive me if I'm making an unwarranted assumption, but I gather you're each...somewhat familiar with this sort of thing? Narcotics, I mean?"

"No point in dancing around it," said Bobby. "We've been to quite a few twelve-step meetings with the Judge, both of us."

"That's good," said Hetford. "Then you know how interventions are supposed to work?"

Bobby shrugged. "Well, we're no experts but, speaking for myself, I've been involved in getting several people into treatment at various times over the years. There's no script, but I suppose you could say there's a pattern. Is he in a state to listen tonight? Or—"

"My wife spoke with him earlier. Let me get hold of her."

A text message and a moment later, Eleanor, with Ruairí on her hip, joined them from another part of the house. "How was he?" she mused in response to Hetford's inquiry. "Well, he was sober. In both senses of the word. We had a good conversation about the past—ours, his and mine, that is. But he made it clear he wanted to be alone. He didn't mention expecting any visitors tonight."

Hetford nodded abstractedly and rose to his feet. "I'm going up there. Yes, my dear, I'm going to risk annoying him because I'm afraid he's thinking of harming himself as we sit here." Amid the concerned exclamations that followed, he hastened to Quirke's room.

His knock was a formality; the ensuing silence could not have stopped him from entering had the door been locked and made of solid iron. He turned on the light and, to the relief of his overactive imagination, Quirke was only lying inertly on the bed, his forearm shielding his eyes.

"Go away, Allan," he said.

"If you thought I was going to stand by while you kill yourself in my house," Hetford retorted, "you were mistaken. Your son needs you. My God, *I* need you; a world without you would be unendurable. Up, up, up, my friend. Don't worry, I'm not going to make a habit of this, I couldn't withstand the excitement." He pulled Quirke's feet off the bed and embraced him, gently scooping him into a sitting position. In the process his chest pressed fleetingly against Quirke's heart, beating through his shirt, through his thin chest wall. The electric sensation triggered another of his episodes of oceanic love-feeling, and for a long moment he could only sit and gaze at his adored object while the adored object gazed back, puzzled. Finally, he managed to say, through the thickness of the emotion, "Your friends are downstairs. As luck would have it, your heroin order couldn't be fulfilled at this time, but I have a better idea anyway."

"Is that so?" Quirke looked at him with doleful amusement.

"We're going on a road trip. I know a place where you can get absolutely divine milkshakes." He fished in his pockets, produced a set of keys, took Quirke's hand, and placed them on his palm. "And you're driving."

Quirke stared at the keys. For some moments, he appeared to weigh his options. Then the balance of darkness and light at last began to shift inside him, and he favored Hetford with the slightest of grins. "So, you're letting a suicidal man drive your Tesla with you in it? Either you're crazy or you must really love me."

"And," said Hetford, "I've been meaning to ask you—in fact, it's why I was waiting for you in the state building the night you never showed up—so, what's being a father all about? God alone knows why Eleanor thinks I—"

"There are thousands of books, Allan."

"Yes, but did any of them ever tell you what it's *really* all about? There; see? Now, start at the beginning."

Eleanor, still holding Ruairí, kissed Quirke on the cheek as her husband and the two friends waited inside the car. "You know how Allan hates letting other people drive his Tesla. I don't know how you got him to do it, but then you've always been extraordinary. Virtually magical."

"Guilty as charged, I'm afraid," said Quirke, getting into the driver's seat. "Don't wait up for us, dear. And goodnight, buddy," he said, blowing a kiss at the baby. "Daddy will see you in the morning."